Time flies

Wynn Wagner

ISBN: 978-1-938964-03-9 (paperback)
ISBN: 978-1-938964-04-6 (casebound)
ISBN: 978-1-938964-05-3 (e-book)

If you spot a character that reminds you of an actual person,

that's me messing with you.

Did you get this story on a biography shelf?

No, it's fiction, man. Try to keep up.

Wynn Wagner, author

Rik Wallin, editor

If you have Coming Out or Bullying issues,
Check out FINDING HELP at the end of this book.

For Sven
Such a good friend. My only living relative.
It's like I've known you all my life.

chapter one
my four men

*"If English was good enough for Jesus Christ,
it ought to be good enough for the children of Texas."*
Ma Furguson (D-TX), America's first female governor (1875-1961)

The four guys in my life were walking down the street in a line. I knew they were headed my way. I also knew it wasn't a parade because of some heroic victory or a fabulous historical event. They'd be my visitors in moments, and it was because of my rooster. Poor little fellow gets stoned on my mom's pot seeds, and he just can't handle his high. I've seen it all before, and I have no idea how to fix it.

Mr. Austin was in the middle of the line. He could afford to live anywhere because he's so rich that other rich people say he's insanely rich and out of their league. Mr. Austin is a straight man, but he usually has his la-di-da shoes on. If you lined up everybody in Waxahachie, Texas, in order to pick the most over-the-top gay guy, Mr. Austin would be way up on your list.

He isn't gay. He's elegant but never gaudy. He's pretentious but not arrogant, and he's over-the-top flamboyant but never garish. He plays to his own stereotype.

If Mr. Austin were a Christmas tree, it would be one of those with ornaments the same color. The lights would match the ornaments with gratuitous precision. He's just like that, without any apology. I think he's kind of cool.

On the far right is Kris, who's one of my two best friends. Kristof Halász is also the smartest man I ever met. We grew up together. We've both lived on the same street forever, but he somehow learned an extra five languages and a species of mathematics that I know was never taught in Waxahachie schools. If Kris were gay (which he isn't), he'd still be way out of my league. The guy could have stepped right out of a haute fashion magazine.

I fantasize about Kris. The things I could do to his body—

One of my great challenges each year was the pool party. I'd find some way to get Kris into a Speedo (fanning face). Let's just say, the last bathing suit I saw him wear was very flattering.

Kris and I have drifted apart a little over the years. There was a time where I'd be at the Halász house, watching soccer on TV or playing chess with his sister.

Over on the left of the line is Mikka Cooper, who's my other best friend. Mikka's gypsy, and he takes that part of himself seriously. He loves being gypsy. He's also a natural gymnast.

Mikka is also the consummate gay guy. He has the limpest wrist in all of Texas. Did he ever come out of the closet? First, he doesn't even own a closet. Second, coming out of one would be redundant.

If you ever wondered about his sexual orientation, he'd be despondent because he didn't swish enough. He hadn't done his job, and the solution would see him make his next arm movement more luxuriant than you thought possible.

No need, though. He's plenty chichi without prodding from anybody. No, offense, ladies… this one's not for you.

Mikka has two tattoos: a State of Texas on a pec and a big 7 on his butt. The state of Texas is just because of hometown pride. The "7" is about the Kinsey Scale. It rates people from "0" (no attraction to the same sex, zero, zilch, diddley-squat). It goes up to the other end of being abso-fuckin'-lutely queer. That's a six on the Kinsey scale.

Mikka had a guy put a big "7" on his butt. He says it's a Kinsey 7. He says it's a "competitive upgrade."

And Mikka's cute. He's adorable nude, which is how I know about his "7". (Not going there right now.)

When there were several ways of doing something, Mikka picks the ostentatious route, and he didn't care who was around to see it. That's a problem in some parts of the world... like, Ellis County, Texas.

Bubbas and rednecks seem to send out patrols looking for gay guys to bully.

It isn't just the hicks: gypsies are notoriously homophobic. Kids should live in a home that's a safe place. Mikka didn't get to do that, and that's one of the saddest thing I ever witnessed. Without a safe place to grow up, a kid has to make his own choices. He has to figure out his own rules for interacting with other parts of society.

With Mikka being Mikka, I'm sure there were conversations in the family. That's guesswork because I've never even seen his house.

I know the local gypsies live in one corner of Mr. Austin's estate. He lets them use the property, so long as they stay put and don't wander. If you aren't a Traveler or Roma, they'd rather not see you near their compound.

I've known Mikka all my life, like Kris.

And then there's Marengo, the fourth "guy" coming toward me.

I was sitting on the front porch, appreciating Springtime in this part of Texas. It's my perk for living in Podunk.

Marengo is my seriously unhinged rooster. It used to be mom's rooster. When she died, I inherited the bird.

Mr. Austin was holding Marengo as far away as possible. Writhing. Twisting. Every feather going in a different direction. Marengo wasn't pleased.

The hens in my backyard heard or smelled their rooster, and they were all going crazy with excitement. The thing is this: the hens were giving poor Marengo the What Ever. They berated their rooster. I swear they sounded like they were laughing at him.

Without warning, Marengo pried himself loose from Mr. Austin's arms. He shot straight up several feet and then did a series of somersaults all the way to the ground.

"Krockle krock swunkle," Marengo screamed.

I lost it.

It was coffee-out-of-your-nose funny, and that's what happened to me. There was iced coffee all over me, the wood swing, and the porch.

"Mind your bird, Andreas," Mr. Austin said.

Andreas: that's me. Andreas Monet. (ahn-DREY-uhs moh-NAY) Really close friends call me André. One kid in elementary school called me Andy. I got sent home after I reset his clock. I swear I didn't hit him that hard, but Mom and dad are the only ones allowed to use that name. They're both dead, so the name is history too.

"Sorry, sir," I said, and I meant it. I've looked and studied and tried to figure out how Marengo gets out of the backyard chicken coop.

"Kwalker-kwalk," Marengo said as I chased him up the driveway.

"Plukker-quantz bluck-bluck," said the hens from the back yard. They laugh at Marengo without any mercy. He definitely has reason to want to escape the back yard. The hens don't take him seriously. I do feel sorry for him.

"He can't handle his pot," Kris said. I already knew that, so Kris got my stank-eye, the one I practiced in front of a mirror.

"I know your mother's marijuana will knock the socks off anybody," Mr. Austin said as I reached the group and picked up the rooster. Roosters don't actually wear socks, but I figured it was a detail best left unsaid.

"You bring the rooster," Mikka said, "I got the dumplin'."

As I trotted up the driveway, the hens gave Marengo twelve kinds of shit. They are relentless.

I think the rooster was trembling when I opened the coop and let him go. I think he was shaking. With Marengo, it's hard to tell. Feathers were every which way.

He took about 3 steps and fell over. The hens hooted. Two of them walked up to kick him.

"Cockly-dwrall-cock-block," Marengo hollered as I walked back to the street. It takes huevos to be the rooster in my mom's brood. I don't know if brood is a real term or something she said to confuse everyone. She was certainly capable of either.

I have no idea how he does it, but Marengo loves to get out of the coop and waddle up to the Austin estate. Marengo thinks he works there too, and he's annoyingly conscientious about showing up on time. The gate up there is always locked, and the entire place is surrounded by a stone fence. To a chicken, it must seem impenetrable, maybe the edge of the earth.

Marengo knows how to overcome all my efforts of keeping the chickens confined, and he knows how to thwart Mr. Austin's fortress. No hen has ever gotten out, only the rooster.

"Kwalker-kwalk," Marengo said.

"Plukker-quantz," said the hens. They laugh at Marengo without mercy. He definitely has reason to want to escape the back yard. The hens don't take him seriously. Poor little guy.

I don't use pot. Not often. It's lots more hassle than it's worth. I don't sell the stuff. I rarely use it. I don't cultivate it. People who use it are the ones who take care of it. Somebody's out there several nights a week: clipping, pruning, weeding (oh, that's funny: weeding the weed), fertilizing, watering.

Everybody knows my rules: (1) don't involve me; (2) no minors; (3) keep the seeds away from the chickens.

I secretly think that somebody throws seed at Marengo. I haven't caught them, and I've looked. You wouldn't know it to look at

11

it casually, but it is probably the most photographed and monitored patch of ground in North Texas.

My bedroom when I was a kid (the one that almost caused Mikka to have a stroke after he jacked me off) had a perfect view of most of the patch, and I had me a brand-spankin'-new shiny digital camera that could take pictures on a dark night without a flash.

Mom once asked me why I was buying so many memory cards. I went and grabbed my shoebox and told her to select a card. We looked. Her jaw dropped way below the floor.

"Young man," she started.

"Just protection," I said. "It's defensive only. You remember how Preacher Jones pushed to get that transgirl thrown out of school?"

She did.

"Remember how suddenly and without explanation, he backed down to the point that he invited her to be a cherished member of his newly-progressive House of Worship?"

"Oh, you did not," Mom said.

I grinned and took the card out of the camera and returned it to its shoebox with just the right flick of the finger. Then I blew on the tip of my finger and put it back in my non-existent holster.

We never spoke of those things again. She knew instinctually that the pictures were defensive only. I'd never considered turning aggressive, using them to start a blackmail scheme. She did suggest that I keep all the memory cards hidden discreetly, in case a burglar hit the house. That would be larger headlines than we'd ever want to see.

She knew I was just working security and that the pot plants were about as invulnerable as it could be (so long as the NSA isn't a player).

My attitude on the undertaking was μολὼν λαβέ.

Μολὼν λαβέ — or *come and take it* — is what Spartan warriors told the Persians (now Iranians) after they demanded Sparta's weapons. Yup, MOLÒN LABÉ.

Here comes me the English major. I absolute love words and how we can chop and slice words. My favorite is to find some stuffy gotta-do-it-this-way creep and take her right up to the literary ledge.

Both molòn and labé are iambs, and that means the accent is on the second syllable. It also shows how sadistic Iranian wordsmiths were. It's really hard to go all iambic on somebody's ass in an argument. It makes your threat sound like poetry or the lyrics of a country western dance song.

Say mo-LÒN la-VÉ. Put just the tiniest pause where I put dashes.

Now, I need to warn you. If you ever say this to somebody who isn't Persian or Spartan, be ready to run. Modern day Second Amendment fanatics tend to know this phrase, and they may take it as a request for a duel. They may try to take whatever it was you're protecting.

Just sayin'. And your mileage, etc, etc.

So, you want to come take the pot? Molòn labé. I mean it: labé your ass over here and molòn mom's marijuana. There's a whole long list of people who may have opinions on your defoliation project. You'll have to answer to others, and I'm not on that list. The State of Texas, DEA, and FDA aren't even on the list. Part of the 1st Army at Ft Hood: they're on the list, and they've got tanks and Howitzers. I see lots of soldiers and other uniforms work the marijuana, and each of them will feel annoyed or betrayed if you try to get rid of the pot. But, feel free to give it your best shot.

And, yes, I have three copies of my photos. One — the originals — is hidden at the house. One is in a local bank's safety deposit box. The other is somewhere else.

I don't want to be an extortionist, but I wouldn't hesitate if you back me into a corner.

Mikka and Kris both work at Mr. Austin's estate. Marengo thinks he works there, too, and he's very conscientious about showing up for his job. The place covers two square miles. That's 1280 acres (thank you, Lords of Google). And it's 5.17998 square kilometers

13

(ditto for our Metric Lords). It's the largest thing in Waxahachie, Texas (a.k.a. The Podunk Central of Texas).

Not everything's bigger here, but that estate is way bigger than it should be. We're in the city limits of Waxahachie.

Who puts a 1280 acre farm inside a town? I never want to see his property tax invoice. When they mail him the tax statement, it takes more than one stamp: that's all I can say about it. Oh, and Texas has what's called the "open records" law, which means that the property tax situation for every property in the state is public record. Some corporations use sleight of hand record-keeping, but if somebody's patient and doesn't mind getting glazed-over eyes, the info is out there.

What I had been doing was figuring out how the Sam Hill I was going to pay both the electric and water bills, but I was interrupted.

Mikka and Kris started walking up the driveway. I know the drill: they were going to see if they could find Marengo's secret.

With Kris, not a single strand of his brunette hair was ever out of place. It didn't seem slicked down, but it was very well trained. No hair would dare to do anything besides what Kris wants.

Mikka was just the opposite: no individual hair looks like it was place anywhere except by chance and DNA. He has a jet-black mop that bounces when he walks. He always grins, but in a way that you think he knows something or he's up to something. (spoiler: he's always up to something.)

Mikka did a somersault without touching the ground. I wish I could tell you the reason he went aerial, but it's just one of life's mysteries.

Maybe the gypsy is related to the rooster. They both like gymnastics. Mikka plans his moves, and Marengo just lets go with a more organic approach to his acrobatics. Marengo does freestyle acrobatics.

"I named him, you know," Mr. Austin said about the rooster.

"Really?" I asked, pretending not to have heard the story a b'zillion times.

"Yup. Marengo was Napoléon Bonaparte's horse. It was fast, couldn't be caught, and it saved Napoléon's skin several times. Marengo was always fast and could avoid capture."

"Sorry," I said. "I'll rework the fencing again."

I had tried everything I could think of, but Marengo could still escape.

My biggest worry: if the rooster could get out, then dangerous predators will find a way to get in. We get the occasional black bear and cougar, but sightings are rare. A bear sighting makes the newspaper. I think it does. There isn't enough money to get me to read the trash that pretends to be our source of news. I'd be more interested in Hitler's cookbook or a Learn the Piano by Pol Pot. The whole Waxahachie newspaper can go sit on a prickly pear, and the world would be a better place. They think they are at the top of journalism, but the reality is that they're printing hateful trash because that's what the newspaper's owners want to read.

There's also the occasional fox, but the real threat to chickens is the coyote. If you don't protect your critters, they will be dog food in short order.

Coyotes live in the nearby hills, and that's fine. I won't go hunting. But if I catch one near my chickens, I will add some fur to my collection. I'm a good shot, up to about a half mile. Sorry, but I protect my kids.

"You coping with it all?" Mr. Austin asked. He was asking about Mom.

She had health challenges for over 10 years. Way back, she had acute pancreatitis. That's just about the most painful thing you can get.

Nothing but strong narcotics let her cope, according to the doctors. They were right about the pain, but they were so wrong about the drugs. What worked was marijuana.

We have a patch of pot. It's been back there longer than I've been alive. Mom said it was already there when my folks bought the house before I was born.

Because my bedroom was on the back of the house, I had a direct view of the garden. When you go out the back door, the right part of the back yard has regular grass, some melon and tomato plants, and a clothesline. Yup, some people still like naturally dried undies.

The chicken coop is on the left side of the yard.

At the far left of the house is the garage, separate building from the house. It's a two-car arrangement for a by-gone era. Cars were lots skinnier back then. If I put my Jeep in the garage, that's the only thing that goes in there. It's about 16-feet wide.

The marijuana patch is behind the garage. That makes it 16'ish x 5'ish feet.

I've had a close-up eye-witness to the whole Community Garden. One of my first memories was the mayor on his hands and knees, weeding mom's hidden garden. I've seen cops, marshals, and deputies. Politicians, Baptist preachers, and cowboys. They all came to garden and to harvest.

I never saw any Methodist minister, even though we have almost as many of them as we have Baptists.

The biggest fireworks I ever saw was when the head preacher from Trinity Baptist found the children's minister from First Southern Baptist. I think they almost had heart attacks.

Mom loved the snapshots I took of gardeners. She hooted and hollered, a rare point of fun in all her pain. She really loved my filing system.

"It's official," she laughed. "Twenty-seven 8-by-10 color glossy pictures with circles and arrows and a paragraph on the back of each one explaining what each one was to be used as evidence."

I told her that I had more than 27 pictures. She told me she was quoting lyrics from the song of a long gone generation.

Mom used my evidence. One time when Mom heard that one of the preachers had given a sermon about gay people, she got him on the phone. He knew who she was. After a few minutes of chatting, the preacher apparently promised to take back all the nasty things he said about queers. He also promised that his church would work to take care of homeless gay kids. Those kids were mostly kicked out of their Baptist parents house for being gay, so the preacher was mostly to blame.

Mom was dead. I gave up my nice job up in Dallas, programming computers. I don't have any qualifications for programming computers. I can add, but multiplication and division are well beyond my ability. For some reason, I'm kind of a savant with computers.

Waxahachie doesn't have many programmer gigs. That's a big city job. And around here, Dallas is the big city. Fort Worth is big too, but Dallas is where programmers make the most money. And Dallas is way more liberal and gay-approving than Fort Worth.

I just don't want to wait tables, like I did in high school.

The pot got rid of Mom's pain. I'm glad we had it for her.

Doctors had removed her pancreas and other stuff you'd think she would need. They have meds that do much of the work of an actual pancreas. It never stopped hurting her, and that was the most horrendous thing to watch.

I'll always remember her as the Mom guaranteed to have a smile waiting for any kid. We went from that to the area of constant burning pain, combined with sharp stabs that easily sent her to the floor, crumpled in agony.

If there's a god, he's going to have some 'splaining to do.

Pancreatitis isn't even what killed her. The final blow was from bacterial endocarditis (a.k.a. BE). See the big words I've learned?

A BE is an infection of the heart valve. I learned that the valves in the human heart have no blood circulation for their own use. The valves are surrounded by blood, but they don't get their own supply. That means you can't fill a BE patient with antibiotics because they can't go from the blood system to the inside of the valve.

17

If you know medicine, you're probably squirming. You are pointing and giggling at my total lack of medical training. Yup, that's me.

Why is it that a doctor's shit never stinks? They have it, and they put their big collection of diplomas on every wall of their office.

I was an English major.

I can translate Beowulf from Old English to German. I'll bet the uppity doctors couldn't do anything like that. But, of course, medicine is so much more important. People wouldn't have survived as a species without trained doctors. Oh, wait... we did survive.

Doctors sometimes kill people. They killed George Washington after he retired. The high-tech cure for everything was bleeding. Doctors really did drain buckets of blood from people, thinking the body would make new blood, fresher than the stinky of crud. Only they were so wrong that they killed the first president of the United States.

So put that in your stethoscope and smoke it.

Sorry, I had way more than my quota of doctors. Nurses are usually cool. They know more about medicine than the doctors. I swear it. They know more because they have to clean up the swath of destruction that doctors describe as "oops."

I took care of her for that last year. She wanted to die at home, so we got a hospital bed and IV stand. A nurse would come several times a week. For the last couple of months, a nurse was on duty all the time.

Through her pancreatitis and BE, I would have been on the streets to find marijuana for her. She had her own crop out back, so that made it easy.

Grass absolutely removed the pain. It did a better job than Butorphanol, Tramadol, Butrans patches, or Fentanyl patches. We tried them all, but pot always worked best.

One nurse told me that he and Mom had chatted about dating and sex. The nurse says Mom wanted him to ask me out. He did. And we did. You have to obey Mom, right?

Mom died last year. Dad had been gone for years. So, I became an adult orphan. It used to sound strange to use that word when I had at least one parent all the time I was in school, but orphans aren't always children. When it happened to me, I felt the loneliness more than I would have thought. Mom was my keel, and life got trickier without her to shake her finger at me. Her main job was to keep me calm enough that I didn't go after somebody, especially somebody who hurt a kid.

Mom was the steam vent on my pressure cooker. I had to learn how to be my own vent, and I quickly learned that (a) it's not all that easy to do; and (b) I'm fairly inept at keeping an even disposition.

When she died last year, I just stayed in Waxahachie. Her house became my house. I like the place, even though it's a little run down now. There's plenty of things not to like about Waxahachie, but I was in my own bubble of friends.

With Mikka and Kris off doing a security inspection of the chicken coop, it left Mr. Austin and me standing on the side of my street.

It was a strange feeling because Mr. Austin didn't ever stand around. He's been a fixture of the neighborhood long before I was born.

He's rich, but nobody seems to know where he got his wealth. I've asked, and he just changes the subject. Others have asked him why he has 2 square miles of property inside a Texas city, but they never got a real answer.

Anatole Austin is the most highfalutin, hoity-toity person you'll ever see.

When he dresses, he does it to the nines. You know how you try to pick a tie or a belt that is compatible with the rest of your clothes? He doesn't do that. Mr. Austin matches colors exactly. If you took his jacket and his socks to a paint store, the color matcher would tell you the two items are an exact match.

Waxahachie, Texas, doesn't have any clothing stores where you can pull that off. Take the test yourself: walk into your local Walmart and ask for a shirt in a medium orchid with a drop of cornsilk. Not happening.

I'm certain he isn't gay. You'd expect him to be gay with such a precise eye for color, but he isn't. Just because it's a stereotype doesn't mean it's false.

"She was a great lady," he said. "Your Mom."

I nodded.

"She always reminded me of Ma Ferguson," he liked to say. I had heard it before. Ferguson was the governor of Texas in the 1920s and 30s, and she was the first woman elected governor of any state. He says he knew both women, but that would be impossible. Do the math: if he knew the governor of the state from 1920, he'd be way too old to be moving around.

Lots of people thought she was corrupt. Anatole said they didn't like to see a woman out of the kitchen.

Gov. Ferguson didn't take shit from anybody apparently. Yup, that's Mom. She was the first female governor elected anywhere in the US. Ma Ferguson fought the Ku Klux Klan all her career. The Klan was the group pushing hardest for that ban on alcohol, Prohibition. She did her best to keep the haters confined and impotent.

That quote back at the start of this chapter is supposedly from the governor. She never actually said it. It was the haters who didn't like seeing a woman in power. It was from politicians who thought she should go back to her house in Temple.

Ma Ferguson released lots of people from state prisons. She pardoned lots of guys who were sentenced for Prohibition violations. She never saw anything wrong with whiskey.

I don't know what she thought of gay kids, but I think I'd like Ma Ferguson.

Here's the deal: Anatole Austin acts like he knew the woman. That, obviously, isn't possible. It goes against everything I know about the aging process.

Entropy always wins.

"Andreas, I have work if you want it," Mr. Austin said.

"What kind?"

"It's my windpump. It started clanking, but then it stopped. It doesn't pump any water. Can you fix it?"

"I'll come look at it in the morning, if that's okay."

"Sure," he said. "I have to be out of town for awhile, so just tell Kris what you need. He'll pay you, if I'm not back when you finish."

Kris will get what I need. How's about Kris being totally naked on top of me in bed? That would be great! He did say anything I need, right? That's what I need.

Kris is straight. Kris is straight. Kris is……

Mr. Austin and Kris turned to walk back to the estate. Mikka took a step toward me. He wanted to stay for a bit.

"Hungry?" Mikka asked.

I nodded.

"Sonic?" he asked. That works for me. We got in my Jeep Wrangler and headed to the drive-in. I headed over to Ferris Avenue, two lanes each direction. Boring street. Flat town. Cowboys with an unhealthy fixation on the Second Amendment.

I was wearing my "At Least I Can Shoot Straight" t-shirt that I made at Zazzle's website. That always gets noticed in town.

Sonic is a regional fast food place. You park and use a mic and speaker to place your order. When the food's ready, somebody brings it out to the car, sometimes on roller skates. I had the top off, so we had plenty of air.

"So, how's it hanging?" I asked Mikka.

"Same old crap. Asshole gypsies are making things rough. I can take them. You know I can."

He could. He and I studied martial arts together. Mikka was always better at it.

"I do worry about Pasha," he said. That was his kid brother who never seemed to fit in around the gypsy compound.

Mikka's thin with curly black hair. I think he traces roots to Romania, but he rarely talks about family. It's a secret or something.

When his family and friends pick on gay people, Mikka really could rearrange their extremities. I don't know why he hasn't done that. Some are really horrible people. I've offered him a bedroom at mom's house, but he never wanted it. He knows I have the space. If there's an emergency, he knows I can help.

Mikka's big thing is getting stuck. That's his favorite word: stuck.

He's happiest when he heads out into the woods, stripping down to nothing, and sleeping under the stars. I have no clue what he does about rattlesnakes and water moccasins. I don't know how he stays away from chiggers and ticks. He somehow avoids all those things, and he won't tell me how.

But the biggest problem for me is what we call "stickers," and I don't mean the decal things you put on the back window of your car.

We have plants that we call stickers. They're a bur grass, and the seed pod has sharp cactus-like thorns. The thorns are so close together that it's impossible to touch the sticker except by the lightest touch around the seed pod itself. We are "lucky" enough to have dozens of species, and each one of those carries the kind of pain you wouldn't even wish on your worst enemy.

The plant uses its thorns to get its seeds stuck on an animal, to grow the sticker population.

If you don't have stickers near you, consider yourself so very lucky. They can make a grown man yell from pain. They even prick you when you're trying to remove them from shoes, socks, and calf muscles. How he walks around out there without any shoes, I may never know.

By the way, a light sprinkling of sulfur powder into socks makes for good protection against chiggers. There isn't any protection from stickers. If you step on one with bare feet, you'll know a level of pain usually reserved for gunshot victims, professional football players, and fight club. (Oh, sorry. You're not supposed to talk about fight club. It's some kind of rule.)

Mikka did tell me about a coyote encounter a year or two ago. It was Mikka vs Coyote, and my gypsy best friend only used his feet. He sent most of the canine flying to the left, but a few important pieces went to the right. He did that with his feet. His feet. Seriously.

Yes, he ate coyote steak that night. No, he didn't bring me the fur.

Mikka can be as scary as the situation requires. He's probably more lethal with his hands and feet than I am with my Glock 9-mil. You don't go into the woods without a gun: snakes, coyote, mountain lions. Even Mikka packs heat when he's out there by himself because there's no way to get help in the backwoods when shit hits the fan. He'd want a gun if a mountain lion came running because kitty is a better runner and wouldn't charge unless cornered or is really hungry for gypsy meat. Whatever bad thing might be in the woods, it's a safe bet they can get to you faster than you can get the police to the boonies.

At the Sonic, I ordered a footlong chili cheese coney dog and a Route-44 cherry limeade. Route-44 means it's the biggest cup they have. The hotdog is so-so, but I love their limeade.

Both of us got messy meals, so we took off our shirts to eat. It wasn't sexual, and we were in my Jeep, so who cares if we ate topless?

Okay, it was a little sexual. He has a nice body. Being able to eat a footlong hotdog while looking at some fetching pecs makes it a great lunch.

Swarthy.

Mikka's pecs look yummy, but they aren't too pumped up. There's a tattoo of Texas on one pec. He doesn't have a six-pack, but his four-pack looks sexy.

There's never been a time where he hid being gay. He's Out. He always has been, and he never cared what you thought about it. He used to say, "What you think of me is none of my business."

Mom's hens absolutely love him. He always takes a second to go to the coop to say Hi. He'd do a dance move or two, and the hens would scream affection. I don't know how Marengo reacted because the hens were quite a bit louder than the rooster.

It's strange, but the first thing he does when he's up at the chicken coop is put his palms together like he's praying. He bows a little and says "namasté."

Mikka avoided most of the mess at Sonic. My lunch took its toll on my chest. Ick.

They didn't make a paper napkin that could clean up all the spilt mustard and chili, so I left my shirt off until I could get to the shower.

chapter two
the fiendish windpump

"Transformation is what happens when we live our life rather than analyze it."
Frank Natale [Professor Trance] (1941-2002)

When I got out of the shower, I was free from Sonic spillage. Why can't I ever eat one of their foot long chili dog?

Mikka was waiting in my bed.

He was dressed like a guy who wanted sex (i.e., he wasn't dressed at all). He was arranged on MY bed like he wanted sex.

Alas, no sex. Damn it. He just wanted to cuddle, and that's always fine with me. No music to set the mood. No gossip chit-chat. Marengo offered somebody his opinion on something every few minutes, but he was the only noisemaker nearby.

Mikka's a good cuddler. I love to sink my head into his chest with one leg between his legs. I'm lots taller than him, but we always make it work. When I sink into his aura, all my cares and worries seem to disappear. He's a 10 on the best friend ranking. I know it, and knowing it makes me feel fantastic.

We cuddled most of the afternoon. The sun was setting when we woke up.

Do straight people have friends who get naked and cuddle all afternoon without having to call it a relationship?

Boys with girls have long lists of what's expected of them. The guy gets on one knee. There are diamonds and tuxedos. That rule isn't for gypsies. He says a gypsy groom's attire is anything with three or fewer unplanned holes.

Dudes doing things with dudes. That area is freedom because we can make the rules up as we go along. That's freedom. We can be sex-crazed men, looking for one thing — and one thing only. That seems a little boring (at least after the first 10 or 20 years). ;-)

We can be best friends who love nothing better than to cuddle in bed for hours on end. That's me.

Mikka makes our infrequent love-making special. We do tumbling with each other. Sometimes we play with gymnastics, but it usually isn't so fancy. The sex between us is a little rare, maybe two or maybe three times a year. n

The most recent time was when I took him halfway up a hill.

"Yee-hah," he hollered. "Ride me, dude."

Did he just say that?

After I got off, he did me on the dam of a beaver pond.

It was what we call a flip-fuck. Both dish it, and both take it.

My guess is that we asked the dam to do things it wasn't engineered to do. Two horny guys need a whole different school of choreography for sex. I'm sure some boy/girl affairs are rowdy sometimes.

The dam's architecture could easily hold up to the occasional passing rabbit. One of Mikka's final thrusts caused a cracking noise deep inside the dam, and I don't think they were the normal sounds of the typical beaver structure.

Beavers were pissed. I would be too.

Best friends… with benefits.

Mikka and I talk about everything, from politics to the cute new guy in science class.

Having friends like that is an amazing thing. Mikka is one of my best friends, but we aren't lovers.

He doesn't want to get stuck, not even to me.

He got dressed and pranced out of the house, after planting one of his juicy kisses on me. M'mmmm, gypsy tongue.

We don't really get much Autumn in north Texas. There are a few weeks where the temperature gets bipolar. Jeans, shorts, jeans, shorts. That's Fall around here.

What I know about Fall foliage comes from magazines. It just goes from hot-as-a-porcelain-kiln to Winter. Autumn lasts about an afternoon here, and that afternoon would be today.

I saw it here once. Autumn leaves. There's a creek that runs through Oak Lawn, the gayborhood of the big city. Turtle Creek has walks and benches and geese and trees. One year, I drove across one of the Turtle Creek bridges, and the leaves stood up and demanded my attention. It was a stunning sight, and I'm jealous of everyone in New England and other places with show-stopping season changes. You are so lucky if you live there.

Rarity: it was a brisk Autumn morning when I took on Mr. Austin's windpump. Actual Autumn weather. There hadn't been any rain, but the world felt damp. A ribbon of fog hugged the ground, and dew stuck to everything. Drops of water clung to the leaves and blades of grass.

You probably call them "windmills." They aren't. There's no mill work here. No wheat. No corn. The guy just wants some friggin' water to shower and to make coffee, and for that he uses whatever water flows under his farm.

Mr. Austin has a windpump. When you go through the main gate, there's a half mile road up to the house. To the left is a one lane asphalt road that goes up a hill. The windpump and its storage tank are on top of the hill.

Years ago, he let a band of Romanian gypsies use one small corner of his farm. There's a big fence across that corner, because he caught some of the Roma redefining the meaning of "small corner." Hello: gypsies.

The gypsy compound was way off in the distance to the left. There are no roads there. You can't get there from inside the farm.

Better said: you can't get there in a Smart Car or FIAT 500, and you're asked politely not to get there in a Jeep.

You're supposed to exit the farm and take city streets over to the far left corner. They have their own gate.

The poor windpump was clanking and thumping and generally complaining. It spouted noise instead of water, probably not what the designing engineers had in mind.

It was a nice hike from my house to the water hill.

I had all my main tools: a pry bar, a gigantic and heavy hammer, a big screwdriver, a can of WD-40, and a roll of duct tape.

Okay, I called it duct not duck. "Duck tape" sounds a little weird.

There was a time I thought the proper term was duct because it was invented to use around air conditioning ducts.

Nope. Not even close. It was invented by the US military in World War II. It was strong adhesive, and it was put onto duck cloth.

My Mom had a motto: if it moves but shouldn't, duct tape. If it doesn't move but should, WD-40. All of life can be managed with those two universal products. They are of cosmic importance.

The windpump has about 15 to 20 blades that spin around in the wind. They were spinning nicely. There are some gears way up top that are supposed to convert the spinning into the up-and-down motion of a pogo stick, or the cylinder of an engine.

The long pole goes into the ground and reaches all the way into the underground water reservoir. Each plunge adds more water to the well channel. The pump brings water up and sends it over to a galvanized steel tank. Modern tanks are plastic, but the one on the farm was old. It wasn't broken, so Mr. Austin never replaced it.

What I don't know is why these country wind-spinners have so many sails. Those electricity turbines in the North Sea and west Texas have 3 blades. That's a huge difference. They're both trying to get turned by the wind. One has so many sails that it looks like a solid disk at a distance, while the other is three toothpicks. Maybe water takes more torque.

I mentioned "Lone Star," and I know why they have that phrase. (Doing the Neener Neener dance here.) They call Texas the Lone Star State because it is the only star on the US flag to have stood alone as a country. In schools here, the story is that the founders of The Republic of Texas were great statesmen who created a magnificent republic. Hooey. The truth is that they started calling themselves a republic to get Mexico to line up for a fight. With a fight going on, they figured that the US would send in troops to help. It didn't work out exactly like he planned, but the US finally reached a deal to let Texas come into the United States.

Texas is occupied Mexico, but don't get all teary-eyed about the poor Mexicans who were brutally ejected from their home by invading Americans.

The story is actually stranger than that. Texas is also occupied tribal territory. There were dozens of tribes here.

Mexico got really tired of the Comanche Indian tribe attacking Mexican citizens. Maybe… just maybe… they would attack if Mexico hadn't declared that all of the tribe's land was part of Mexico. Comanche Indians are a little on the ruffian side of things, but Mexico was playing a dangerous game.

So anyway, Mexico "invited" families from the US to come live. It was supposed to be a band of whitey families with the idea that the Indians would attack these new families instead of doing damage to Mexican citizens.

Texas is the land where guys get all puffed up and plan on using non-combatants to accomplish combat-type objectives.

Don't worry, the test next period will be open book.

I just think the story is cool, especially when the real history is so different from what they teach in Texas schools. There's a reason Texans are considered idiots outside the state. We are idiots who were taught subjects out of textbooks that revise events. Texas schools don't teach kids how to think; they make up fairy tales about all the good Christian immigrants who were brutalized by everyone.

Sorry, I'm just a kid with a cowboy education, and I get curious. It doesn't pay to be curious in the Lone Star because being a Sunday School teacher carries more weight than measurement, and experimentation to prove or discredit the theory at hand.

We're taught what to think. Only a few kids in private schools are taught how to think.

Texas textbooks: a whole special Dewey Decimal for lying to kids. There's multiplication. Experienced, not thought. Texas is enormous, so they buy gobs upon gobs of textbooks. The sales volumes mean book printers can lower the price.

So kids all over the region are taught science by book authors who believe creation went poof over a six day period. I mean, literrally six days.

Texas puts Sunday School fake-science into textbooks, and it's cheaper for other states to get the same textbooks. They're killing their kids' minds, but Texas makes it cheaper to do so.

Somebody, please fix this! We need kids who know how to think.

So my blades were spinning, but somebody in the gearbox was complaining loudly. I kept hearing the voice of Curley from The Three Stooges: "I tried to think but nothing happened. Bwoop. Bwoop. Bwoop."

Could they have put the breakable stuff lower to the ground? I think so, but I was just an English major.

The gears were up with the blades, and that meant climbing a rickety ladder up about 30-feet. It seemed like about a mile and a half.

Galvanized steel. Don't let somebody tell you that galvanization prevents rust. There was rust all over the windpump. Maybe it resists rust, but it certainly can oxidize.

About halfway up, the hammer fell. Clank. Clank. Thud. Bang. Dratz.

I saw it crimp the tower in a couple of places.

I thought about going back down to get the hammer, but I just wanted to get the whole thing done.

Up, up, and up. And I'm getting too old for this, I think. This will sound sad and strange, but I have to report that the subject of heavy hammers and galvanized steel are totally missing from the coursework in American Literature of the 18th century. That's what I know about. Everything else is guesswork. A few times, I guess right.

Anybody okay with rusty ladders at dizzying heights? Let me know, and I'll call you the next time somebody offers me a sweet deal like this.

Truth: I was trying to figure out how to pay the electric bill and my property tax statement. Mr. Austin's offer came at just the right time. The trouble is that I never asked what he was going to pay me.

Here lies Andreas Monet.

Murdered by a rusty ladder.

And he never got paid for the job.

And the gear case was bone dry. Even a Beowulf translator who can't find work in his chosen field will tell you that metal against metal only works when everything is oiled or greased.

I applied the windpump's brake.

That isn't accurate. I tried to apply the brake. Nobody'd touched this particular brake since Moses discovered the North Pole and claimed it for Portugal. Something like that.

My pry bar convinced the brake's arm to turn, locking the sails.

The clanking stopped. Sweet silence.

If you're an engineer, shut up, please. I know you want to laugh at me. If you've lived or worked on a farm, you might have worked on one of these machines.

Go ahead and laugh at my explanation. It's okay to wag your finger at the way I worked.

Laugh.

But... and this is the important point... can you translate Beowulf? I don't think so. Not only can I do that, I can translate the Olde English into iambic pentameter in friggin' Australian English. Go smoke on that.

You might even bring up the fact that you'd be translating English to English. One of them is Old English. I say, go for it. Take a gander at what Old English looks like.

I do my best, with what I have to work with. What I have here is a useless hammer on the ground, a mess of duct tape, a can of WD-40, and a class of smart ass engineering students who think they could do a better job.

I got a chuckle: they probably could. But I got the job, so neener-neener.

So I got all my tools and the broken gear to the ground, after slipping a couple of times. Everything was so damp that day.

Climbing a ladder on a damp day has lots more things to do than climbing it in a drought. For one thing, it's damp. For another thing, Andreas — Beowulf expert — decided to work way up on a rusty ladder wearing street shoes with a leather sole. Who knew that could be important?

And... oh, you know how you work things out in your head where you are the absolute hero of every situation? Yeah, me too.

In this case, I was pretty sure that I could conquer everything that mother nature threw my way.

So I was completely surprised that my walking down the asphalt road from windpump hill resulted in me on the ground. Sure, it was a little slippery. It wasn't ice. It was dew.

It happened so fast that I wasn't able to deploy all my Ninja acrobatics to save me from falling. Nope, I was walking, and then I was flat out on my back with the back of my head being totally fucked. (Excuse my language, but it really hurt.)

Ouch. I mean really really really Ouch. I don't even remember going down. I don't know if I even tried to slap the ground like my Sensei taught. Twist like a cat. Slap the ground. It would all be okay.

But none of that happened.

"You okay?" Kris said as he walked up.

"Does it fucking look like I'm okay?"

"Stay still. I'm calling 911."

"Don't," I said as firmly as I could.

Damn that hurt. I mean daaaa'yum, mother of pearl, hog slap hurt.

In a minute, some of the laborers at the ranch showed up. Most of them tried not to laugh. I made mental notes of the ones who didn't have self restraint... like...

"Et tu, Hank?" I murmered.

They got me stretched out in the back of Kris' car, and I was so embarrassed.

I told them I could get up and walk.

"Cállate, tonto," Hank said with a big grin. It means "shut up" in Spanish. And he wasn't calling me the Lone Ranger's sidekick. It's how they say "silly" around here.

"Ok," Hank said. "Vamos, kemosabe."

So, maybe Hank didn't mean *tonto* as *silly*.

I may have been addled, obviously. That's an awesome word. It means my head isn't working, but in Old English, it ("adele") meant the liquid that comes out when you have diarrhea. Is it a full change in its definition? Or just a realignment? I love words, especially using scat words to describe my brain function. No, wait…

Kris' car became my makeshift ambulance, and we then had the arduous trip back to my house. The drive lasted about a minute and a half.

I sat up in the back seat and stumbled out of the car. Kris was there to help, and I got a hardon. I'm not proud of that, but Kris is the most studly guy in the universe. He's tall with light brown hair.

He is soooo straight. I've drooled in his wake for as long as I can remember.

Kris walked with me all the way to the bedroom. There's no way I was going to pull off clothes, not with my hardon. No amount of counseling could ever relieve that level of shame. You just don't get a hardon around your best friend… straight best friend.

Kristof Halász is 6-feet tall, with dark hair and dark eyes. His chest is nice but not pumped.

His family left Hungary in 1956, when tanks from the Soviet Union rolled into the country. After World War II, Hungary was in the part of Europe "assigned" to the USSR's sphere of influence. Apparently nobody asked the Hungarians about it.

Eventually the locals got uppity. When Hungarian liberties started sloshing around beyond the USSR's comfort level, Moscow (a.k.a. Warsaw Pact) sent in the military to restore the love of all things Russia. Some families had enough and started to bail. They left.

I doubt Kris' parents were the ones that left, but grandparents or somebody upstream wanted out of Eastern Europe and headed west to Austria. Up in the mountains (hills, actually), they were spotted by a soldier from East Germany. The soldier was there to stop precisely what the Halász family was doing.

"Nicht scheißen," somebody screamed toward the soldier. They probably hollered the same thing over and over. It's possible they did some jumping up and down while they screamed.

The soldier started laughing so hard that he almost fell into a creek.

What the savior of the entire Halász bloodline was shouting was "don't shit."

So there's an "ei" in the verb for shit. What they needed to be saying was "schießen" with an "ie."

Sheeesen. It was sheeesen. Shē-sen, not Shī-sen.

The soldier was laughing so hard that he signaled for the group to go on.

This was the only time a Halász messed up anything involving a language. Kris speaks English, Hungarian, Spanish, German, Japanese, and who-know-what else. School days weren't enough for him, and his parents did a kind of home schooling after our regular studies were done for the day.

English was first. Hungarian was family. We all learned Spanish in school. German so the Halász family could avoid making soldiers fall into a briskly-running creek. Where did Japanese come from? One day, maybe I'll ask.

I sat on the side of my bed. Kris had ducked outside for some pot, and he put a bud into a pipe he found on a side table.

"Here," he said.

"No thanks."

"It wasn't a suggestion," Kris said. "Here."

Damn, he's pretty.

"Damn, you're pretty," I slurred after a few puffs. Oh, the shame. I don't remember much after that, but the concussion stopped hurting.

Growing up, I always found some kind of sports on TV at the Halász house. It was never American football. They had a bunch of sports channels on satellite that brought in soccer, rugby, and other exotic sports. Exotic to me anyways.

Soccer was okay. They called it football or "association football." It was soccer.

Players were adorable. They didn't wear much in the way of padding. I assume they each had a cup under their fairly-flattering shorts.

Soccer is way too polite. Gratuitously polite. When a player accidentally makes the ball go out of bounds, he raises his hand. He fesses up to his gravely serious crime before anybody throws allegations.

I mean, who does that?

They also watched Australian football. They play in the Fall (here), which is Spring there.

"Aussie rules" is a sport at a level of loony not found anywhere else. The playing field is huge and oval, similar to a cricket field. They have 4 goal posts on each end, and each team sends about 20 players on the field at any given time. So there's 40 players, 8 goal posts, and a few officials. This is athletic pageantry to make Cecil B. DeMille proud.

The ball looks similar to an American football, but it's bigger and more rounded on its two tips.

In Aussie football, they have to kick their ball through the goal posts, with different point levels depending which of the 4 goal posts you go through.

It's about kicking because it's called football. They can hold the ball and run with it, but the rules say they have to dribble the thing every few feet. Let me say that again so we're clear: every few feet, the player carrying the pointed ball has to dribble it like in basketball. I never tried to bounce an American football. Pointy ball going bouncy-bounce. I suspect you'd get laughed at if you tried it in Waxahachie, Texas.

Go run up to a running back with the New England Patriots and tell him he has to dribble the football ever 15 yards. I think he'd be sorely tempted to set the ball down and come remove the hangy-down part of your left ear. Just sayin'.

Oh, but the nutty Aussie rules aren't running up the bizarre index even more. The rules say it's okay to climb up on the top of another player in order to catch a ball that was kicked from somewhere else. You can climb up on any player, even those on the other team.

"Excuse me, other team, I need to borrow the shoulder of one of your guys to pull down a ball kicked so high by my teammate. And thanks for paying the salary of my make-shift scaffold."

Not only is this okay, but the rules encourage it. If you catch a ball while you're up on the back of an opposing player, the game stops, and you get a free kick toward the goal.

It's a big field, crowded with too many players protected by little more than their jersey and shorts, and nobody wants to do sensible things with their strangely shaped ball. It's batty.

The game that's encased in insanity is rugby, which is the child you'd get by mating soccer and cage match wrestling.

I was watching a rugby game at the Halász house a few years ago. I was a virgin to rugby games. The players still don't wear much padding, but this is a game where a little protection would be the smart thing to do. Rugby rules were compiled by psychotic adrenaline junkies, so padding is completely out of the question.

Where the players in soccer and Aussie rules are often adorably cute, the men on a rugby team look scary. I don't want to run into any of these guys without (a) me being inside an M1 Abrams battle tank or (b) them restrained in a titanium cage.

While I was watching my first rugby game, a player did something and got a whistle. Shameful.

The official called it a knock-on. I took out my phone and shimmied over to ask the nice folks at Google what a knock-on was. Nothing about it. I had to work for it, and one rule explained the knock-on by going on and on about some other unexplained rule. I needed breadcrumbs, body armor, and a salami sandwich. I was going to be awhile.

Basically a knock-on is a forward fumble. Seriously. Why they couldn't just say that is a mystery. The game and the rules are both deranged.

It took me another half hour to find out whether a knock-on is a good thing or bad. Why would this tidbit of information be so secretive? I didn't know. If I knock-on, am I cheered, jeered, chased off the field, or suspended from the game by a pack of Rottweilers with foamy drool?

I would have said that crawling on top of the opponent's players would be frowned at, but Aussie football thinks that's hunky-dory. So a forward fumble is... oh, hell...

A knock-on is a bad thing, not the worst thing but it's apparently something players are supposed to avoid.

Rugby has weird rules like soccer does. Like Australian football does.

The players seem to follow the rules, for the most part. If the rugby crew wanted to shave off the top of a rule, I'd just let them play on. Look at the players. They don't seem as polite as soccer players. They all look angry. Let's just say that if a rugby player knocks you down by kicking you in the cup, they seem the least likely to apologize or help you up.

Kristof grew up around this kind of thing. I was at his house lots, so I had some exposure. Kristof was immersed in it year after year. I wonder if anybody did studies on which sport gave kids the most warped personality. Smart money is on rugby. I think I'll wager golf.

And then there's American football, where over-bulked millionaires dress up like M-1 tanks and run after each other. Yes, we call it football, but there's little actual kicking compared to the other football types.

After each score, there's a massive celebration at the scoring end of the field. All they did was run a little or catch the ball inside the end zone. Nobody even has to dribble the damn football every 15 yards like in Australia.

And they're all liars. When a defensive player makes the wrong move to keep somebody from catching a pass, the entire defensive team waves its arms like an official's signal for an incomplete pass. It's the power of numbers, convincing the referee that it was just incomplete. No defensive pass interference. Nothing to see here, ref.

It never works, best I can tell.

The officials pretty much know the rules. The league asks them if they understand pass interference, and you don't get to wear zebra striped shirts unless you say that you have a fairly good understanding. They study about interference actions. They have dreams about tough calls. They practice.

So why do the players lie? They all do it. It convinces nobody.

Did I mention that Kristof is smart. I mean, his smartness is genuine, and it didn't come out of any official Texas textbook. He wasn't part of the whole Sunday School paradigm of fake science education. He was more like a saboteur embedded in the system.

In high school, Kris intercepted the school's bell system. He found the wire up in the attic. Why was he in the attic? I have no clue. He just was.

He spliced into the wire and inserted a timer to shave off a few seconds from each period.

They brought out engineers, but they couldn't find a problem. They said the master clock and the bells were all working fine.

They brought out the friggin' manufacturer of the clock, but they were just as clueless. They were in some danger of losing the clock contract with the whole school system because they couldn't tell what Kris was doing in the attic.

They turned off the clock completely. The bells still rang.

They unwired and isolated the clock. The bells still rang.

Nobody ever found the timer. After he proved his point about being superior to all the other engineers, Kris removed the timer.

Ego? Sure, why not?

"You ought to ask Kris out," Mom said several times.

"He isn't gay. That's the big reason."

"How do you know without asking?"

If Kris were gay, he'd still be out of my league.

I relit the joint that Kris made for my concussion'ated head. We chatted between tokes.

I told him the mayor had stopped by overnight. He asked if I'd seen Maximilian from the Dallas Cowboys.

"Dallas what-boys?" I laughed. "They drug test."

"Maybe he was quitting or outside the season," Kris said.

"And how do you know all this?"

"We were dating."

Brain explosion.

This is how my entire world collapsed in on itself. Kris -- the Adonis of Texas — was dating a pro-football player. We were best friends, and I didn't know he was dating a professional football player.

Three little innocuous words: WE… WERE… DATING. All the mental pictures I had were rendered invalid. I suddenly didn't know what was left and what was right. I knew forever and a day that the only thing keeping Kris out of my bed was that he liked girls. I thought it was a kind of icky thing to like for sex, but I couldn't argue with his sexual orientation. He was what he was, and what he was was heterosexual.

Now?

He's gay? All I could do was stare at one of the posts on the front edge of the porch.

"You're gay?"

"All my life," he said.

"ALL? Why am I just finding out about that today?"

"You never asked," Kris said in a matter-of-fact tone.

When I asked who he was dating now, he told me that he wasn't dating anybody. His job was too much. Mr. Austin's farm is more important than getting into the Spandex of a tight end?

[Short pause in my story to let you go through all the 'tight end' jokes.]

Oh, no, no, no. This can't stand.

"Can we go out sometime?" I asked.

"On a date?"

I nodded.

"No, probably not," Kris said. "You're cute — really cute, and you're smart. I'm sure you're great in bed. Here's the thing: I'm all about tricking from time to time. You would be a boyfriend, not just a trick. Boyfriends mean attachments."

"Now you're sounding like Mikka."

"Don't go there," Kris warned. My two best friends never got along. Not really. They tolerate each other when I'm around. They even work together, which has to be a burden to Mr. Austin.

41

"At least I knew Mikka's gay," I said.

"How could you not?" he asked. "Don't dwell on it. Move on."

Mikka could put Kris down with nothing but his hands and feet. Kris knows how to rewire the bell system in high school buildings. Mikka does martial arts. Kris know everything in the universe.

Kris didn't want to date because he didn't want a boyfriend. He refused to trick with me. How could somebody not want to trick with me? I tried to imagine the kind of parallel universe where that made any sense. I'm a nice guy, and I've been told that I'm really good in bed.

"Okay," I said. "I won't dwell on it, but I want you to know something. I want you to know that having sex with you would be one of the great events of my life."

I was dwelling on it big time.

He tried to shush me. Dwell. Dwell.

"I've been in love with you since I sprouted pubic hair," I cried. "Maybe before that. I've imagined you in bed, on top of me."

I saw a tear start to race down his cheek, but he turned and walked away.

Every thing that I thought about him growing up… it was all wrong. He didn't even care enough to talk about it.

I live out in the sticks, where I'm surrounded by hateful fucks in cowboy boots. The school system never did anything to protect me from bullying. The local government passes laws with the sole purpose of destroying any decency in my heart. And now, the most gorgeous man in the world says he's gay but never wants to trick with me.

He's one of my best friends ever. I've known him all my life. But apparently I didn't know him at all. I felt like a failure at the whole BFF thing.

Wow. How the hell do you start to process all this? My head was ripped apart, and I have no copies of *Pud-Whacks for Dummies*.

chapter three
state-sponsored terrorism

Be yourself; Everyone else is taken.
— Oscar Wilde, Victoria's ex-con (1854-1900) —

If you have Coming Out or Bullying issues,

Check out FINDING HELP at the end of this book.

I need to vent. This is me, Andreas. Not the publisher or anybody else. Don't get snippy with them.

I can't imagine what it'd be like to have skin darker than mine. Not in the US. Not these days. I won't pretend to figure that out. Let's just say, there are lots of black folk who are much more polite than I'd be, considering how they're treated. I'm full-blood Scandinavian, and you just can't get whiter than that.

You know, Texas used to be part of Mexico. The US swiped it, and now a Mexican citizen can get into trouble (or be treated as sub-human) when they cross the Rio Grande River. That's messed up.

Of course, parts of Texas used to be the Comanche Nation. Mexico stole it from them. Before them, we had the Clovis people, who came here for a romp on the beach and some tasty wooly mammoth au poivre served on a sizzling rock.

So why can't Texas be a place where we respect every shade and hue? It seems simple, considering the history of the land under Texas.

What I know is being gay, growing up in small town Texas as a screaming queen. In some ways it's better than it was, but that's just by degree.

There's this guy — a well-meaning gay guy — who has a campaign to spread the news that "It Gets Better." It's a moral feel-good approach for LGBT kids. He's Dan Savage, and he's one of my heroes.

I have no idea where he hid all my life, because nobody in Podunk, Texas, got the memo about "better" even being one of the outcomes, with a micro-smidgeon's possibility. Now that he's noisy, maybe the bubbas will at least hear about how lousy they are as human beings.

The adults around Waxahachie hate me (for reasons that were never explained). They berated gay kids in front of their own children. That was hater training school. Their kids followed their parents' lead, even those poor souls who were gay and having to pretend daddy wasn't savaging the kid's own spirit. I'm told that I'm supposed to love everyone. I'm told to treat others like I want to be treated. If I were being the main source of torment to my own children, I don't know how to reconcile all that.

I'm sure other places are as tough on gay kids as Waxahachie, TX. But this town has preachers who do little other than bible-thumping malice, and they are some of the most disgusting people in the world. Literally.

The only thing I can come up with is that these preachers had a youthful crush on another student or a teacher, and they were let down badly. Maybe they have emotional scars and need a therapist. I don't know. It shouldn't be on our list of things to worry about, but there's nobody standing up to these Schweinhunds, who claim holiness, claiming to know what god's all about. No. They are either intentionally throwing around prevarication or they made no higher than a D- in the seminary classes that taught what's in the gospels.

If you know a gay kid, let him or her know it's okay. You DO know gay kids, but they may be hiding in the corner of their closet. Afraid. Feeling like they're the only one who swoons over people of their own gender.

To the haters:

Hey, preacher, the word is LOVE. That's what Jesus taught, you babbling moron. Love yourself. Love your enemy. Love your neighbor. I am doing my best to love you too, but you make it so I have to strain so much that I wonder if you are even worth my effort.

And that love-the-sinner-hate-the-sin is a bunch of malarkey.

Your Master said LOVE, no footnotes, no exceptions.

Yes, Jesus turned over the table of some currency exchangers in the Jerusalem temple. I have a few issues with him attacking small businesses, but I don't see anywhere about hating those guys. He just wanted them out of the Temple. Fine, venue-based hatred. If you want to preach against gay people, make sure you're clear that it only applies to adherents of your own flock. Don't preach it to me, even if you think it's some grave error. Keep your boneheaded notions out of my skull.

One more vent, please.

Hey, kids:

When you hear an adult spew hate your way, you have my permission to run and tell somebody that you've been bullied. Get away from that adult if you can. Talk to a counsellor if you can't. You don't have to put up with invidious, homophobic bullshit.

So, Andreas, tell us what you really think.

I know there are plenty of closeted gay cowboys from my days waiting tables. So just go away with your idea that men in Waxahachie, Texas, don't watch other guys. They do. I've seen it.

Every time these rednecks elected a politician, they always picked somebody who wanted to throw as many roadblocks as possible against gay kids leading a normal life.

They say that gay men can't love other gay men. They say we are freaks of nature. They say rapists are better members of society than gay kids or transgender kids.

Society — at least in my small town — has nothing to hold up for LGBT kids. We don't get any role models, so we have to figure out relationships without any guidance from the adults. We have to make up our own rules in dealing with other LGBT folk. We have to find our own moral framework.

It's all guesswork. Sometimes we guess right. Sometimes we make a mess out of things.

Straight society is fucked from my standpoint. I don't really like saying that because I'm not a mean person. But here in my small town, it's all I see being presented.

They're going to hate anything we do. In other words, society doesn't really care whether or not we figure out morality on our own. It will all be evil.

My own experience is that it was hit-or-miss. I did a few things that make me cringe today.

Some things were good, some were embarrassingly bad.

In my case, it did get better. Society had nothing to do with that. Adults — most of them — worked hard to keep things from getting better. They threw roadblocks down. Constantly.

I had a mother who paid what little money she had to get her kid trained in martial arts. No adult in any of my schools stepped up to protect me. I was gay, and they were redneck adults. Their best approach was "kids are just going to be kids."

I had Mom, and I had the best two best friends in the world: Kristof and Mikka. Kris has a razor-sharp mind (and a sizzling hot body). Mikka is the craziest guy ever, but he has a strong sense of protecting his own (i.e., me). We all love each other, and we'd probably die for each other if we had to.

It got better only because we finally figured out how we could make it better.

There was no "it" — no "it gets better."

No, we made it better.

Some days, venting is all I have.

Queen Victoria was on the thrown when Oscar Wilde was thrown into a barbaric prison for being gay. That resulted in *De Profundis*, one of the most haunting and wonderful books of all time. Queen Elizabeth II was on the thrown when the best mind in digital technology — Alan Turing — was shot up with so much diethylstilbestrol (synthetic estrogen) that he ended up killing himself. The Nazis would have won World War II without Turing's work on encryption, and we certainly wouldn't have anything like a personal computer. Fact-check this!

After WW2, the Allies quickly threw out the Nazi's barbaric laws, until they got to the anti-gay laws (around since 1871). That's the one Germany decided to keep. Gay sex wasn't off the books until 1969.

Is anybody okay with all that?

Yes, it happens elsewhere. And yes, England is a constitutional monarch. Big deal: a society that consider itself modern should be ashamed to those cases.

Gay kids are there to witness what's going on. They see their government, which is supposed to protect them, causing the greatest of harm to others just like him. He sees them as their future, and how they react to what they see is always dicey.

Wow. Mom's pot is truly kickass. I was tripping lots, and I was basically unconscious from noon one day to early the next morning. It wasn't a true unconscious state, but I was ridiculously unsuitable to be around anybody (except Marengo).

Dwell. Yeah, I was still thinking about Kris. Dwell. Dwell. Oh, and the electric company's blood out of a rock division was getting downright testy. Dwell. Dwell.

Sometime in the evening, I saw Mikka come into the bedroom. Beats me what he said, but it was nice to see him sitting in the bedroom.

He snuck in without making too much noise. He just sat.

When I woke the next morning, Mikka was still in the overstuffed chair in the bedroom. He hadn't moved.

Awww.

Mikka Cooper is gypsy. I think the proper word is Roma. Sometimes he thinks "gypsy" is a rude word. When he thinks that, there's always something else going on to push him into a corner.

He says his name as MEEE-kah.

The top of his head is about the same height as the top of my shoulders. His hair is jet black, and it has its own idea on where the part should be.

Mikka demands freedom. Being free is the opposite of being stuck. He's lived in Waxahachie all his life, but somehow he isn't stuck to the town. He doesn't commit to anything.

And he just disappears for a few days. He told me that he heads into the woods of Mr. Austin's ranch. He loves to sleep under the stars or even the rain when it's warm.

There's nothing Mikka does that says straight guy. He's always been flamboyant as hell. If you like those "straight-appearing straight-acting homos in polo shirts" who call themselves secretly gay, you just aren't going to like the way Mikka comes across.

That doesn't mean it's okay to cross the guy. You do that at great peril.

Let's just say that when he runs off to the woods and takes off all his clothes for the day, he's still fully protected. If I were out there, I'd have a snakebite kit and maybe snake-resistant boots. I'd be armed to the teeth with guns: at least one serious handgun. There are animals out there who think people look yummy.

Shotguns, rifles, and knives are "goop" or "glue" would just hold Mikka back. Absolutely everything in sight is a weapon if you know how to use it. He really is like that, and I've never heard of that quality in anybody else.

To Mikka, the entire world is a weapon that he can press into service. Carrying a billy club or switchblade just slows him down. Pray to whatever god(ess) you feel that you never see him in action.

I have my own bully. His name is Cooter Keith. I secretly think he turned into a bully because of his first name: Cooter. It's his real name, not just a nickname.

He caused me to get suspended once in high school.

"Fag," he screamed in the hallway as I was walking to biology class. "Homo. Sissy. Fag. Fag."

"Could I interest you in switching to decaf?" I asked, which is when he tried to throw a punch at my face. I deflected it.

"Oh, come on, Cooter," I laughed. "Is that the best you got? And why do you have to embarrass yourself at least once a year?"

Incoming, I thought as I saw his fist coming my way. This time, I stepped away from his blow. Then I threw a jab at his face. He was still pulling tooth parts when security arrived. This time, I agreed with the principal's stern sentence. No school for 2 weeks. Sweet! Cooter got the same suspension, but his came with a dental bill. Public school in Waxahachie is soooooo much fun.

Cooter and I have history that dates to elementary school. He said he hates sissies. I wasn't even aware that I was a sissy. I thought I was plain old Andreas.

I got bullied. It wasn't "gay bullying" because we were just in elementary school. Nobody knew what "gay" meant, and we certainly didn't know who was and wasn't gay.

It happened, and I didn't like it, so Mom bought me some self-defense.

"I'm here to buy some proper self-defense for the kid," she said. She enrolled me in a martial arts school. I didn't even know Waxahachie had such a thing, but there it was. By the time the next school year started, I could hold my own against any kid.

Cooter came up and tried to knock my books to the ground. I stepped back and gently placed my books on the ground in a nice stack, while he stumbled into the lockers. Poor Cooter. I just stood there, looking at a completely embarrassed Cooter. The other kids who had assembled for their first show of the new school year were laughing at my bully, which didn't go over well with the kid.

I waited. He got up and tried to throw a punch. I deflected it into the wall. (Ouch!)

This is my favorite part to this day: he tried to kick me, so I just reached down and grabbed his ankle and pulled up as hard as I could. He screamed as he spun in the air. I think he landed on his back or hip.

I got marched to the principal's office. Mom was called. The rent-a-cop who was guarding the school was there.

"He injured a fellow student," Ms. Smith said.

"Was it Cooter Keith?" Mom asked.

"That isn't relative," the principal claimed. Even as a kid, I knew the principal stumbled into one of mom's traps.

"It most certainly is," mama bear roared. "He bullied my child all last year, and you never did anything."

"But—"

"He beat my boy last year," Mom said calmly. "Do you have your records on how many times that was reported to you? I have a list at home. Each attack on my child is listed. I will be happy to get it and review it with you, the superintendent, and board. Did you record the measures you took to protect him? The list of actions you took is quite a bit shorter."

"We protect all our children," she said.

"Stop," Mom said. "Just stop. I had to send Andreas out to learn martial arts because you failed to do your job. You said nothing against bullying. When it happened, you gave me something lame like 'kids will be kids'. So you need to take yourself down a few notches. You may can play Mr. Helpless with other parents, but I know when somebody is just lying, when somebody is doing a lousy job at what he's paid to do. What are you going to do about Cooter Keith? If you do anything like last year, Andreas knows how to take up your slack. He can protect himself, and I've told him to do so."

Cooter Keith got suspended for a couple of days. There were statements read in every homeroom in the school.

About once a semester, the bully Cooter had a memory lapse. I was armed with martial arts and was always available with a refresher course.

Okay, maybe I went full bore on his ass when a glancing blow would have done. In my defense, I never sent him to the hospital.

My mother cemented her place as #1 Mom in my books.

After the kids saw me take on Cooter, all the other bully-wannabes took note. My street cred was established.

Mikka took notice. The other guys at the gypsy compound were giving him trouble. They always did because gypsies are assholes about gay guys.

He somehow put together enough money to come take martial arts. He was a natural. In short order, Mikka took his skill far beyond anything the rest of us could do.

I think we were in the 2nd grade. Maybe 3rd.

About the same time, Mikka discovered tumbling and gymnastics. He can do flips without touching ground. I've found him just standing on his head on my front porch or against a tree. He said it was relaxing.

My front yard has a 4-foot chainlink fence that was put in when dinosaurs roamed this part of north Texas. He can jump up without showing any effort and land on one of the fenceposts. You don't see him squat down first. He just stands, and the next second he's somehow airborne. I couldn't perch on a fencepost if you built me a ramp.

"Will you live?" Mikka asked. "An answer of NO isn't a showstopper. I got your obit ready for the newspaper."

"The Daily Beacon?"

Mikka nodded with a big grin. He knew I'd have a comeback.

"Please," I said, "when I die, I don't want a single word in that hack. It's like the worst newspaper in history. They pick the most hateful bubba running for office, and that's their pick."

"No, I was thinking the Dallas Voice or The New York Times. GQ works."

"Awww," I laughed. "You spent the night?"

"Yup," Mikka said. "Can't pull anything over on you."

"Won't your folks be worried?"

"No," Mikka said. "Leave that lie."

In other words, he didn't want to talk about it.

He put a box of donuts on the bed. I don't know when he got them. Maybe he dashed out when the grocery stores opened. Maybe he already had them.

"Thanks," I said.

"Boss wants to hire you full-time," Mikka told me.

"For what?"

I couldn't imagine. It's not like he has old copies of Beowulf lying around that need a new translation.

Years ago, I waited tables at a steakhouse.

And don't even try to tell me there aren't gay men in Podunk, Texas. I had a pair of jeans that were so tight, you could read my MasterCard number through the back pocket. When I wore those pants to work, my tips freakin' doubled. Almost doubled.

There's bubbas who like guy-butt. High school boy-butt. It's there, and it's real. I've experienced it over and over.

I'm not proud that I did that, but I needed the money. Cowboys were more than willing to give it.

Of course they go back to their wives — Wanda Sue or Peggy Lynn — and they talk about how the homos are ruining 'Merica.

"Did you bring an application?" I asked.

"Anatole doesn't do stuff like that."

Anatole. So they're on first names now? Oy.

And with that, Mikka sprang up into the air. He landed on the bed in a hand stand. He had one hand on each side, so he was upside down with his head closest to me. Mikka slowly bent his arms, so he moved closer and closer.

We kissed with him standing on his hands.

We kissed with a bit of tongue. I like tongue, but he doesn't ever do that, so I gave him plenty of reasons to know I was liking what he was doing.

Mikka and I have had sex for years. We're best friends with benefits.

This was just a kiss, but it was different. He lingered above me — tongue dancing inside my mouth — for quite a while.

When he was done, he just did a kind of sideways wheel and ended up on his feet.

Mikka left for work, and I staggered out to the front room. There's an overstuffed chair out there. It has real wood accents that were worn beyond their design. It still felt good. Some people have comfort food, like chicken and dumplings or biscuits and sausage gravy.

Mom's recipe for dumplings kicks butt. I think it came from her Mom.

```
Find an old hen that's stopped laying eggs.
Wring her neck. Pluck. Dress and cut up.
Cover with water in cast iron pot.
Add garlic. 4 sprigs thyme. Salt. Pepper.
Simmer covered for an hour. Let the pot cool.
Combine 3c flour, 1/3c shortening or lard.
Dash of bacon drippings. 1c buttermilk or milk.
Remove cooled chicken. Separate bones, skin.
Chunk up meat. Set aside.
Bones & skin for later stock.
Boil chicken water.
Roll out dumplings. Add one at a time to boil.


At serving, add chicken and a little cream.
```

When I was just barely learning to read, Mom caught me making fun of the writer for spelling it thyme. That work couldn't possibly exist, right?

You can do everything but the last line way ahead of time. I sometimes freeze it: chicken in one bag, sauce and dumplings in the other. Before serving, I get everything to temperature and stir in some cream (or some butter).

As her end grew near, she knew it. But she was still Mom inside. Her curiosity never faded.

After she read about vaping, she gave me a shopping list to take to our local vape store. You inhale a vapor instead of smoke.

First came the concoction:

```
Grind a gram or two of pot, as fine as possible.

Put it in a mason jar.

Cover with food grade vegetable glycerin, about an
inch over the powdered pot.

Put the mason jar in a slow cooker.

Add enough water to come about halfway up the out-
side of the mason jar.

Turn the crock to low (but not "stay warm")

Cook for 4 to 8 hours

Squeeze through a mesh filter with holes not much
bigger than 1-mil. If the resulting VG tincture
has grit, you need a tighter filter next time.
```

Then you have to turn your VG tincture into e-liquid. I'm not sure what the "e" is about. I just accepted it and went on to do other stuff without accusing the vape industry of being freaks.

VG isn't runny enough to use in a vaping device, so you have to dilute it. You can't use alcohol or water, but you can use propylene glycol. You can get PG in flavors or with nicotine. Mom wanted nothing but the PG.

It's roughly 2/3 VG tincture and 1/3 PG. Or do half and half if you're squeamish. Mom liked two parts kick to one part runny.

In the back yard, I heard Marengo giving his morning orders. The hens just laughed.

Poor guy.

To use my high-tech doorbell, you just come up and scratch on the screen. As technology, it doesn't have a rich set of features, but it is really robust. Power goes out, some people don't have a doorbell. Mine always works, even in a hail storm.

[scratch scratch]

"Come in," I hollered. My head was still tender. It wasn't on fire like yesterday, but I knew something bad happened to it. Brain wasn't ready to let me forget.

"Hi, Andreas," Mr. Austin said.

"Good morning, Mr. Austin," I said.

"Anatole," he said. "Call me Anatole."

"Okay, Mr. Austin," I said. He gave me the stank eye. I grinned.

"Your mom's weed sure can take the raw edges off a concussion," he said. "Just promise me you'll be careful. You don't use weed, so be careful."

"Okay," I said, "you mean, don't try to drive."

He laughed and said, "No, son. I meant try not to walk. I've heard from guys who smoke something every day of their life, and your mother's weed knocks their tukus for a loopus, all the way to Lubbock. That's way too far a drive to pick up a tukus."

Anatole Austin is older than dirt, yet he doesn't have big issues with marijuana. He owns 2 square miles in an urban (sort of) environment.

He walks like a gay guy. He squawks like a gay guy. Not gay.

He's about my height (6-feet).

"Will you survive this plunge of yours," Anatole said, "or should I send around my friend to measure you for your casket clothes?"

"I'm over it, but thanks."

"Okay," Anatole told me, "but you'll pardon me if I don't believe you. Just stand down for a few days. Okay?"

I nodded.

He sat down. He never sits down. He's always in and out. He says his piece, then it's all gotta-go gotta-go.

"There's a position at my compound that's just about right for you."

"What's that?" I asked.

"I can't tell you," he said, watching for how I'd react.

I didn't react. Just to show him I could play at that level, I absolutely didn't say anything — not in New or Olde English — nor did I flench or any of other "tells" I've catalogued.

"If I ever find out what the job is," I said, "I have to shoot myself. Right?"

"Not quite," Anatole said with a grin. "There's confidentiality involved."

I nodded.

"Anyway," Anatole said, "you wouldn't have to worry about shooting yourself, because we have groups of hired professional ruffians on retainer to do whatever shootings and other detonations we require."

"Detonations," I said with a flat tone.

"Exactly," he said in a close match to my tone. "Now you're getting it."

And I almost lost it. He's funny when he does that, but I don't think he realizes anything is anything but ordinary. Or if he knows he's bat-shit cray-cray, he just doesn't give a freckle's pube.

Wait. He totally dead-panned what he said about ruffians, and that was a complex sentence. Nobody but Anatole can put that much grammar together on-the-fly.

Shakespeare had the best flair in history, but that was when he had his quill handy with plenty of time. At the pub, he might have sounded like Yosemite Sam reciting "Caged Bird." Anatole was doing word magic on-the-fly, with no do-overs.

"I brought a check," he told me. "It's your first year salary. If you take the money, you are bound not to tell anyone anything. You just work for me. You can make up something, but you can't tell anyone what you do. Period. If you stop working for me, you still can't tell anybody anything."

He let all that sink in. Anatole was good at pacing himself.

"What happens if I don't like the job, or you want to fire me?" I asked.

"You will be okay financially," he told me. "It isn't slavery, so you can walk any time you want. But your agreement to keep secrets lasts forever."

"And if I squeal like a stuck pig?"

"Don't," came the answer. "Just don't. You know how pigs end up around here."

"Yup, and according to them, they want more folks who keep Kosher."

"Shall we continue?"

I took a minute. I knew my answer, but I wanted a few seconds to see if any of my unconscious brain cells wanted to send out flares.

"I'm good with it," I said. Anatole handed me a check.

$282,966.37

Crois moi…

Okay, first of all, humans are all susceptible to heart attacks. Anatole took me right to the edge of that, and I'll be damned if he played me like I was an oboe, complete with a double-reed vibrating inside my concussion. It's really hard to laugh when you hurt.

Second, how the Sam Hill did he come up with that number. In addition to being more money than I ever thought of, it didn't seem random.

"Thirty-seven cents?" I asked.

"It is what it is."

He knows exactly where all my tickle-buttons are.

It was the kind of deal where one of my eyebrows wanted to shoot up in a tall arch.

"Uh," I said. See what an English major can do for a conversation? All those days crouched over research in a library were finally paying off.

"Interested?" he asked.

"Uh............," I said and thought.

"Let's do this," I finally announced after a few seconds..

Anatole gave me the check. All I could do was stare at the damn thing.

"So everything about my property is between us. You can talk freely with Kris and Mikka but only when you are behind the walls of the farm. You say nothing here in your house, or anyplace else."

I nodded.

He waited.

"Time flies," he said.

"Ahhh, *tempus fugit*," I said, happy to have something I know about on the table. "It's a quote from the poet, Virgil. I think it's from Georgics. Could be the Aeneid, but I—"

"No," he interrupted. I felt dejected. He hits on something I actually knew, but then he slammed the door on that conversation.

I waited, but Anatole seemed to be waiting too. He was probably waiting to see if I said anything else stupid. I just waited too.

"You know that screened-in area behind my house?"

I nodded.

"First, you are never to go close to it. Don't try to look inside it. Just stay away."

"Okay," I said.

"Time flies," Anatole continued, "are creatures from somewhere. They aren't flies, of course, but what they do could destroy the entire planet."

"Why?"

"They eat time."

It was the kind of pause in a conversation where there's still a ton of noise inside the brain, whirling scratchy noise. If there'd been a shooting on the porch, it would have sounded like a hollow bass drum.

My mind was running full-tilt. What do you say to a crazy person who just gave you $282,966.37 and says he has whole groups of ruffians, armed so completely that you don't even see a banshee coming too close.

"Hopefully, you won't ever have to deal with them."

I had to come back to the conversation. What a I dealing? Oh, time flies, the single, most ridiculous thing I ever heard.

"But you interact with—"

"I do.", Anatole said. "You don't."

"So what am I supposed to do?" I asked.

"Kristof tells me you're pretty good with programming computers."

I nodded, but I bristled when he said that name. Kristof. Again, I have to deal with Kristof. I'm not proud of that, but that's what happened. Mr. Austin was dragging a new scab with a wire brush.

"I have a gun," he said. He isn't threatening me. Is he?

I'd seen the thing. Sometimes Mr. Austin has it slung to his back with a sling. It's a gun, but it doesn't look like anything I'd seen before. It's a long gun, not a pistol. It isn't a hunting gun, and it isn't an assault rifle. It's its own deal.

The thing is over 4-feet long. (For the non-gun folks, that's really long.)

It has a little thing on the butt to put against your shoulder. He has a sight that looks more like a big telescope. That's about all there is to the gun. There's really nothing that jumps up and down to make the shooter seem cool or mega-tough. If you're close enough to see how simple the rifle is, then you're not the target. Probably. YMMV. My point is that if you are close but about to die, your assassin will be using something more conventional. I think.

When you're up close, you see there's some kind of gizmo on the muzzle that makes the whole thing look like an uppercase T.

It is clearly the biggest and strangest-looking thing ever to wear the title "rifle."

"I don't like guns, though," I admitted. "Sorry. I guess I'm off the case."

Bummer. I hated to turn down the work because it seemed such a sweet deal.

"I understand," Anatole said. "I'm looking to hire you as a programmer, not a marksman."

"I never heard about programming a gun."

He laughed. Okay, laughing isn't what you want to hear from an employer who just gave you $282,966.37.

"Ballistics," he said with a grin. "The time flies can't be killed by a regular bullet. I never got close enough to figure out why, and you don't need to find out either. Point is, Kristof" — slight pause to dwell on Kris for a second — "Kristof builds me special bullets that explode near the time flies. That does it nicely."

I had no idea Kris built bullets. No idea. The secrecy around Anatole Austin was solid. On the other hand, I never knew Kris was gay either. Dwell. Dwell.

"Their ballistics are just enough different from regular bullets that I miss too often."

He wanted me to program a computer to help with aiming. He has to be both accurate (hit the target) and precise (you can hit it first time, every time).

So we talked about ballistics.

I won't repeat everything because your eyes are guaranteed to glaze over. It's fairly dull stuff. Dealing with wind and distance will get you an accurate shot. At a non-trivial distance, you aren't necessarily precise. It might take you a shot or two to get close enough.

To be precise, there are some other players. I kid you not about this: the Eötvös Effect. When you drive through a corner above the suggested speed, you get smushed into the door. That's the Eötvös Effect. Coriolis, the rotation of the freakin' earth, moves bullets ever-so-slightly.

If you're a plinker or if you take down the occasional coyote about to chomp down on your nicest hen, you don't have to worry about gravity or the earth's rotation.

If you are trying to hit a time fly that's 1 1/2 miles (2500 meters) downrange, you have to deal with friggin' everything.

chapter four
the hidden sore

If at first you don't succeed... so much for skydiving.
— Henny Youngman, itchy violinist (1906-1998)

If I ever get arrested and have to stand trial for something serious, they're going to hire somebody to get inside my head. That person will go back through everything I've done or said. I have no way to tell if that last chapter will make me seem sane or insane, but the "I need to vent" section is something the shrink will spend extra time reviewing.

So, I hate guns. Yes, I already told you about it. Maybe I just need to retype it because my work just took a surreal turn. Anatole's project (if true) would fall under my "okay to use a bullet to protect the kids" policy. There wouldn't be much difference between me killing a coyote attacking the hens and Anatole killing a whatever-it-is to protect the planet.

"Crock-el," came the unmistakable sound of Marengo doing his morning thing, but something was different.

"Srok, crock," the rooster said. I was hearing one noise every five or six seconds. It went on and on.

I turned in bed to look out the back window. The rooster was flat on its back.

Every five or six seconds, a hen would jump off the top of the coop and land on Marengo's stomach.

"Crackle," Marengo said. There's a wooden ramp up to the top of the egg laying part of the coop. Hens were lined up, queued to jump on top of Marengo.

I couldn't believe it.

I'd been thinking about Anatole and his farm and his strange story about time flies. Best I can tell, something suspicious is going on there, and the time flies thing is a cover.

Eating time. Really? That's the best story they could think up?

It was a day for housework because I needed to think. Anatole wanted a non-gun guy to come work on ballistics (counter intuitive idea) against time flies (nucking futs). The last train to sanity just called "all aboard," and after it's gone the whole arch of my life will be on an irreparably different curve.

Laundry: done, folded, and put away.

Floors: done.

Windows: don't get pushy.

Job: great money for something I can't put on my resumé.

I needed a drink.

The Hidden Door is my regular go-to bar in Dallas. It's a denim bar (read: nobody cares what I wear). Because it's away from the main strip, it's mostly for locals. I'm not exactly local, but I'm close.

There's always an armed guard outside, and he always greets me. Friendly.

The ceiling seems too low. It's been around for a long time. When it first opened, they kept the door locked, and you had to have a membership key to get in. That stopped, but then they'd collect underwear from customers to hang over the bar. I'm sure the Health Department wrote a letter or two, offering extra thoughts on having dirty underwear over the ice machine. Just a guess.

They don't let you smoke in bars in Dallas anymore, but the whole inside looks and feels like it went through decades of smokers. The smell is fine, just the looks of the paneling, make the decor seem out-of-date.

It's way too cramped inside for me, so I get my booze and head out to the back patio. One guy off in the shadows is giving somebody a blow-job. That's a first: I've heard about that going on from time to time, but I never saw it. It seemed like desperation. Why would anybody do that? Maybe they are proving themselves to the audience (me) that they have some merit. Somebody wants to put their dick in his mouth. Somebody wants the guy, regardless of what I might think. That's warped.

I was on my third drink, a rum and coke. I was staring at the back wood fence when I felt a gentle hand on my tush.

"Hey, there," he said. "Why don't I know you?"

"I'm André," I said.

"Carson," Carson told me. "That guy over there is my lover, Jesse."

Jesse was a picture-perfect Latino with a gorgeous smile. He wasn't the most masculine tusk in the herd, but he fit in nicely.

The three of us talked most of the night.

I was about to leave to find a hotel room (too drunk to drive) when Carson invited me to his place.

Yes, it was a 3-way. I'd read about them but never experience it. Carson and Jesse seemed comfortable with each other, and they were willing to let me come inside their tent to play.

When it was over, they fell asleep right where they lay. I put on my underwear and went to the living room sofa.

The next morning, Jesse was all bubbly and friendly. Carson seemed gruff, like he regretted sharing his guy. I don't know why: I never fucked Jesse… just the opposite. Carson took Jesse, and Jesse had me.

They had dynamics in their coupling that I wasn't ever going to understand.

I felt Jesse and his telephone pole all the way back to Waxahachie the next morning. Ouch. It was a 40-minute drive from Carson and Jesse back to my place. Dallas and Waxahachie are close by car … but it's like time travel to the Dark Ages. I hate the boonies some days.

Ouch. Jesse is hung. He was a bit effeminate, but he knows what to do with a guy's ass.

Thanks, Jesse… I really needed that, I thought.

I needed it, but I felt like a floozy. I didn't need Carson's attitude the next morning, but riding Jesse was a hoot. Do straight people have a whole level of society that does that?

Casual sex. Condoms, of course.

"So you went to the Hidden Sore without taking me?" Mikka accused from outside the front screen door.

"How'd—"

"I have my http://en.wikipedia.org/wiki/Romani_people spy network, dude. Gypsies know things."

"You know things?"

"So, how was he?" Mikka asked. "Spare no details. Hung?"

"There was no HE," I insisted.

"Liar."

"No, there was THEM, not HIM."

66

"Ooooooo, kyrie eleison, child. Who the hell are you, and what have you done with my sexually skittish friend, Andreas?"

I laughed.

"What got into you?" Mikka asked.

"Everything dumped on me at once," I said. "First the time flies—"

"No," he said. "Stop."

"But I can't process all this stuff. Kris—"

"Stop it," Mikka said. "I know it's a lot to take in," Mikka said as he sat next to me on the living room sofa. He pulled my head to his shoulder.

"You've known all this all along?" I asked. He did, and I was hurt. He said the rules were in place to protect everyone. Yeah, everyone but me.

I told him that I had been in need of a drink, and that meant the Hidden Door (or Sore to use Mikka's name for the joint). I didn't mind driving to Dallas. Waxahachie doesn't have a gay bar. It's too small a town. And if somebody opened a gay bar there, I didn't want to know which cowboys have sex with other cowboys. It'd be T.M.I. If we had a gay bar, the *Beacon* newspaper would have churned up a froth of cowboys to get the city council to pass a truckload of unconstitutional laws to make my life miserable.

Jesse and Carson just happened. I wasn't trolling for sex. We were just chatting, and one thing led to another. It was better that I drive a couple of blocks to their place than get a DWI trying to get back to my place.

"Did the cops find out who tagged your place?" Mikka asked as he came in the next morning.

"What tag?" I said.

He took me to the front yard. Somebody had written FAG in huge letters on the roof of the house. White paint.

I hadn't seen it.

A call to 9-1-1 brought the police, although I didn't see how they could do anything without evidence beyond the paint.

The pair of uniforms called a pair of suits. They all wanted to hear everything.

Everything. Repeated incessantly. Questions asked relentlessly.

Yes, I had to go look up the address of the Hidden Door. Yes, both Foursquare and Yelp know about "The Door." The bar even has its own website with pictures. No, I wasn't in any of the pictures. I checked.

They quizzed me. They asked when Mikka first saw it. The way the police talked, they thought Mikka and I were a couple. I didn't correct them. Screw that.

By the time they left, they had a paint sample from a splotch on the ground. They had a few hundred pictures. They went around to see if all my doors and windows were locked.

Then came the big lie: "We're on it."

That was one of the suits. He said his fib as they were getting into their cop cars. I knew I'd never see any of them again.

"Hey, Windex makes an outdoor glass cleaner," I said.

"There's a special one for outside? How does it know you aren't cheating and using it inside?"

"You screw it onto a hose," I explained. "Runoff doesn't hurt the plants."

"Let's go."

I don't like going to Walmart because it feels like I'm hurting home-grown businesses. This time, we went to the big guy.

After getting lost a few times, I found the garden chemical section. Of course it wasn't there. And would a clerk know where it is? Yeah, fat chance. I tracked down the household cleaners, and there it was: Windex Outdoor window cleaner.

On the way back to the front, the biggest asshole in the world. It was the jag-wagon that tried to bully me in school. I slapped Mikka's arm, and he saw him too: Cooter Keith.

"Can I go cut him?" Mikka said, bouncing up and down. "Please!"

"Shhh," I said. "Look at his right cheek."

"I can't. He has pants on."

"Face. Cheek," I whispered, pointing at the cheek on my face. "What's on it?"

"Bengalo pula," he said. Don't ask: I have no idea. I was hoping the rant wasn't for my benefit because there wasn't a footnote or glossary in sight.

Mikka finally spotted what I was talking about: two drops of paint — white paint — on Cooter's cheek. My bully from Elementary School is the twittlefuck that painted FAG on my roof.

I got us both out of the store without causing an incident, and I got Mikka to promise that he wouldn't go after Cooter alone. He assured me he'd have half his gypsy clan, but I made him know that I didn't approve of anything.

"He doesn't respect you," Mikka said. "He has to respect you."

"He doesn't respect anybody, mon cher."

"I'm moving in," he said. "I'm protecting you, even if you won't do it yourself."

We grew up together, Mikka and I. We've been almost inseparable since we were kids. Now we Mikka is moving in, so we'll be living together.

"Are we a couple?" I asked when we carried the last box from his car to the house.

"You and me?" Mikka asked.

I nodded.

"You're gadje," Mikka said, "but I'll go along."

"Do you love me?" I asked.

"It's complicated," he said.

"Complicated," I said. "You have a mental list of everything that I've been told in just the past couple of days?"

He nodded.

First it was the time flies. Then came a job building rifles to kill the time flies. Kris is gay, but he wants nothing to do with that around me. And I got Carson royally pissed at Jesse because Jesse stuck his schlong where my sun don't shine.

Anatole is so old that he's been around since the early 20th century, maybe 1910. Something like that. He hasn't aged like somebody that old because he's worked around time flies, and they literally eat time.

All this got dumped on me over the span of a week. I think I'm being very restrained and "together" for having all that crap flying through my fan this week.

Then there's Cooter Keith. In school I thought he fell out of the stupid tree and hit every branch on the way down. I'm not proud of thinking that, but that's the way it was. This fuckwad moved up from elementary school psycho-douche to painting obscenities on the roof of my mother's house.

I swear that's his real name: Cooter. If they'd done something like this to me, I would have hauled my parents into court.

And that really is his family name: Keith. So this piss-ant pickle-fucker had a first name where his last name was supposed to be. Cooter Keith.

Truth: his name might have been a shock that unhinged the kid from reality. Maybe we should all hold hands and hum Kumbaya. (That's funny!) [sound of a fuzzle, coffee spew from laughing face]

No adult in school tried to do a damned thing when he bullied me in school. I had to take care of myself, and I did that. I wasn't expecting anybody to get him this time either.

And now, Mikka — the guy who decided we should live together — says loving me is complicated. Really?

I wadded myself up on the bed. Knees at my chin. Hands in fists around my shins.

"We should talk," Mikka said. "Come on, babe."

"You say you aren't my lover, so you don't get to call me 'babe'."

"I love you, Andreas," he whispered as he wrapped me in his arms, "but don't you have enough to think about right now?"

And at that, I lost it.

We just sat there in bed. Me balling my eyes out. Mikka holding me tight.

chapter five
gaming the system

I just think if you're 44 years old and you're not smarter than you were
when you were 35 years old or 25 years old, just stay in your room.
— Keith Olbermann, meddler, fired from the best news outlets (b 1959)

There's nothing routine about working at the Austin compound. My first day was a tour of the main house. It all looked like a normal house in rural'ish America.

When I first walked in, there was Mikka. He had one of those feather thingies for dusting. He was in the front room, working on shelf after shelf of chachkies.

And there was his leather bustier with chrome spikes.

"Really?" I said.

He has an infectious smile.

"Anatole didn't like me in cutoffs," Mikka told me.

"So you went full-boar…," I asked.

"It's malicious compliance," Kris interrupted at the doorway.

"Ma-what-shus?" Mikka stammered.

"Malicious compliance," Kris repeated. "No cutoffs, so he's not in cutoffs."

"Only he insists on making his point."

"Exactly," Mikka said. "Alrighty then: malicious compliance it is."

When I looked at the doorway again, all I saw was Kris' back as he headed to another part of the house. I keep thinking about how I reacted to Kristof saying he's gay. If your best friend is out-of-the-closet, isn't it okay to talk about you being gay too? Is there a down-side that Kris was avoiding? Did he assume I'd take advantage of the information? (I probably would, but that's a whole different topic.)

Mikka started walking away. When he got to a door on the far side of the room, he motioned for me to follow. We walked down a long hallway that was decidedly different. Where that first room had lots of wood and shelves for chachkies, we were in an area of the house that could be a hospital or school. It was decidedly industrial.

We went into the last room at the far end of the hall. It was full of lockers.

"Here's where you can stash stuff," Mikka said as he rapped on the front of locker "69."

"69," I said. "Subtle."

"Bring a lock if you want."

In a minute, he was nude, for reasons he didn't explain. I like it when he's nude because he has a really nice body. When we were in high school, he got a Texas tattoo on his chest. There's big "7" on his butt.

Mikka isn't hairy, but he has a little bit of fuzz across his pecs, and the sexiest Treasure Trail of soft hair that runs from his sternum down to his pubes.

He fumbled with clothes. When he finished, Mikka was wearing white pants, a white satin shirt, a bow tie. He put on a red and white striped seersucker jacket and a cane. He did a wide swoop with his arms, kind of a grand reveal.

"Which do you think?" he asked as he held up a top hat and a straw boater.

I pointed at the top hat.

"Why?" I asked.

"Your tour of the huse," he said. "I have to look like a tour guide."

"You dressed like a cheating carny."

"Gypsy," he said like that would explain everything.

"What kind a wardrobe is a gypsy supposed to have?" he said. "If I don't know carnivals, what else would I know?"

He walked to the door. With a quick spin of his cane, he motioned for me to follow.

"Really?"

He just smiled. It was all okay. Mikka has that kind of smile. I wondered if the smile is why gypsies are so good at peddling.

"The hawkster," I said.

"Hawk?" he said. "Oh, no, no, no. This is merchandising, *mon cher*. It's technical. They teach the basics in school."

"Hawker," I repeated, "and stop calling me 'Cher.'"

Sleeping quarters were all along that hallway, according to my tour guide.

He showed me one room that was jammed with car batteries. I didn't count, but it had to be hundreds.

"We don't have city electricity," Mikka said. "It's all solar. When the batteries get low, a generator kicks in. I don't hear it often because we have a ton of batteries, but I test the system once a week."

"You do the test?"

"Yup."

Every room has a skylight of some kind. I guess it reduces electricity use, but I don't see how all that plastic survives our Texas hail storms.

The kitchen is a tiny bit larger than most home kitchens. All the appliances are commercial, stainless steel.

"Droboy tume Romale," Mikka said to the woman in the kitchen. She raised an arm to wave. Smart money will be on that woman is gypsy, like Mikka.

Mikka pointed to closed doors. One was Anatole's office. Another was Kris' bullet factory. The third was to be my office.

He showed me a workbench in my room. There was a notebook computer still in the box. I also saw a long box with "Remington" on the outside, so I suppose it's one of the rifles I'm supposed to... beats me what I'm supposed to do with it.

There was also a box marked as "NightForce" — whatever that means.

"These are yours," Mikka said. "Rifle, scope, computer, and some little stuff."

He told me there's Wi-Fi with the password being 4S&7ya. The way to remember the password is "Four score and seven years ago," all lowercase except the first letter. Clever.

I finally got to see the cage at a distance. It's in a room that looks something like a sunroom on the back of the house. Instead of a nice backyard, it has a metal wall with one door. There are about 10 round windows, like you'd see on an ocean liner. The door has a combination dial, like it's a safe or vault.

Mikka let me go up and look through one of the windows. Big deal. So what. It looks like a thicket that has screening on the sides and top.

I didn't see any flies or anything else.

"See that huge rock on the left?" Mikka asked.

I nodded.

"That's about where your dad was killed," he told me.

I couldn't move. I couldn't think. No words.

"We were just kids," Mikka said, "so I wasn't here, but that's the spot Anatole says it happened."

That's bullshit, of course. My dad was Special Forces and was killed overseas. I once heard the word Turkmenistan, which supposedly is where he was killed. That would have put him into the Middle East, between Iran and Russia. I didn't know any of those place names, but I made sure I became an expert because of my father.

He died bravely, the government had told Mom. He was a hero.

It isn't like they create a whole new story for each death. Right?

I pulled away from the window. The image of that big rock was seared into my mind.

After standing there for a minute or two, not looking at anything, I turned to the front door. Mikka called and called for me to stop. I didn't stop or even slow down.

I went home.

Instead of dad being killed overseas, he died down the street from our house? No. Can't be.

Instead of having a secret ninja father, dear old daddy was just a guy with a fly swatter?

Dear old daddy.

Back at mom's house, I sat on the sofa and stared at the floor.

After an hour or so, Anatole scratched on the screen door. I really didn't want to see anybody, but the man just walked in and sat in the chair that's closest to the couch.

"I was inartful," he said finally. I think that's what he said. Truth: words that hit my ear had a hollow reverb to them. I couldn't parse sentences.

He let me stew.

"So he wasn't a secret sniper," I insisted.

"Oh, he certainly was that and more," Anatole told me calmly.

His words came out with reverence, if reverence is possible in this kind of chat.

"Your father saved the world more times than I can count. He was the best tracker I ever knew, and he was a fine marksman. Your dad's gender fluidity never got in the way of protecting you."

Wait. What?

"What the fuck is 'gender fluidity' ?"

"Oh, sorry," he said. "I thought you knew."

No, apparently I didn't.

"When you're ready, I'll tell you— ."

"I'm ready," I said. "Tell me now."

I wasn't ready. How the fuck can somebody be ready for phrases like 'your daddy was gender fluid' (whatever the fuck that means) ?

Gender fluid means somebody changes gender. It's mental. You don't actually swap out your dick for a vagina for an afternoon. The person can't control it. They can wake up male or female or something in between.

"Did Mom know?"

"I thought you all knew," Anatole said. "Sorry, but I don't know how to answer."

"Who are you people," I said, standing up.

I walked outside and up the driveway and just sat on the curb. Anatole let me sit for several minutes before walking outside. He sat on the porch swing.

Let's review. I hate guns, but I have a job programming a ballistics computer.

I don't like smoking pot, but I have a marijuana patch used by preachers and cops alike.

My house has "FAG" painted on the roof by one of the local bullies.

The straight guy I've drooled over my whole life has been gay forever, but he just doesn't want to fill me with his babies.

The gypsy guy who just moved his stuff into my (our?) house is wearing a leather bustier with chrome studs and insists that a relationship with me would be complicated.

And (drum roll please)… dear old daddy was a lesbian who was swatting flies (only they apparently swat back).

Did I miss anything? Yup, it's all way up there on the complicated index.

I heard Mikka come in really late. I didn't move because he was really trying to be quiet.

It was okay because I fell back to sleep quietly.

I was within seconds of reaching over to give Mikka a blow-job. We hang out and sleep together, but we don't have sex all the time. He worked long and hard, so I figured he'd enjoy an hour or so with my mouth.

We didn't do that because all hell broke loose outside. Later for the entertainment.

The noise woke up my bedmate, but he didn't panic. I was about to run outside in my… I sleep necked, so that would have been a show for the neighbors.

"Relax," Mikka said. "It's all good."

When I got outside (in my bathrobe), I saw the machine. Somebody had moved a cherry picker to the drive. I recognized the guy way up in the air as being one of the workers at Anatole's estate. He's the guy who called me "silly" after I slipped and fell on slick asphalt on Windpump Hill.

The man had a power washer, and he was squirting "FAG" that phlegm-bag Cooter painted on the roof.

"Wow," I mouthed. The man smiled from his cherry picker cage over the house.

"They had the boom lift out for something else," Mikka said, "so I asked if they could swing by."

"I guess it means I'm officially out of the closet here," I said.

"Oh, ya' think? Anyway, Emiliano's brother is gay, so he always has our back."

I ran in the house and came back out with the pot of coffee that had brewed itself on the timer. I came with sugar, and fake creamer, and some donuts that I bought yesterday.

"How much money should I give him?"

"None," Mikka said. "Friends help friends."

My roof was de-Cooterized in about 15 minutes. As Emiliano got the cherry picker ready to tow back to the farm, I walked up an put 3 $20 bills in his hand.

"Nope," he told me, "I got your back on this."

My work at Anatole's place took me places that I never thought I'd see.

I started smithing my new Remington rifle. Guns here aren't used on people. They're necessary if you want to get off the trail and head into the woods. I've never killed a living anything… except to protect the girls (chickens) from a coyote.

My Remington 700 was chambered for 6.5mm Creedmoor. The same rifle can handle bullets of different sizes. You have to change some of the hardware, but it's possible to do. Some of those things — like the barrel — are expensive.

A 6.5mm Creedmoor bullet is a little puny. Skinny. It's only about a quarter inch wide, but the cartridge is really long, so I ended up with a lightweight bullet being pushed by a ton and a half of powder. It's "smokeless powder" not "gunpowder" as I learned the first time I said anything.

The powder inside most bullets doesn't explode, not like old-fashioned black powder. New powders fizzle, but they do so really fast. The powder is effective only when it's triggered in a tightly confined space.

There's a ton of different powders. Some are granules; others are like dust.

I spent several hours on the firing range every day, and I got to be a good shot.

Plus I was able to murder lots of paper targets.

The range had marks at 25, 50, 100, 200, 500, and 1000 yards. I only used the first three, but I knew that I was going to have to figure out what to do with the NightForce scope.

Remington doesn't even put a crappy sight on their model 700. I had to do that myself. Dollar here. Thousand dollars there.

I learned something interesting about the gun industry: they make a big deal on where something is made. By far, the largest area for factories is domestic. Everybody makes gun shit in the United States, and they make a big deal about it.

One company says it isn't just their products that are domestic. They make their products only using machinery that's made here too. Good for them!

A few brands do sleaze-ball tricks. Springfield Armory sounds American. The Massachusetts firm supplied weapons to the American Revolution. Only they closed up here. You can only get a pistol from Springfield Armory that's made in Croatia, one of the areas that used to be part of Yugoslavia. I'm sure they are really nice people. I'm certain that they try their best. Point is: an American company with a long history of employing people in Massachusetts is now paying people in Croatia.

Another company — Glock — was started as a Swiss / Austrian company, but Glock now manufactures some of its semi-automatic handguns in Smyrna, Georgia, in the south eastern part of the USA.

Don't get me wrong: some gun people have bizarre politics. Bizarre to me. They cross over into hateful sometimes.

I have t-shirts: "At least I can shoot straight" and "gun-toting liberal."

I have a couple of silly shirts too: "there's no such thing as too much ammo (unless your house is on fire)". And my favorite: "I reserve my right to arm bears" with a picture of a heavily armed Smokey Bear.

You didn't buy this as a gun reference, so I'll spare you the minutia. It's like they gave me an erector set, and it's so cool.

The goal is to get the sight to be absolutely parallel to the barrel, and mount it so the rigorous jolt of firing the gun over and over can't dislodge anything.

I used epoxy to mount my sight! Epoxy, and it's not for stickability.

So there's the rifle that has four little screw holes drilled in the top of the barrel. I needed to get rings mounted on the barrel. One company has rings with mounting holes to match my rifle, but I figured (correctly) that this option would hold up to the most violent jolts. It was also unable to guarantee me the perfect alignment. We're going for perfect here, but I want to get out to 1000 yards on the range. Not only that, I wanted to make sure Anatole could go out further (like killing a can of root beer on the moon on the first shot).

Guns have widgets. Rails are one kind of widget. I decided to put rails on the top of the rifle. They have rings that plug onto the rail, and NightForce scopes can be held really steady by the rings. I wanted to lock down the scope without using glue to keep it still.

It has to be absolutely parallel to the barrel, and it can't move even a micron, on the 5,000th firing. It has to be able to handle an explosion kicking the rifle around.

It took me two days, but the result is amazing.

I put some natural shoe polish onto the barrel. That's important because I don't want any epoxy sticking to the rifle.

After the shoe polish, I removed the four placeholder screws. It's where the rail was to go, but I wanted to make sure I didn't get shoe polish into the pre-drilled holes in the barrel.

Then I got the rail. You have your Weaver rail system, and you have the Picatinny rail system. To tell you the truth, they look exactly the same. (Note: don't send me mail about the differences. I really don't care. The main thing is that I love saying "picatinny.")

The rail is a series of notches. Companies make things that clamp onto the rail. In my case, we're going to clamp rings.

When I laid my Picatinny rail onto the barrel, I could rock it back and forth… just a little. Almost right counts in horseshoes, not ballistics.

First, I put 4 pipe cleaners into the 4 predrilled holes in the barrel.

I then mixed about a tablespoon of epoxy and spread it onto the underside of the Picatinny rail. Picatinny. Picatinny. (Sorry. Words are soooo fun.)

Once the epoxy was spread evenly, I pulled out the pipe cleaners.

Next I gently put the rail onto the barrel and pushed gently. When the screw holes were all lined up, I screwed the rail to the top of the gun. Finger tight, as they say.

The day's last step was to wipe away the ooze. Some epoxy decided it didn't want to play with the others, so it crept out of the tight space. I didn't want it there, so I wiped off the extra.

Picatinny. Picatinny.

The next day, the epoxy was cured. I removed the four screws and pried the rail free.

"Free from epoxy?" you ask.

Absolutely. The shoe polish on the barrel was a kind of releasing agent. It formed a tiny layer between the epoxy and the barrel. The glue couldn't bond with the shoe polish.

So I had this rail that didn't just fit my rifle, it was an exact match. My rail was formed with no other rifle in the world. The whole process is amazingly simple.

What I love the most is that none of the college kids who invented epoxy knew how abusing their compound would end up as the most amazing science project ever. Using a non-stick bonding agent is the kind of process I like. Bedding a rifle scope isn't covered by the directions on my epoxy packaging. Nope, because I was breaking the rules.

Next I took off the rail to get all the shoe polish off the barrel. It was natural polish, so it didn't leave any black or brown residue.

I had rings that bolted onto the Picatinny rail. I also had a foot-long pipe that was exactly the same diameter as the scope (30mm). I put the pipe through the rings with a little bit of grit. People in the know call it lapping, but I'm not really in the know. After a few twists of the pipe, I could see that some parts of the inner rings were worn away. Ah-HAH, the rings weren't exact. Left alone, they would have scratched the $2000 optics. Plus, lapping the rings would give them a snug fit. And comparing my rifle against yours gives me a smug feeling.

That night, Pasha was standing on his head on our front porch.

"Are all the Cooper men weird?" I asked Mikka.

"Pretty much. Is that going to be a problem?"

"You won't take me to meet your folks, so probably not."

"Let's go. Right now. Don't ever say I failed to warn you, especially after they put 12 gauges of shot through your chest."

"Hey, lovers," Pasha said.

"Hey, roach," Mikka said as I unlocked the front door.

We all went in, with Mikka and me flopping down on the living room sofa in each other's arms.

"Awww, that is so sweet," says the roach. "I got a question."

"Congratulations," Mikka said. "We have answers, but nobody guarantees that any of our answers are going to be anywhere related to your question."

"How do you know if you're gay?"

It stopped both of us. I wasn't touching it.

"I don't know, lady bug," Mikka said. "You just know. You're watching a movie with the latest Hollywood star, and you see you got a hard-on. You want to buy a cucumber to... no, never mind that."

Pasha waited. Considering things.

"I'm a fag, bro."

"Please don't use that word in my house," I said. I was as calm as I could be.

"Sorry."

"You are gay?" Mikka asked, staring out a window.

"I never did shit, but yeah, man. That's me."

"You know what dad's gonna say," Mikka warned. "He will kill you if he finds out."

"I'll leave," Pasha said with that teenaged invincibility. "I'll go up into the woods."

He started crying. When I moved closer to hug the kid, he got up and ran out the door.

chapter six
opus: the project

"How should I know if it works? That's what beta testers are for. I only coded it."
— Linus Torvalds, digital pied piper —

"Send code."
— A SmartAss BBS programmer answering a request for a new feature. —

The editor says I have to warn you about the shoe polish in the previous chapter. What I used was wax. You can get polish that's waxy or liquid. The fancy schmancy liquid polish doesn't work. Don't use that because it isn't a releasing agent. Use the old fashioned wax polish.

And while I'm on the subject, why the Sam Hill are you taking gunsmithing tips from a romance novel? You are supposed to get your rifle training off YouTube.

Thanks for putting up with me going on and on about gunsmithing. I'm really not one of those "gun people." I'm not!

The National Rifle Association used to be cool. It was founded in 1871 because the founders were shocked at how poorly the kids could shoot in the civil war. Truth: the Union Army reported that it took 1,000 bullets for each Confederate soldier killed. They could march up and down a field, but they literally couldn't hit the broad side of a cow's ass with a 2x4. Horrible shots.

The NRA was founded by some Union generals to teach kids how to aim. They had competitions and other events. They offered patches and trophies.

It was all fine for a hundred years. Then in the 1970s, everything went to hell. Some goofy rightwing politicians took over. The NRA began to present itself as a hateful and unbending lobby group. They don't understand the concept of compromise.

Fact-check me on this. Go ahead.

In short, they are acting like they want the whole country to turn against them. They seem to be sabotaging the Second Amendment... to convince the country to repeal it.

Work. Home. Work. Home.

Sound familiar?

Mikka dragged me out to one of those home improvement stores. He bought us a washing machine and dryer. I helped plumb and wire an area on the back porch. He talked about creating one of those all glass rooms, but it hasn't happened so far.

Every few weeks, he'd had enough of Waxahachie and would head into the woods for a day. Rain or shine or snow: he didn't seem to mind any weather.

Saturday brought great weather to Waxahachie. Mikka and I opened all the windows and let nature air out the house while we goofed off on the porch. Goofing off is serious business, and the took our goofing as the most important job in the world.

"I like having you living here," I told him. Mikka smiled as a reached out to squeeze my shoulder. It was more mushiness that usual. He's usually a ball of kinetic energy that turns flips and handstands.

"Yeah, me too."

The hens cackled. They weren't reporting any problem. They weren't picking on Marengo. It was just a nice day, and the girls were enjoying it.

"I love you, Andreas," Mikka said softly.

And the world as I knew it stopped.

Go back and read that line up there... the thing that Mikka said to me. It came out mellifluously. Gentle waft of phonemes and pheromones. They were the words that my heart had dreamt all my life.

The only word that popped into my head was mama. I knew she was smiling down at me. She'd be grinning with all her pearly whites glistening. Mother would be so happy, so proud of me.

He said, "I love you, Andreas." What the fuck am I supposed to do now? We didn't cover this in social studies or even sex education. We sure the hell didn't talk about it in the boys' bathroom at school.

A man — a good man — the sweetest man I ever met — told me that he was in love with me. He didn't have to do that. Lord knows there wasn't any family pressure from the Roma for us to be with each other.

We knew each other all our lives, and Mikka was my best friend. But we could have stayed friends, and he could have slept with me for as long as he wanted. We could have done that, but it's not what Mikka wanted. He wanted more.

Nobody ever said that to me. Mom did, but that was different. He and I were close, close friends. We were THE CLOSEST.

"Yoo'hoo, earth to Andreas," he said, reaching out to close my lips together. I had been standing there, not saying anything, not doing anything. I didn't even sway back and forth.

"You got stuck," I told him.

"I did," Mikka said. "Any objections?"

I just smiled and shook my head to say No objections. None.

He pulled me down, to lie on the porch, and he climbed on top of me. We kissed. Oh, did we ever kiss.

You may play out this kind of thing all the time. It was my first. A grown man… my best'est friend ever… just went opposite of everything he holds close, and he said he loves me. He got stuck, and I'm the reason.

It was the first time I felt like I could let go of everything. I got lost inside his eyes with his black curls brushing across my face.

Mikka cupped his hands behind my neck and pulled me closer. We were already close, so it felt like a hug — the most loving hug ever.

In a smooth change, he pushed himself to stand up. He moved his hands to behind my shoulder blades and pulled me upwards. When we were standing, he started pulling me into the house.

"Sastimos, Meeks," a voice came from the sidewalk.

"What the fuck does he want?" he said. Mikka broke free from me, and went over to talk to the kid. The boy was a teenager, 15 or 16 years old. Pasha and Mikka talked for a minute, then the kid turned to walk away.

Mikka was back, pulling me inside.

He closed and locked the door behind us. I never used to lock the doors or windows. Mom took me on a weeklong vacation one time and left the door standing wide open. With hateful pricks feeling their oats in Podunk, I had to start locking everything down. Mikka even got a tiny video camera that mounted on the wall of the front room. It stored whatever happened onto a little plastic card, about half the size of a postage stamp. I could put the video camera's plastic card into a computer to watch. It worked like the card that I used in my digital camera over the years, only the new gizmo gave me video clips, not just stills.

"It's a room," I said the first time I saw the recording. "Exciting plot to the movie."

We got out of our clothes as fast as possible. He was kissing me, which made stripping difficult. I didn't object.

He picked me up and put me onto the bed, and then he slowly eased himself on top of me. I felt his warmth engulfing my entire body.

Mikka gently moved my legs out of the way. He took me, with no lube other than saliva. I've never had a guy in me who was so gentle. Mikka moved so slowly.

I never felt like this before. He always has some internal metronome. His head has his own beat going on. Not this time. Somehow.

It wasn't a testosterone bam-bam. He felt me, every part of me, and he was so into it.

We both got tested, so we ditched the rubbers some time ago.

It was so slow that I should have missed his climax, but I didn't. I felt every drop of Mikka inside of me.

He stayed inside but we rolled over onto our sides, and we stayed there for 5 or 10 minutes. My fingers did a circle-8 on both pecs, and then I traced the soft hairs of his Treasure Trail all the way down to his—"

"You got stuck," I whispered.

"Totally and completely."

"Me too," I grinned. "I got stuck too. I love you, Mikka."

When Mikka unlocked the front door, his brother was still here. He was at the screen door.

Jet black hair: gypsy… check.

Standing on his head on my welcome-mat: relative of Mikka… check and check.

"Whacha need, Pasha?" Mikka asked. I think that's the name of one of his brothers.

"I smell you, bro," Pasha said. "I smell both of you, and it's intense."

"Focus, Pasha."

"Y'all just had sex. I can smell it. Let me in: we need to talk."

I put on my cutoffs and started to walk to the kitchen.

"Come join us," Pasha beckoned. Beckoned. Really?

"One of you is Andreas," Mikka said. "The other's Pasha. You guys can work out which is which."

"Wow, the boy toy," Pasha said. "Very pleased to have the name, gadje. Oh, Meeks, dad's gonna shit. Payo in the family. I love it. Not even raklyi. I gotta be there when you tell—."

"Nobody's saying anything. Got that? GOT THAT?"

Pasha nodded.

"Good," Mikka said. "Don't drift away from English."

"Delicate gadje," Pasha said. "Good to know."

"I mean it."

"When are you guys getting married?" Pasha asked.

"We...," I started to say.

"I asked him," Mikka said (a lie). "He hasn't had the chance to answer 'cause there was this crumb-crushing gypsy standing on his friggin' head at the door."

They both looked at me. What was I supposed to do?

"Yes," I said to Mikka. Both of them turned backflips in the living room. It's a tall ceiling. But still....

Mikka came up and planted a really wet kiss on my mouth and halfway down my throat. He even squeezed my butt... same butt he just used so tenderly.

No, wait. If he was caressing my ass, why does he have both arms around my back? I moved away from Pasha's eager hands.

"Pasha," I said. Mikka figured out what was going on really fast. His arm moved so fast, you could hardly see. He backhanded his brother, who fell back onto the sofa.

"He doesn't mean to be rude," my new fiancé said. "He's just happy for us."

I smiled at the kid.

"More or less, gadje," Pasha said from the sofa. "I'm hoping Meeks shares with his—"

"Not happening," I said.

"Which of you is the woman when you fuck?"

"Pasha!" Mikka threatened, but I calmed him down.

"Good question," I said.

"Stupid question," Mikka corrected. "We're both guys. It's the whole point of being gay."

"Wow, you used the word," Pasha said. "That is so cool. Used to be he wouldn't label himself. Labels would get him stuck on one image of himself."

The whole gypsy thing with being stuck… I still don't understand any of it.

"I want to be gay too," Pasha said with a wide grin.

"No," Mikka said. "You don't choose to be gay. You either are, or you aren't."

"I wanna be Andre's woman," Pasha announced. "I want to be gay for him."

I could feel Mikka's blood pressure rise.

Time flies. There's a book about that.

I told you the title but immediately went off in another direction. We have time flies. We really do.

But… when you found out this was about flies that eat time, you rolled your eyes. Admit it. You were ticked that I suckered you in with an outlandish plot object in a science fiction tome that would give Kilgore Trout a hard-on.

And then I poured it on thick by writing about everything other than flies or their dietary restrictions. It's almost bait-and-switch.

I've never seen a time fly, but Anatole swears they exist and their dangerous. They killed my father. who might have been my mother at the time because of… you know… I'm not going to litigate dad's gender thing.

I mean, how the fuck am I supposed to work through all this shit? They said my dad was actually a trans-woman, I think I could work through most of that, assuming I understand what the underlying issues are and how they present themselves. A counselor would help. Dad has no other relatives who are still alive, so asking next of kin is a non-starter.

Time flies.

So… my dad woke up lesbian some days.

Mom lived five years without a pancreas, and that ought to be some kind of record. Yeah, mommy!

We have the most awesome patch of the demon weed that's been growing since before I was born. Everyone from cops to politicians to preachers and rabbis tend to the plants. I do nothing.

When my house was under attack by the most homophobic pigeon fucker in town, the cops did nothing. Maybe I should have shown them pictures of them tending the garden, but I didn't. I'd probably have to destroy the pot afterwards. We didn't get to that level yet. I gave them Cooter's name, but nobody was going to have my back. They never have any gay person's back. Welcome to friggin' Texas.

I literally hate guns, but gunsmithing is how I earn money. I've become a crack shot with long guns and pistols. I study ballistics until I dream about the stuff.

On my own, I practice fast draw. I'll never need it, but it's fun.

I like tending my farm, but the rooster is a pot-head who breaks loose that mounts daring daylight raids on my employer's farm… targeting the… uh… I have no clue what he wants at Anatole's estate.

My lover has been my best friend all my life. He's stuck on me, which is serious for a gypsy. Every part of Mikka's body is a weapon, and he knows how to deputize sticks and garbage cans whenever he needs extra tools to control a situation.

Lover's kid brother wants to be my woman. I'd explain that we'd both be bottoms, but I'm not sure he'd understand.

It's my life. It's confusing. Parts of it are maddening.

What I really can't figure out is how do I process this shit?

And how do I make room for time flies?

The first time cum came out of me like a big geyser (lie: it kind of squirted like it was the last little bit of a tube of toothpaste), it was into Mikka's hand. He was terror-stricken. He jerked his hand away like I doused him with sulfuric acid.

It spooked me too, because I didn't have a clue what just happened.

That wasn't my exact reaction. I didn't know what happened. I didn't want anything bad to happen to Mikka, who by now was cowered in the corner of the room shaking. The thing of it is: I really really liked the way whatever-it-was felt.

I wanted to figure out how to make it happen again. Mikka had jacked me off, even though we didn't know that word. We were just stupid kids, looking to have some fun.

When you're sneezing, there's a splinter of a millisecond where the world goes away, and your sneeze is all-consuming. That's what my first ejaculation felt like. Trippy.

Mikka had been telling me all about this secret thing guys can do. He wanted to show me. We talked about it for a week or two. We talked about it so much that I thought I was going to have to pop him in the face to get him to shut up.

Mom was out of the house, so we had the place to ourselves. We went back to my bedroom, and he showed me. It got big. It felt

95

really good. I didn't want him to stop, and then… holy fuck… wow. I mean WOW.

I had no idea what just happened, but I wanted to do it again. Right then.

When I got my eyeballs down from the roof of my head, I saw Mikka — panic-stricken. He was trembling and crying against the far corner of the room. His mouth was moving but nothing was coming out. He shook violently.

Enough build up. It was a major scene. It was something that neither of us would ever forget.

I had my first wonderful, magnificent orgasm.

Mikka thought he broke his best friend's dick.

It was all grown-up ejaculate. We'd never seen anything like that. We never hear that's what a dick might do if you rub on it a certain way. It was a first for both of us: agony for my terrified best friend, and ecstasy for me.

"I have a whole new Happy Place, man," I told him with the sweetest giggle ever.

"You don't want me to call an ambulance?" he asked shakily.

"No, I want you to do it again."

We stared at the blobs on my stomach for awhile. We had no clue what they were.

I touched it and then tasted it. So. So.

Mikka did the same. He loved it so much that he licked my stomach clean. I saw him peek up at me once or twice to make sure I wasn't about to die or have a stroke.

We continued to be best friends after that, only we were friends with benefits. There never was anything about romance be-tween us, but we sure knew how to play each other's body like the well-hewn machines they became.

"Happy birthday, Andreas," Mikka said.

Wow. Top that for a 13th birthday.

It's be years before I could really do what we just stumbled into. I didn't do it with another person until, maybe, 9th grade.

Oh, the memories…

There's a theater up in Fort Worth — the Scott Theater — where they do plays from time to time. The place is fairly small. It isn't a huge concert hall to have Broadway musicals. Scott is cozy.

Mikka and I got walk-around money by doing odd jobs. Theater is hard work and not for the faint of heart. You know all those pretty lights that come in from the highest part of the theater? You know, about 178 stories off the ground?

Unrelated: why are "green rooms" never green?

Some fancy lights (read: expensive LEDs) are motorized, so the theater company doesn't have to hire crazed kids who are stupid enough to endanger their lives for minimum wage. So what if it was a job that would give any OSHA inspector a stroke? Somebody (raising hand) had to point all the lights suspended hundreds of feet off the ground.

Mikka and I did the job. We needed the cash, and it's always fun (if not treacherous) working with Mikka. And — in case I didn't mention it — we really needed the cash. Well, I needed the cash. I didn't know it then, but the gypsy was well-off more or less.

This one night, we finally got finished at about 4:00 in the morning. The place was locked up tight. Fortunately, the stage door is a crash door, so we knew we could get out. That's far from the most festive exit. What we actually did was go outside from a secret door up in the control booth in the far back of the theater. There's a spot of roof there. It's flat and covered by tar and gravel. It shows 30 years of wear from all-nighters. We went out and scaled down a pipe. That's much more fun than exiting from some stupid door. Note to thieves: no, you can't get back in that way. Crews are careful with their toys, and that roof certainly qualifies as toy (Andreas clears his throat innocently).

Back to the lighting job on the death-defying walkway over the seating area (the "orchestra" as it's called). Anyway, Mikka decided this would be one of our 2 or 3 sex days of the year. He was holding onto my pants as I leaned way too far off the walkway. It was the only way of pointing one light because somebody forgot to bring the stick.

He left me hanging after the light was done and let his free hand explore my butt through my shorts.

"Honeydew," he said. "Used to be tomatoes."

"Please get me back on the walkway," I pleaded.

"So plump."

"Motherfucker, I'm not kidding. My body language will confirm that. Get—"

He reached between my legs.

"Ooooo," he said, "baby needs that thing worked on."

"Mikka, I swear I'm going to remove your spleen and force-feed you with it."

He finally pulled me back. With me hanging onto the 9 inch walkway, we made love. I had one foot on a fresnel and the other on what was probably a leco (a.k.a. ellipsoidal, for the purists). Sorry that I didn't do a good inventory, I was kind of busy. The "bed" was only a 9-inch wide board that was dusty and creaky. Oh, and one wrong move would put an ugly hole in the top of the theater. It was a fall of, maybe, 20-thousand feet, so I might make the local newspaper (which just has to be better than the rightwing crap I get at home).

That was our weirdest and dustiest sex-backdrop so far.

I've never seen Mikka frown when we're having sex. I hear about guys putting on their game face. I'm manly, man, so I need to look tough.

He doesn't laugh or anything. I rarely see teeth, but you can always tell that he is having the time of his life. I'm usually happy to help.

When our eyes make contact during sex, we both smile. Big smile. There's no better way to say "I love you" and "This feels totally awesome." The first of those messages is the one that sticks, but I'm a big fan of both.

chapter seven

tattoo texas

I tell you, we are here on Earth to fart around,
and don't let anybody tell you different.
— Kurt Vonnegut, Kilgore Trout's literary agent —

It was a rainy day in Waxahachie. So that's the day I picked to go to city hall to pay a tax bill that'd been overdue for months. Afterwards, we were going to the range to practice with my 9-mil handgun.

I also needed to get an updated registration sticker for the Jeep. Mikka hopped into the passenger side because he wanted to grab lunch before going to shoot.

I always like being with him, so he didn't have to beg.

It was the first of the month, so all the lines were longer than usual. The rain wasn't helping anybody's mood.

They definitely have the technology to make lines move more quickly. They only need to hire a few more clerks. Guess what that takes? Money. Tax money. You get what you pay for, and none of the rednecks in town want to give government a nickel.

Rain. Slack-jaws. They all talk in a dialect that reminds me how hateful they are.

Get me in. Get me out. I don't like being in city hall. The locals hate queers, and I'm less and less fond of them every minute.

The line at the tax office moved slowly, but at least it was moving. My property was all paid for... all the city services, like hiring people to find the douche-cracker who painted FAG on my roof... like that's ever going to happen.

The clerk — Wanda, according to her lapel pin — smiled sweetly when she stamped the tax bill PAID.

Mikka and I were walking through the crowd to get over to vehicle registration. Here in Texas, it isn't DMV or DPS. Car license plates come out of the local tax office.

It was all under one roof.

Mikka took the Jeep paperwork and headed to the bathroom.

Then pain. Mouth. All of a sudden. No preliminary anything. No warning.

My mouth was holding too much of something. I didn't know what, but it really hurt.

Stench, too. Ick.

Then slap. Clack went my skull as it hit the cinder block wall behind me.

More pain as the back of my head was slapped against the heavily-painted cinderblock wall.

Commotion. My attacker rustled around. My arms were flailing a little, and I didn't see Mikka nearby. I hope he was okay.

There was a fist inside my mouth.

"Hey, faggot," Cooter Keith said. Ah, okay. That explained the smell. He hasn't used mouthwash since Milton Berle was president.

I wanted to respond, but there was a dirty fist in my mouth.

I responded the only way I could.

"OUCH," Cooter said as I chomped down on his fingers. Poor baby. He might not have considered this as a possible retort. Don't forget that he was my bully when we were little kids, and I went to martial arts school to learn how to protect myself in most situations.

In all fairness, sensei never instructed us on any scenario that had an entire fist in my mouth. We had no class on handling fists in the mouth. Why would anybody do something like that? Cooter had to derive some meaning from it.

With one hand he slammed me back against the wall. I didn't try to stop him.

Ouch. I was just getting over the concussion that I got falling on a slick road at Anatole's farm.

"Ouch," I said. "Stop it. You're on the edge of pissing me off, oh, ye of little dick."

He put his bloody fist back in front of my mouth. This time, it was just for show. He was trying to be intimidating.

"Hey, faggot," he screamed as people moved back to give us plenty of room.

Deputy sheriffs were there. Did they come help the gay kid? Oh, heavens no. Nope. No how. No way.

Gay kid was on his own: not a problem.

"So asshole," Cooter said in a tone he probably thought was menacing. (Spoiler alert: it wasn't menacing at all.)

"What's to keep my fist from taking out all your teeth?"

"Oh, that would be the Glock 43 pointed at your goobers," I said. My 9-mil had been in a holster in the small of my back. I always keep my shirt tail out, so it was really simple to pull out the little Glock. Nobody ever knows I'm packing heat. They don't need to know because I hate guns, and I never use guns. And....... there is now an exception to my rule.

"GUN!" somebody screamed. There was a mad dash to the exits.

He pushed his fist. I pulled my finger.

Boom.

Fuck, that's loud when you aren't wearing ear muffs. I always wear ear protection, and I had never been next to a pistol firing a 9-mil bullet.

Fuck.

Damn it. I was aiming at his leg. At the last minute a woman – who looked like she came from a knitting circle – delivered a hand full of fingers to the side of Cooter's neck. Dang!

A straight woman in small town Texas stood up for somebody called out for being gay. She had to be all of 5-foot 4-inches tall and weighing in at, say, a loaf of bread.

Dang.

"Sorry, kiddo," she said. "Nobody gets to do that to somebody, not when Paula's here."

"Uhhh," I said.

"Sorry I messed up your shot," she said with a grin. "I'm Paula. Paula Brown."

A grin? Really?

So, I threatened to blow his balls off without really meaning to do anything other than put a hole in his leg to get him to stand down. I guess it was his nuts on the firing line.

No more little huevos on Cooter. I'm sorry if you were pulling for him.

Huevos — the Spanish word for eggs. It's what I always called balls.

Cooter had no eggs. You could see them over here... over there... oh, and there's a red thingy all the way over on a kiosk with posters bragging how peaceful Waxahachie is.

His eggs were cooked, and I was the chef.

I scrambled his huevos.

Get it? Scrambled?

Too soon?

No goobers. So no little Cooters in the future. Again: sorry if you were pulling for the bully. It isn't going to work out to your liking this time.

I held my Glock by the muzzle with my other arm away from my body. A deputy took my pistol, and popped out the magazine.

The magazine clanked as it hit the floor.

"Don't just drop it," I said. "You know how much those things—"

"Stand still, sir," the officer said.

She pulled the slider a few times to remove the round that was still chambered. She put it into a bag with EVIDENCE written in enormous letters. The deputy and I went to the far side of the room.

Cops were all over the place. Asshole newspaper came. Cell phone flashes were everywhere.

Two suits appeared soon enough, and they wanted to know all about what happened.

The cops put me in plastic handcuffs. Cooter was completely free from restraints, except the restraints brought on by seeing your testicles strewn about in a few hundred little chunks.

There were questions for me. More for Mikka. They talked with Paula Brown for quite a long while, too.

Officers were also talking to people who saw it or heard it. Notebooks with tall skinny pages. Lots of writing and scribbling.

A Glock 43 is a tiny gun. For the past few years, I rarely leave the house without some kind of weapon. Mikka thinks pistols are silly because he knows how to use whatever's lying around as a weapon. I'm not that handy, and we have far too many kooks in Waxahachie. In the woods, we have seriously dangerous animals.

The 43 is an awful gun to fire. It's so small, it doesn't fit my hand. It weighs so little that the recoil isn't fun. Most of the gun — most of all Glocks, in fact — are plastic. A solid and heavy gun is the one you want at the gun range. The tiny plastic number is what you need to carry around.

I really can't say why I put the Glock in the small of my back. I just did. I'm usually gun-free.

When you see me, you have no idea that I'm carrying or not. It's called "concealed carry" for a reason. It's not because I'm trying subterfuge. I'm just trying to be nice and not scare the kids. I never use my guns (until today). I never shoot living anything (until today).

The feeling of having protection is palatable. I would have laughed at you if you tried to tell me that a year ago. No hunk of steel and plastic could possibly change anybody's attitude. That's surprisingly wrong. It changed everything. I became confident that I could go to and from the grocery store without being beaten up. I could go pay my friggin' taxes without getting a fist down my throat.

Serious truth: nobody is helping gay kids. Nobody protects us. Some days in the backwoods, it feels like nobody cares. Then I see people like that short woman who knows all about karate jabs.

And there's at least one gay kid (raising hand) who decided to protect himself... to protect his property and the ones he loves.

Paramedic got bug-eyed when they first saw my work. My 9-mil bullet apparently exploded both poor Cooter's manhood. The earth will never see a Cooter Jr.

They put a neck brace on my bully.

"It's okay, everybody," I said loudly. "I think a dentist might be able to fix my teeth. Thanks for being concerned."

"I'll kill you, motherfucker." Maybe I should have aimed for his larynx. That might have been more of a public service.

I was on the receiving end of a big stank eye.

They took about 2 hours to document everything. They only took about 10 minutes to piss me off thoroughly. I was ready to leave Waxahachie. There's fag-bashings in Dallas too, but the cops up there seem to try.

"He tried to put his fist down his throat," Mikka said from across the room.

"I'm not talking with you now, gypsy," the suit said. Wow. Racism is alive and well, and it isn't even disguised.

"Cooter tried to put his fist down my throat," I said (almost the same words as Mikka). They didn't seem to mean anything to the law.

"It was self defense," I said. "I was protecting myself. And Mikka's my fiancé, so you'll talk to him if I say so."

"Yup," the officer said finally as he cut off the handcuffs.

"We all know the Monet house," another detective said. "Don't you worry, kid. We got this."

Really? When did that start?

"What happens to my Glock?"

"You'll get it back, eventually," a detective said. "If it were me, I'd buy another. Or maybe I'd wait at your house until somebody drops one off for you."

To say I was astounded would be the understatement of the century.

It was also the first time I used the word "fiancé" in public. It felt really good.

As Mikka and I were heading out, one of the clerks hollered at me.

"André," he said. I stopped and turned around. He ran up and put a kiss right on my lips.

"I am so proud of you," the guy continued. "Asshole picked on the wrong gay guy."

Sure did.

"Wait," Mikka said as he pulled me to go down a hall. It was packed with people, but they all moved aside when we got close.

Mikka dragged into the county clerk's office.

We got a marriage license.

Our friend, Monique Thompson, was working the counter.

"Hey, Mo-Mo," Mikka said.

"Hey, White Trash," Monique jabbed, "Y'all do all this?"

We nodded. She smiled.

"Don't go mess with my whitey boys," she said under her breath. "Crackers sometimes mess back."

When we were about to leave, Monique said: "I bet you guys will have no trouble remembering this anniversary.

She was right.

Mikka and I grew up with Monique Thompson. Somebody in the Thompson family really messed up when they decided to move to this part of North Texas. Almost no other black family thought it would be fun to raise kids in Waxahachie.

Waxahachie is so white that the Pillsbury Doughboy looks Mexican. The town is over 60% white here. Latinos make up about 25%. That leaves just enough unused digits for the Thompson family.

Most of my energy went into fighting homophobia, but I saw some of the shit our God Fearing white folk threw at the Thompson family. I'm always going to fight against homo-hate before anything else because that's my shit. There's plenty of other stuff when time allows. There are politicians in Washington and creepy guys with bombs overseas, but home is where the hate starts. Home is where young gay kids are having to face politicians who want to turn the entire penal code against us.

Mikka and I helped Monique out of a jam or two. We didn't go out of our way to help, and that's not something I'm proud of.

When little Monique (maybe 2nd grade) got pushed to the ground outside the school, Mikka tripped up the racist twittle-dick who did it, sending him face-first into some mud. The boy's dad — Mr. Twittle-Dick — goose-stepped his way into the principle's office, demanding Monique's immediate suspension. That didn't work, so he demanded Mikka be expelled. Mikka was suspended for a week.

When I threw a hissy fit over Mo-Mo's suspension, I got kicked out for a week too. That's such a crappy example of a circular squiring squad. It's epizootics of the blowhole, and it's a dandy example of how The Man tries to get all his underlings inside a tight-swath tube of irrelevant… hey, did you know they could line both sides of the blow hole with cranberries and totally fix the problem of not having cranberries that are sweet enough to serve.

"You guys lookin' to be Cracker of the Year for getting suspended?" she said. "Not happening, by the way. My Halloween costume has saltines all over it, and that's the cracker award for this year."

Mom was so pissed that she went to the superintendent. I don't know what she said, but all three of us got back into school the next day. The principal who suspended us just disappeared. I don't know where.

I did see her talking to Mo-Mo's dad a few months later. We were at the grocery store. I don't know what was said, exactly. I did hear Mom saying "try to keep my whitey men to pay attention more." If you can figure out the context of that, you're better than me.

Remember the windpump and its broken gear?

The company that made Anatole's windpump went out of business. The broken gear was so old, nobody could find a replacement.

The boss decided to get a whole new setup, including a new tank. It meant I didn't have to go traipsing up that rickety ladder. It was my job to get it done, but Kris was all over it because of the guy in charge. I think he was the contractor, but I'm not completely sure what title he used.

Kris and Windpump Dude laughed and carried on. So, *that's* Kris's type: tall, preppy, with an Armani fetish. He was all over La-coste too.

I was feeling better about myself. Kristof and his fancy foot-ball games, and the count of languages he knows (hint: Graham's number), and all his impossibly coiffed hair… finds Windpump Dude the summit of genetic accomplishment? Dude, he sells fucking wind-mills and plastic water tanks for a living.

May they have a blessed life together with lots of little Hun-garian windmills running around crushing every crumb in the house.

Freakin' wow. It was the most bizarre eye-opening spectacle I ever saw.

To celebrate not getting any teeth knocked out, Anatole told Mikka to get me down to the gulf for a week. Mandated vacation is one of the things on my bucket list, and you just can't beat Galveston.

There's a kind of bug in south Texas that locals call "love bugs." It's their name because you never see just one of the bugs. There's always a bug pecker inside another bug. I assume that most of the insertee bugs are female.

Whatever. We were kind of like love bugs in Galveston. It is so wonderful to be in love with your best friend. We grew up together, and now we're growing old together.

They let me drive my Jeep right onto the beach. We made sure that we didn't destroy any sand dunes. Some seemed set apart for bog-ging.

"Weeeee," we both shrieked as the Jeep went airborne. We almost rolled it a couple of times. That wasn't a big deal because… well… it's a friggin' Jeep for gods sake.

I have a frame around my license plate. It says NO PROBLEM on the top, and PROBLEM on the bottom. The bottom word is upside down, to be read easily when the car is upside down. Get it? Ha Ha Ha.

We went crazy eating fresh everything down there. My favorite fish in the world is redfish. Some people call them red drum or channel bass. That's all a bunch of gobbledegook: they're redfish.

Fishermen have to be careful because redfish population is down. They are expensive to buy, but they are soooooo good.

When I'm cooking, I put buttermilk, salt, pepper, Old Bay powder, garlic, and minced onion in a bowl and use that as an overnight marinade. The next day, it's just a matter of patting the filets dry and cooking them in a cast iron pan with a little oil. You always cook fish skin side down. Always do that. It just takes five or six minutes per side.

Why do I always put skin side down first? It's the way mama taught me, and that method was never broken. I didn't need to fix it.

There's a restaurant right on the seawall in Galveston called Casey's. It's right next door to another restaurant named Guido's. And don't go giving them a yankee accent. It isn't GWEE-doh. It's GUY-doh. I have no clue about why they do that, but I can tell you they get supremely touchy about it.

So these two restaurants — Casey's, Guido's — are connected. There's just a wall that workers can fold away. Guido's has cloth tablecloths. Casey's is just regular. Guido prices reflect the hoity-toity tablecloths. The food all comes out of the same damn kitchen using the same recipes.

I can't imagine how they both stay in business. The property is right on the gulf, so it isn't like people are coming in for a formal occasion. They're coming from the beach, and they have sand in their flip-flops.

The world is bizarre.

We went over to Port Bolivar for an afternoon. The only way to get there from Galveston is by ferry. The state of Texas runs ferries that cross the entrance of Galveston Bay (which is an enormous body of water). The ferry crossing is free because it's part of the state highway system.

The Port of Houston is one of the largest ports in the country, and it's all up somewhere inside Galveston Bay.

We went to Bolivar, which is a thin strip of sand. Texas has a barrier island that runs across most of the shore. Bolivar -> Galveston -> Matagorda -> San Jose -> Mustang -> Padre Island. That's a long list of islands, but Texas has plenty of shoreline. Some of the islands are the home to endangered critters, like whooping cranes.

You just thought you were buying a stupid romance novel. My story is an educational experience.

We stripped down to our swimsuits and ran down the endless beach. I did keep the Jeep keys on a jiggly thing around my wrist. We got sand into everything.

"I love that fluff of hair around your nipples," I told Mikka. We were relaxing in the motel room after a strenuous day of goofing off.

"We should keep a memory of places we've been," I said.

"Like a travelog?"

"I was thinking of brightly colored thumbtacks," I said. "We need to get some. I'll start by putting one where Galveston is."

As I said that, I touched Mikka's tattoo of Texas right where Galveston is. I gave him a huge grin.

"You will meet with an untimely, yet richly deserved, demise," he said. "We gypsies know how to do things."

We spent a few hours locked up in our vacation room. Man, it's a lot of fun being in love with an acrobatic gypsy.

This is going to be hard to describe. Don't laugh if I screw it up.

One wall of the motel room was cinderblock. It had one of those foldable suitcase benches. Mikka folded up the bench and moved it to the closet.

He stood in the niche with his back against the righthand protrusion. When he jumped, he clamped himself to the wall. Legs were tight against the left side, and his back was to the right. So he was about a foot or two off the floor, held by nothing other than pressure between his legs and back.

He somehow got a little higher with jumping and squirming moves.

And — oh, by the way — he was naked. Totally au naturel.

What came next was pure Mikka. He pointed his fingers at me and motioned for me to come over to where he was. It was that "bring it" motion you sometimes see before a fight.

"Nekkid, please," he said. I did.

"Lube," he said. When I gave it to him, I assumed I was to jack him off. He still has cum left inside? I didn't see how that was possible. We spewed from one end of Galveston to the other.

He lubed himself, and then reached around and pulled me up by the tops of my arms.

Mikka got me positioned, and he lowered me slowly onto his penis.

I kid you not. It happened exactly like this. Cross my heart.

He made love to me suspended in the air. I can't imagine how much muscle that takes, and he did the entire act without breaking a sweat. He didn't strain or wince.

Mikka wanted me, and he wanted to take me in a way only Mikka could do. It sounds bizarre, but it was the most loving thing I ever experienced. (My word processor is having to deal with tears of joy as I type this.) We were off the ground, defying gravity. Okay, Mikka was defying gravity with me along for the ride. Life with him has always been one hell of a ride.

I wish we had pictures of him making love to me up in the air in that brick niche. Without a photo, I don't think I'd ever get a straight person to understand how phenomenal gay sex is.

It was gentle. Defying gravity means we couldn't do thump-thump sex. He moved inside me, and I loved every second. When he came, he let out the longest sigh ever. When I looked down, I came too. It was all so wonderful that I didn't realize it.

When he's in me, my orgasm isn't just letting my rod be a geyser of cum. I feel him. I know he's about to give me the most personal thing he has: semen. He usually tips me over when it reaches into my prostate. Every thrust rubs it when he gets close to shooting. It's like the tip of his penis knows just where it needs to be, and I see stars. It's so intense.

When all those feelings are on the table, don't bother me with creating a mess of goo that we have to clean up. I did that, too, in that Galveston motel room, but it certainly wasn't the main attraction.

All those glancing blows against my prostate make the most intense orgasm ever.

We stayed in our perch for a minute. I could have stayed there forever, but Mikka was starting to show strain. He was doing all the muscle work.

"Ready?" he asked with a grin.

"Yup."

"Okay, hold onto my arms," Mikka said after he put his arms against the wall behind my armpits.

It was so fast; you could barely follow. I think what happened is this: he broke the tension and got his feet on the floor with me holding on. He then lowered me to the ground.

We stood and looked into each other's eyes.

"I love you, gypsy."

"Right back at you, gadjo."

"I think I did okay for myself, mama," I thought.

Then I thought of Kristof: "Suck it, Izod."

chapter eight
cheeky chicken

History, despite its wrenching pain,
Cannot be unlived, and if faced
With courage, need not be lived again.
Lift up your eyes upon
The day breaking for you.
Give birth again
To the dream.
—Maya Angelou, poem was written for B Clinton's first inauguration (1928-2014)
(She was the only one who can read her poetry on the same stage as Shakespeare and
not get booed)

To catch you up: I get so pissed at straight people, but then I run into folks like Mo-Mo and Paula Brown. For vastly different reasons, they both scare me.

Before we left Galveston, Mikka had one more surprise. He brought out our marriage license.

"Let's light this candle," Mikka said. "I'm ready, if you are."

I hugged him. I was ready.

He got us inside one of those wedding chapel that dot the tourist parts of town.. Unfortunately they were booked solid for the next 3 days. They told us of another chapel close to where the big cruise ships dock.

With a quick phone call to our Plan-B venue, we were about to be married.

Mikka took us into one of those souvenir stores that mostly has shells collected who-knows-where and plastic junk from China. The only thing that made any of these things about Galveston was the machined stamp that said "Galveston."

When we left the store, we were in matching skirts. I had about a zillion beads strung together as a necklace. Mikka bought two half-coconut shells (plastic), worn like he had boobs. He bought some lace to be our tops. We had tons of glitter, which the wedding chapel banned. (Thank you!) And the amazing part is he somehow found matching top hats.

"Not happening," I told him.

"Wha?" he answered with an innocent grin and a flick of one eyebrow.

"I'm not wearing any of this shit," I insisted. "You can, but you got too much just for you."

"Gypsy," he said. "I am gypsy. Every pore. Every synapse. Everything. I go along with a lot of your gadjikane shit my whole life. I love you more than life itself. Give this to me: I am gypsy, so I'm having a gypsy wedding."

"And that means 14 tons of kitch?"

It did. And that was that.

I wasn't sure I wanted to drive the Jeep in all this stuff, but he reminded me that I used to ride my Honda dirt bike in a kilt. (Blushing)

"I'm gypsy, man," Mikka said. "We gussy up for weddings.

The chapel is in an older part of Galveston Island. The sidewalks were wooden as were the awnings to keep rain off the sidewalk. I doubt the lumber was the original, but it definitely wasn't new.

It happened: Do you? Yup. Do you? I do. Do you have the rings? Nope.

By the power... yadda... yadda... y'll are husbands for life.

Boom. Boom. And Boom. We were married.

All of a sudden, Andreas went full-tilt gooey. I became totally assimilated. Syrupy sentimentality dripped out of every pore.

So I figured we'd head back home to some consummating. That ought to tell you two things. First, my figuring really sucks sometimes. And second, I still don't know jack-shit about my new husband. We pulled into a liquor store. I sat in the Jeep.

Then we went to Walmart. It's a strange location in Galveston. They put Walmart right on Seawall, the street of prime real estate that runs along the shoreline. They made one point, I never need to think to know where the Walmart is. We got a couple of the biggest plastic tumblers.

I drove down to Stewart Beach. It isn't an all-gay beach, but it's the friendliness in town (unless you head way way up to the boonies, where the sandpipers (birds) don't seem to mind anything).

While I adjusted my top hat, Mikka was making drinks. Forty ounce tumblers full of hurricanes. I mean, holy shit, that's a lot of rum. He also tied a string with noisy metal thingies and a sign "Just Married" that dragged along with the metal stuff.

We got to the beach. He held my hand, and he sang, "You put your left foot in...."

"Oh, no," I said, "I am not doing this on Stewart Beach."

"Gypsy family," he giggled. "You are part gypsy now, man. Feel it. Be unstuck from everything."

"Unstuck from reality? Sanity? Self-respect?" I asked smiling.

"Yup, if that's what it takes."

So there we were, full of camp, doing a kind of swagger duck-step, singing the "Hokey Pokey." After a few seconds, I heard the deepest voice in the world going "bomb bomb ooooo" as a base track. People started singing and laughing.

Drunkards all. I loved it.

Toward the end of the Electric Slide (yes, we did all of them), some guy with an alto sax joined the party. Whoops. Hollers.

I noticed we got the attention of the Galveston Police. One stood up on the seawall. The other was with us on the sand. He was feeling the moment, and for reasons I'll never understand, he knew all the words of "Macarena" but in Spanish. About a third sang along with the coolest cop in Texas. Everyone joined in with "Heeeeeey Macarena."

And because it was Texas, we had to do Cotton Eyed Joe. I'm talking about the sometimes-famous line dance. Lots of it is instrumental, but we had a sax player, a human bass guitar, and somebody doing strange consonants. Plus, we were all pretty buzzed by then.

If you have no clue what I'm talking about, head over to YouTube and look for "cotton eyed joe texas line dance." Most everything there is lame, but you'll get the idea.

When things started dying down, the cop took over.

"Hey, ever'body," he said loudly. "Can we give it up for the newlyweds."

A cop in Texas actually said that, and I felt a happy tear trying to escape my eye.

"Nobody had glass containers," he said, "so thanks for that. But make sure you leave the beach the way you found it. Or, cleaner if you can."

Galveston police are notorious for not cutting anybody slack. Things change, and sometimes they really do get better.

We were there on Stewart all festooned like a gummy bear fell into a tchotchke store, and they were all happy for us. It was one of our Rites of Passage. They weren't celebrating "gay marriage." Nobody even used the word gay, not that I heard. One guy used the word gypsy, but he was brought up to speed quickly on how dangerous that line of discussion might be.

We were so much in love that day, and every day since. With the cops watching the party, we just walked across Seawall Blvd and got a motel room to finish getting married.

Wow. Stewart Beach flash party was the best wedding reception anybody ever had, and I still cry sometimes when I remember. I even found some vids on YouTube. It was amazing. Me in a grass skirt. What the hell, Meeks says I'm honorary gypsy, at least to him.

Thanks, Galveston.

All the years of growing up, I told everyone that I didn't need to assimilate straight culture. I didn't need marriage. I didn't want it. If I had it, I wouldn't use it.

I was gay, and we did things our own way. We didn't need anything from straight people.

It was what I really believed, and that belief was one of the stupidest thoughts that ever got inside my head.

Once I was married, so many things happened. First, I get to live with a real looker who's great in bed. We're best friends as far back as either of us can remember. I don't have to worry about wills and contracts to keep the Cooper family away from me, if anything — god forbid — were to happen to Mikka.

And on and on.

The result of me getting married was literally the first time I knew that I was 100% American. Before, the haters beat gay people: second-class, sinners. One of the TV money whores said HIV+ guys wore rings with sharp points to run around infecting others. The US Representative of my district actually wanted federal concentration camps. Bunks full of horny gay men: what could possibly go wrong.

I wasn't trained on how to act or react to marriage. The institution that was denied to me all my life just turned my life upside down.

It had meaning, and the meaning was a message: Andreas Monet is a valued participant in America.

Not being able to marry was keeping me separate and unequal. I was here: born, taxed, schooled, and everything else, but I wasn't really part of the team. I'd always be the outsider.

It seems like so banal. Humdrum.

What it ended up being was my welcome into the world. I was part of something. I was of value. I thought that just as I walked by a mirror that showed my top hat and shells and lace and so forth. Baby step, Andreas.

Yup: value. Top hat and everything else.

It's always my Bible-thumping neighbors who try to do mean crap against others. I searched the King James translation — which one guy swore is the one Jesus read — looking for a exception to the neighbor rule. I didn't see one. Neighbors are neighbors.

If we're supposed to love our neighbors as ourselves, we must hate ourselves as the pond slime we appear to be.

Southerners are bullies by inheritance and by training.

They're dicks. They've always been dicks.

Guess who the south supported in the Revolutionary War. If you think they wanted the revolt to succeed, that would be wrong.

The south had slaves, and the slaves made products (like cotton) that was always sellable in the King's England. So, guess who southerners wanted to win. When you say a Confederate family were patriots, it means they are loyal to the king of England. In the Civil War, the so-called Rebels were actually Loyalists.

Slaveholders in the south only flipped sides when the market for their evil products went haywire.

When you hear bubba doing loud (and often off-key) shit about being patriotic, remember that their patriotism wanted to see George Washington and Thomas Jefferson swing at the end of a rope.

They don't teach that in schools here, but just go look it up. You've been taught lies about what patriotism means.

They don't like black people here. They don't like Latinos, either. They certainly don't like gay people.

To tell you the truth, I've never figured out why southerners are so insecure. They have no need to bully anyone, and yet they do.

They passed laws that made it illegal for a black woman to have a white husband. The only thing that proved was that southerners were complete dicks.

I do have a few good things to say about laws. Society says it's just fine for guys to run around topless. Pecs are on full display. Nipples are okay, so long as they are male.

This is exactly the correct position. Pecs and nipples are wonderful. When I go to the swimming pool or the beach, I am usually drooling within three minutes.

So, thank you, society. Thanks for the pecs. Thanks for the nipples.

If I knew who invented Spandex, I would send him a Thank You card every year.

Woops. I'm married now. Do I have to stop drooling at... yeah, whatever.

On the way back home, I pulled into a self-service car wash. Our personal belongings consisted of one of those really big, blue IKEA bags. All our clothes and lube fit nicely. Mikka got out with the bag. I got out and fed money to the car wash. On cue, the wand popped. It was full of water and ready to go.

We opened all the doors on the Jeep, and I got busy. Sand was in everything. I spwooshed out the inside. (If it isn't a word, it should be.) If the inside had anything not bolted or glued by the Jeep factory, I sent it flying off into space with the rocket-powered squirt wand in my right hand. I also sent gallons of intense water jets to the undercarriage. And I nailed my honey just for good measure.

"Be ready to die," the gypsy foreshadowed.

"Always ready."

When the coins were all used up, we started pulling off body parts. The top of the jeep consists of three pieces: two over each front seat, and a bigger top over the back. No, I don't have one of those 4-door guys. Mine's 2-door, like god and the US Army intended.

There's a winch up front, but that's my only add-on.

We put the three parts that make the roof into the back and rode open air all the way to Waxahachie.

Houston was the first major city we came to. Hell, it's the only city between Waxahachie and Galveston that's wider than a piece of toilet paper. I see no purpose to that town. It smells awful from all the oil refineries. They get some extra tourist coins because part of NASA is in a suburb. The yankees probably hold their noses all the time they're walking around the rusty Saturn V rocket that lies on its side there. I know they tried to restore it, but it's still skanky, and the whole town stinks.

The rest of the drive was smooth Interstate travel, a few hours of it.

Marengo and his ladies were all excited to see us.

"Hi, girls," Mikka said. The rooster lost his balance as he jumped up and down. The hens followed Mikka around as he worked putting the top back on the Jeep. We were all properly sunburned. I was, at least. I think gypsies don't burn.

He pointed his melon-shaped butt toward the hens and shook it. They went wild, screaming and hooting and cackling.

I just stood aside and watched.

The big IKEA bag and I headed toward the front door.

When I stepped on a board closest to the front door. It was a bit loose, and the noise it made isn't something you ever want to hear.

CLICK — a deep and loud click. It was a switch that had no sound deadening anything. The click got picked up by the yellow pine that had hardened into the sound amplifying floor of my front porch. The click was the loudest thing in the world.

"Mikka!?!" I screamed.

"What is it, love?" he said as he came running.

"Don't come up here," I said. "Could you call 9-1-1 for me? I think I just tripped a bomb."

He did, and he stayed right with me. I had to threaten him so he kept a little distance.

"If the bomb goes off," I said, "there'll be a fraction of a second when I see that you're about to die, and I'll hate you for it. I'll hate you because I didn't take care of you. Is that what you really want?"

He moved back.

I didn't know if there was a bomb under my foot, but I didn't want to find out. And the reason sounds so mushy: I wasn't done with Mikka yet.

You know that I made it off the porch. Otherwise, I couldn't be telling you about it. So quit being all nervous. The bad guy(s) will get what's due, and it will be a method that only the most psychotic gypsy could approve.

While we waited, I tried to figure out who'd be coming. Waxahachie is a redneck town of 30,000 people. It's in Ellis County, which has 150,000 people. Those are tiny numbers. Nobody there wants to spend a dime on government because they're assholes who don't care about anything but themselves and their church picnics.

Who do they send to a bomb situation?

Everyone, apparently.

Waxahachie police have a S.W.A.T. division. Ellis County has deputies with a bunch of equipment they don't get to use often. Somebody even called the Texas Rangers (law enforcers, not the baseball team.

I was approached by a guy dressed like a gray Pillsbury doughboy. He had a robot sidekick that looked like a dog on tank tracks.

"Tell me what you heard," the man said through the foot-thick padding.

"Click. I heard a click."

"Don't move your foot."

"Really? You thought I'd stay motionless until you came and then just walk away?"

"Sir," the man said, "I'm the one who's gonna save your ass, so please don't try to make me laugh."

"Yes, sir. Sorry."

The man got down onto one of the steps and drilled a hole in one of the step risers. He then put a long pole into the hole.

"I'm looking at the... oh, there you are. Yup, what we have here is a bomb. Nice work too."

He stayed back at his hole for about 5-minutes (seemed like several hours).

"Okay, that's it," he said. "Come off the porch."

"Really?" I asked.

"Are you saying I don't know how to clip wires?" he said. "No, you wouldn't say that at all. Not if you're nice. You're nice, aren't you Andreas?"

"You know me?"

The man said, "Yup, ever since you tripped and spilled your milk all over my arithmetic homework. That was 3rd grade, I think."

I pulled up my foot. No boom.

I ran off the porch.

"Campbell?" I asked.

"Yup."

"I love what you've done to your wardrobe," I said.

"Still the class clown," Campbell said.

When he took off his helmet pads, I ran up and kissed him on the cheek.

"I still don't play for that team, man," he told me.

"I always kiss people who save my life," I told him.

"Third grade," I said. "Really? Still carrying that around? I apologized to you way back then. I even let you score a soccer point when your dad was there to watch. Move on, Campbell. It was just milk."

"Whole milk," Campbell needled.

"Do you remember Mikka?" I asked.

"Sure," Campbell said. "How've you been?"

"Married to Andreas," Mikka said with a broad grin.

"Group hug," Campbell started to say. "Group hug after I get out of my work clothes here."

We all moved back to let him get out of the padding.

Police were busy taping off my porch. Crime scene people were there. Who knew Ellis County had gotten so urban?

Campbell, Mikka, and I stepped to the side of the house on the driveway side.

"They'll call me when they get down to bomb shit," Campbell said.

"Bomb shit?" Mikka said.

"That's our technical lingo."

"So, are you married?" I asked him.

"No, Raylene left to join the Navy."

Raylene and Campbell had been an item all through high school.

"Sorry to hear that," I said. "Y'all were special together."

"Yeah, except I mysteriously kept getting the clap," he told me.

"Mysteriously?"

Campbell just smiled. Briefly. It was obviously a tender topic, or he was just trying to be coy.

"You sure are looking good," I told him. "They got a real nice set of teeth for you."

He lost all his teeth in 7th grade (roughly) in a motorcycle accident.

I said, "I could make that a real selling point in getting you a boyfriend. You'd be surprised the mental places you can send another dude when your mouth doesn't have any teeth."

Mikka slugged my shoulder.

"I apologize for that," Mikka said.

"Andreas has a way with words," Campbell said with a grin. "I thought about that, actually. Maybe I'll go try it one day. I'm not into the whole relationship thing, but a hookup could be fun."

It could be fun. Campbell's really cute. Not my type, but there are plenty who'd go for him in a flash.

"Let me know," I said. "I'll get some pom poms and put together a cheering squad."

"Dude," Mikka said quietly, "they call it 'on the down low' because it's supposed to be down and low."

And with that, the porch guys were ready for the bomb expert.

He was up there for a couple of hours. Step one: take apart the bomb, so nothing can explode. Step two: keep all the pieces as pristine as possible so he can find DNA and fingerprints and maybe even a bomber's signature.

Investigators were going to find out what Cooter Keith was doing over the past day and a half. Their working theory is that he was miffed at the state of his testicles. Maybe.

I was a media star, of course. The homophobic newspaper sent photographers and reporters. I wouldn't let the camera guys on my property, and I referred the reporters to Campbell. They asked me why I was being a hard ass, so I unloaded about a half hour of reasons on their ass.

The paper did their typical hatchet: Homosexuals Attacked by Citizens. What a load of hooey. By the time they were finished, the good Christians of Ellis County were going to be lining up to buy bomb stuff at the hardware store.

The paper also rehashed the devastation of Cooter Keith's now-severed sperm knobs.

Fuck 'em.

I bought some video cameras, pointing them at every corner. Inside. Outside.

Motion sensors caught all movement and stored it for a month or so.

This is precious: one of the douche-canoes who do editorial work for the paper sent me email saying they were going to do a big exposé on my illegal marijuana business.

I sent a quick note to the publisher of our sorry-excuse for a newspaper. The letter skipped over the sorry-excuse for a reporter… skipped her sorry-excuse for an editor… and went to the douche-canoe publisher. The current publisher was the bible-thumping grandson of the douche-canoe founder of what we call "newspaper" in give-or-take terminology.

My letter said the report on that the marijuana garden would be fine. I don't use the pot. I don't make money from the pot. It's just wasted space as far as I could tell. That said, an exposé of the garden would give my property an uncomfortable amount of publicity.

Maybe I enclosed snapshots of the publisher, the editor, and the religion reporter all picking more than their fair share of marijuana. Most of the pictures dated back to when I was a pimply-faced kid who slept in the back bedroom. That kid happened to get a nice digital camera for Christmas one year, and he'd been documenting the marijuana patch ever since. Maybe I enclosed some of what that camera saw over the years.

The last line of my response: Bring it.

They didn't bring anything. I was old news in a hurry.

Somebody told me they toned down the hate. That's good for gay kids. I don't personally give a rat's ass.

Death threats started after I did my 9-mil castration and public humiliation of Cooter and his testicles. There was a note taped to the front door. Somebody stuffed my mail shoot with what looked like cow shit. I mentioned all of them to the cops. After the poop, I put up a couple of video cameras, but that's when the death threats stopped.

And it's quietest just before the big storm. Right?

chapter nine
the king of patriotism

A lot of hacking is playing with other people, you know, getting them to do strange things.
— Steve Wozniak (most righteous hacker ever born) —

Mr. and Mr. Cooper. Or Monet? Were we going to change names?

Yup. We'd be doing that. Mikka wanted out of the Cooper charade. Almost every Roma in the area is named Cooper. None of them are really Coopers. They don't try to pretend.

It's none of my business what their name is. They're probably right about that, but it seems a little weird for a whole band of people to call themselves Cooper just because they can.

Mikka asked me if I'd mind if he changed his last name. Mind? I cried a gallon on the spot.

"I think your Mom would like that," he said. I just nodded and smiled.

It was surprisingly simple to make the change. We just went to the Department of Public Safety (DPS) office with his current driver's license, our original marriage certificate, and 11-bucks. Bam and bam, there's a new Monet in the world.

How fucking cool is that?

Texas still hates us. Politicians still do anything and everything they can to make our lives miserable (for reasons I'll never understand). But we got married, and the assholes aren't allowed to say we aren't. We're somehow part of the citizenry.

Did I mention in passing that living in small town Texas is dicey? Oy.

Mikka and I fell into a rhythm, working at the farm. Nobody ever talked about the cage. Nobody ever mentioned flies or fly food or anything related to what makes the place so interesting.

Ignorance is the most blissful thing ever. I don't really want to know about time flies. I don't want to date one or have sex with one. I don't even want to be in the same room with one.

Once or twice a month, we'd do a weekend in the woods. I was terrified the first time because one of the first things was to get rid of everything. Everything means everything. Okay, almost everything. Me being gadjo, he let me keep my sneakers. Tender feet.

The main thing was firepower. I hate guns, but I always have a couple handy when I go back into the woods. We have mountain lions and coyotes and snakes. I want total and complete control of the situation when an apex predator is part of the equation. I don't know when I might run into one, so I have guns within easy reach.

I wouldn't kill one of those great animals unless it didn't give me a choice. I'd much rather run or hide or something, but the main skill of a cougar is tracking down animals that don't want to be tracked down. I resemble that kind of animal. Hence, the ace up my sleeve.

But no.

We had no snake bite kit either. He told me that it'd be okay.

I'm telling you all this because I want you to know how much I love this man. Love. Trust. I trust Mikka with my life. He says he can take out whatever needs to be taken out, and he swears it's not just gypsy exaggeration.

We run and jump. We climb trees and swim in the river, one of the forks of the Trinity River to be exact. We hug and kiss and play with each other's body for hour after hour. I've loved him all my life, but I never knew really really loving him could be this much fun.

Every time he reached over to touch me, I'd get a big wave of warmth. He loves me, and he doesn't mind showing it.

We spent our entire lives getting to know each other, falling in love with each other. Now we were spending hour after hour learning each other's body. I taught him some moves that oh-my-god send me over the cliff.

There's this place near my taint that will make me shoot a load in less than a minute. I had no idea that somebody could even do that. He can. He does.

What got me totally hooked on the woods was sleeping next to Mikka on a dark, dark night. The stars are amazing outside of the city. You can literally see the star clouds. They almost look fluffy.

Country guys are laughing now. Waxahachie is Podunk, but there are just enough street lights to hide the most subtle shows of the cosmos. Unless you get out into the real darkness, you just can't see the galactic center of the Milky Way.

I still consider that view to be one of the best gifts he ever gave me.

He taught me how to catch fish with my hands. Sorry, but it's too weird. My husband (love using that word, by the way)… my freakin' HUSBAND got all the protein. He sometimes finds crappie and buffalo fish, but I don't like either. He once showed up with a gar, but I chased him out of the campsite. It's like a scary snake with fins. My favorites include catfish and bass.

Mikka let me use the pocketknife that I always had in a pocket. We're in the buff with almost nothing (no pots, no tools), but I have my Swiss Army knife. I can scale a bass or skin a catfish in almost no time. I pull the meat off the bones, and I'm ready to go. It doesn't take long to cook a fish filet on an open fire with no pan or grate.

I do a mean prickly pear side dish. It's easy to get hurt. It's cactus, for crying out loud. With my trusty knife, I get all the pricklies off and slice the meat. It tastes a bit like green beans. Green beans are probably better, but I never saw any growing in the wild around here.

We have gayfeathers and farkleberries too. I don't know how you'd eat them, but I love the names.

Go farkle your berries....

There are some wild roses and onions, too.

I wouldn't say that we feasted out there, but we weren't there for the culinary experience. We were there because there's nothing I like better than watching my husband get naked. I could watch his balls flap around for weeks or months. We only have a night here and there.

Pop. Pop. And pop.

That's what got us up the next morning.

We just knew we had to hurry.

One gunshot means HEY or ALL CLEAR HERE.

Two gunshots means absolutely nothing, unless there's a Navy SEAL double tapping somebody.

Three gunshots means shit has hit somebody's fan.

We dressed on the run, leaving everything we didn't absolutely had to have.

I was panting like there wasn't any oxygen left in Ellis County. We ran back to the main house. Mikka's careful in the woods. He taught me how to look for big cats and apex dogs around every turn and up every tree. Not this time: none of those wild troublemakers would have to catch us.

"It's Pasha," Kristof said through the driver's window on his car. "Come on."

On the way, Kris said that Pasha Cooper was in the hospital. That's the only information we had at the Austin farm.

Kris had his car waiting. We piled in and raced to the hospital.

I could see Pasha in one of the treatment areas. It was the loudest part of the emergency room because there were gypsies. They're always screaming about one thing or another.

They didn't know me. I didn't know them. But they were all smart enough to figure out that it was me who's been fucking Mikka. I doubt any got the wedding notice.

My husband stayed calm. You get to do that when you know that you could put any of them down with one kick or hand chop, and you're pretty sure the police would come to help him. I sound really smart when I'm reporting on what happened well after-the-fact. My head was racing that night. I'd never met any of the family, except Mikka and Pasha. From the looks of things, I wanted to keep things that way. The men were disheveled and covered by splotches of oil, grease, and street grunge. They did spectacularly lower class things to their facial hair, with mustaches poking outward and upward, and side burns pointing forward, downward. There was at least one big, gray, lamb chop in the family's repertoire of facial hair.

We made our way to a grouping of cops. I knew some of them.

"Mikka Cooper?" one officer asked.

"Mikka Monet," my husband said. "What happened to my brother?"

"I don't know exactly," the officer admitted. "Where were you for the past 6 hours?"

"Camping in the woods with my husband. When can I talk to—"

"We're still trying to piece this—"

"Clear out the family," Mikka said. "If you think one of them did this, they shouldn't be in there."

"We're handling this," the officer said.

133

"No, you're not," Mikka said. "Clear the goddam room of the gypsies. Let me talk to him alone. He'll tell me."

Some officers talked for a minute or two, and then they started moving family out of the niche. I would have preferred they were moved out of the E.R. As it stood, the police were moving all the Coopers over where I was supposed to stand.

I held tight to Mikka. He got me into the niche, next to Pasha.

"Hey, jailbait," Mikka said.

"Hey, Meeks," Pasha said through the tubes and wires.

"We're right over here, Mr. Monet," an officer said quietly. Mikka nodded.

"Monet?" Pasha asked. "Da-fuq?"

"Meet your new brother-in-law. André and I got hitched."

"Holy fuckin' wow......."

The next few minutes were in Roma, and I never did find out exactly what was said. I could make some shit up, and I bet I'd be close, but that's not the way I do things.

Bottom line: Pasha came out to his parents. Mommy Dearest threw a cast iron skillet full of boiling grease at the kid. Loving father then picked up the skillet. Daddy picked up the skillet, pulled down the kid's pants and started fucking him with the handle.

Wow. That family's a piece of work.

When Mikka told the officers what happened, they moved all of them out of the E.R. and away from Pasha. (finally!) When I stepped out a half hour later, no gypsies were in sight. Mommy and daddy were arrested and in jail.

DFPS (Department of Family Protective Services) were called because Pasha isn't quite old enough to be on his own. Mikka stepped up and became his guardian.

For those keeping count: I got married and became daddy to a teenage boy in the span of a week. I'm actually his guardian, but we plan on adopting him if he mows the lawn. While all that gets sorted out, "daddy" works fine. It makes me feel older, but it's okay.

I'd defend that kid just like he was mine. The fact that he's on record as wanting to strip me and be my "woman" is a whole different topic.

Over the next few days, Anatole Austin won every accolade in my book. He got all parental ties between Pasha and the Coopers thrown out.

The kid was emancipated. It felt good. Pasha was in love with Anatole because nobody ever gave a flying crap about him. The only thing an adult ever did for him was hit him.

Anatole got a strong restraining order keeping the Coopers away from Pasha, and Mikka, and me, and our house. The lawyer explained all that to us.

We became the kid's legal guardians, after a short court hearing.

"Can I paddle his buttock?" I whispered to Meeks. (I kind of like that nickname.)

He stepped on my toes. So, I guess the paddling will be negotiated later.

I took flowers to the kid one day.

"Awww, you ARE sweet on me," he said, so I turned around and gave the flowers to a nurse.

"Mikka's parking the car," I said as I sat in the chair on the far wall. All my memories of Mom in that last year came swooshing back into my head. I didn't like any of it.

"Look, do you know about the pot growing—"

"Everybody in Ellis County knows about it," the kid said.

"Thanks to you, there's a police cruiser parked across the street. It's there around the clock. The pot's going to take over the yard unless somebody can get back there with a machete or some agent-orange. Something."

"Hey, jailbait," Mikka said. "How's it hanging."

"You don't sound like any father I've ever known," I said. "And I can't be part of this parent or guardian gig."

They both just looked at me.

I waited, hoping they'd understand. Alas, no.

"Wardrobe. I have nothing to wear to P.T.A. Meetings. And if we have a cake sale, the only thing I can cook is marijuana brownies, and I don't really know how to do that. It'd be guesswork."

"Sweet," Pasha said.

"Shut up," the Monet couple said in unison.

WAIT. I want to type that again: the Monet couple.

Oh, man, that feels so righteous.

chapter ten
the trill of a lifetime

In real life, I assure you, there is no such thing as algebra.
Fran Lebowitz, world's only confirmed fan of Checker Cars (b 1950)

So, I am the proud new parent of a 15 year old Roma kid who was savagely beaten when he tried to have a conversation with his parents — the very people who were supposed to protect him. He was coming out of the closet to his family, only that's like the son of a Baptist preacher running off to be a Buddhist monk. It was a troublesome situation.

I married my best friend who took my name. Family support was diluted by the fact that it would have come from the same alleged parents who just tried to kill their younger kid for being gay.

My parenting skills are... wait... I don't have any parenting skills.

Fifteen years old. I think that puts him in the ninth grade.

"What school does Pasha go to?" I asked Mikka.

"School?"

Oh.

On a positive note, this means I won't have to figure out anything about any prom dates.

My mind tried to manage all the new whirlpool of swirling responsibilities. We had ourselves a gypsy reject who didn't know his hypotenuse from his pentameter. I had to do something about it, but what? How the Sam Hill can I fix a kid who's never had anything go his way? And I'm supposed to be able to jump on everything that needs jumping on without training or tools or talent.

I am already planning my next book: Figuring Shit Out for Dummies.

"Whacha doin'?" Mikka called from the other side of the spare room.

I was way in the back of a room that some architect felt would be a nice bedroom. It has never actually seen a bed. It's the storage room.

"I'm looking for my 9th grade chemistry notebook," I said, like it was the most obvious thing ever.

"You're a crazy person," he told me.

"I am not," I protested. "I am being contentious. We just got thrown a bunch of responsibilities that I can't handle. I don't know anything about educating a kid. If he comes out of this family, he will have a certain level of education."

"Crazy person," he repeated in a sing-song tone. It was a mocking tone.

What I wanted more than anything was my mother. She'd know what to do.

The hubby and I took turns going to the hospital. We tried to stay valuable employees of Anatole's fly ranch, but family comes first.

Pasha was just a doofy kid, but he'd been abused so badly that I wanted to hold him and make things right.

When I was at the hospital, I took school papers. I read everything about the ninth grade. There were books on getting a G.E.D. and home schooling.

In one of my papers, I found a report I did on farting. No, really. Just… stop sneering, please.

I was in high school, and the assignment was to write a paper on strange publishing. I picked the good old razz. The cartoon character "Bill the Cat" spelled it out: "Thhpptpt!"

According to my paper, the term raspberry dates to 1919. See, this is serious stuff. The US's film censorship panel, Hays Commission, officially banned the noise because of children and delicate viewers. USA! USA! USA!

Don't try to tell me English majors can't have fun.

While I was going through the edit process, one editor sent me a link. Somebody actually did time lapse photography. Go to YouTube and search for Time Lapse Raspberry Blowing. It's a great time to be alive.

The good people on the committee that's responsible for making an E look like E or e… they have a fart character. Oh, yes they do.

It's formally called a voiceless linguolabial lateral fricative, a trill. The character should be available to you in the more complete fonts. Check me out on this, but razzing has come to a word processor near you. Make sure your font can handle the Mehri language of Somalia.

That's the glyph on the right.

You're welcome, America.

I can't wait to tell Mikka about it. Pasha's going to get the best home school education ever, and I plan on being totally prepared to convey what I know to the mind of an innocent child.

Okay, "innocent" might possibly be a bit optimistic.

Damn, I love this stuff.

"I'm gonna kill them," Pasha said. It's his favorite sentence lately.

"No, you aren't," Mikka said at the door of Pasha's hospital room.

"It's my—"

"No, jailbait. I got this," Mikka said calmly. "Your job right now is to heal. My job is to protect you."

"And educate him," I said.

"Yeah, Meeks," Pasha said with a big grin. "He's been telling me all about trills. I ain't certain what that is, but it sounds really sweet."

"Over trill," I said.

"Over dale," the kid said. "I forgot to ask: who's Dale? And do you think he wants to fuck me?"

"I just talked with the doctor," Mikka changed the subject with a resolve that told me there'd be no negotiation. "We're taking you home."

"No, I can't," the kid said with a jerk in every muscle. "I'll kill the motherfuckers."

"Stop," Mikka said strongly. "I got that situation. You need to concentrate on getting well. I won't let anything happen to—"

"I think the kid's confused on what the word 'home' means," I said. "Our house is now your house."

"Huh?"

Mental note: work on the kid's vocabulary before anything else. "Huh" is the best word he could find here? Oh, no, no, no, no.

"You're our kid now," Mikka said.

"Can daddy let me play with his junk?" he grinned.

"No," Mikka and I said at the same time. We were presenting a unified front. How cool is that? He doesn't need to know that I know nothing about taking care of a kid. He doesn't need to know that.

Fake it 'til you make it, Mom used to say. So the house now becomes ground zero for shenanigans.

"Pot any time I want. Amazing."

I reminded him that there's a police cruiser watching the house around the clock.

Maybe it's time to get rid of mom's marijuana patch.

The first night of Pasha living with us was tense. For one thing, he kept trying to take my pants off. For another thing, the officer in the police cruiser called me at 3:00am. Somebody was trying to sneak up to the house, but the cops saw it all. The officer warned us to stay inside with the window drapes closed and all lights off. We knew the drill, but this lockdown had the most ominous feel of them all.

All the time the cruiser was out front, I'd been called when they spotted anything alive: deer included. False alarms happened just enough that we got a little complacent. This was different somehow.

The police have an attachment that clips onto a cell phone. The Flir One turns their phone into a thermal image camera. All they had to do was let their phone wander around the neighborhood. At night, a person with macular degeneration could spot a child from a block away. The cops weren't worried about kids or old people with vision problems. They just wanted to know if one of the Cooper assholes were up to something.

Since they got the thermal doobie, the false alarms stopped completely.

The cops got the daily double: Mikka's dad came there with Cooter Keith. Daddy must be out on bail from the original attack on the kid.

Both had several guns. Neither looked like a sales person for Girl Scout Cookies, and nobody needs to be peddling magazines at 3:00 in the friggin' morning.

It was nice to see Cooter was out of the hospital. I'd pay good money for a picture of his private parts. He doesn't have much, since I blew off his nuts with a 9-mil a few months back. The term "full recovery" wouldn't apply.

The police cruiser just sat there, and the uniform was most likely incredulous. The two bozos acted like sneaking around was the most normal thing in the world. Add them both together, and you're still several screws short of a hardware store.

Mikka wanted to run outside when he saw his father.

"Wait," I whispered. It got me an icy stare.

We waited because we had no idea what was going on. The police seemed like they were being way too lax. That's from our point of view. Any time you see two people coming your way with hate in their eyes and firepower in their hands, anything short of seeing the 1st Cavalry from Fort Hood is going to seem flaccid.

The officers had been silently busy. They made a few calls. They know people. Other cops, mainly. Uniforms know other uniforms. And all of a sudden, the neighborhood lit up with every light owned by the city of Waxahachie. We had flashing colors and strobing white lights that went round and round.

Most people would understand the situation. The police knew they were there, and they had a whole brigade of officers with handguns and long guns. Who knows what else: tasers (probably), flame throwers and Howitzers (maybe).

Did our two late night rocket scientists see the police?

No, apparently not. They ran up to the side of a neighbor's house and squatted down low. They squatted because it's a well known fact that thermal imaging doesn't work when you are squatting. Seriously. What were they thinking?

We didn't have a good view of the excitement. They were up along the side of a neighbor's house, and they were at the bottom of the class on being stealthy.

Cooter stood up, an officer told us later.

Here's a free tip: if it's in the middle of the night but you're lit up like it's the sunniest day of the year, it's possibly an error in judgment to raise your pistol with the business end pointing toward whoever has the lights.

One shot. And another. Then the nighttime exploded into a completely one-sided shoot-em-up.

My first thought: the chickens. It was impossible to ignore the sounds, and I was convinced I'd see some of the girls dead from heart attacks.

No, the chickens were fine.

Cooter: not so much. They wouldn't let us go over to where they made my bully porous enough to be a colander. Part of me wanted to see it.

The sad part was my reaction, and I swear this is true. I only wanted to know if they would bury Cooter's balls and pecker with the rest of his bullet-ridden body.

I'm not proud of that reaction. I'm okay with it, but not proud.

A guy just died in a cloud of bullets. The thousand year old man who lived in the house probably had to see a doctor and hire people to clean the shit off his mattress. I can't imagine how I'd react. Sure I can imagine it. I would react about the same way Mr. Watson reacted: poop all over the damn place.

I did not take the high road. I didn't even look for the High Rd exit. Nope. I just wanted to know about his testicles.

Cooter Keith was dead. I continued to smell gunpowder for days.

Milosh Cooper took a few of the bullets intended for Cooter, but it wasn't life threatening. Knowing that his co-conspirator was just a glob of perforated skin didn't even slow down the elder Cooper.

He got up and started walking (staggering, actually) toward our house. He needed to restore honor to the Cooper clan, and that means it was his mission to kill his youngest son.

It was like a cheaply made movie with a crappy script.

Police reacted to Milosh quickly. Obviously. Milosh acted like his IQ could fit on a BINGO card. Who does this stuff? What is a person's mind like for this night to seem like it's a good idea?

When I looked at Pasha, tears were gushing. He was trying to process all this input: the disgust in daddy's eyes. His own father was hobbling up to kill the kid with a handgun. The kid's semen-donor had stopped being a father a long time ago, but the kid had all those memories. He watched the man most responsible for keeping the kid safe. That man had turned against his son. It was weird and sad to see a man dishonor a teenager.

Pasha was going to live with that vision for the rest of his life. This wasn't simple rejection; it was guttural cruelty at its worst.

Milosh Cooper was the most depraved and immoral man I ever saw. Cooter was just a sick fuck all his life, but Milosh was supposed to be a father. There's no excuse for what he did to Pasha year after year. I blame him, his family for not getting Milosh help, and the law for not throwing his sorry ass in the slammer years earlier.

Somebody should have taken care of Pasha. Mikka tried over and over, but Milosh was too much for one person. The police didn't listen to gypsy problems, according to Mikka.

Everyone failed Pasha. Everyone. I'm ashamed of the whole thing.

Sure, there were the physical pain and the emotional torment, we all robbed Pasha with the most important thing a gay kid needs: hope. He didn't have any because we all were part of the outrageous injustice.

I was suddenly okay with Pasha's plan to liquidate daddy. Maybe they'd let me blow off his nuts before they kill him.

And, oh my god... it was the first and only time in my life that I really wanted to use a gun to take a life. That stopped me cold. That's not who I am. I was going to make sure that it wasn't what Pasha was either.

That was then. I'm daddy now, and my kid's going to be okay, even if I have to tie his wandering dick in a knot.

My rage against Milosh Cooper is just as strong as ever, but I can't give in to it. I'm better than that, so I have to throw away those feelings. But how the fuck am I supposed to pull that off? And how am I supposed to teach Pasha and set a good example for him when all my hatred is smoldering just below the surface.

I needed to smoke a joint. I settled on Scotch. This whole adult stuff isn't easy.

This whole thing of being an adult is really hard stuff.

They took Milosh Cooper away in handcuffs. I saw his bugged-out eyes, so full of malice. He tried to burn a hole in me with his eyes. I did the best thing I could do: I smiled sweetly at him, and I blew him a kiss.

"Never a dull moment," Mikka said.

The State of Texas had already filed a long list of charges, mostly felonies. A judge set bail at $50,000.

The insane thing is that somebody paid the bail. After a month, Milosh was out of jail.

And that's the end of what I know about Milosh. I have my suspicions. If you told me Mikka or Pasha did something to make him disappear permanently, I wouldn't be surprised.

A judge revoked his bail, so somebody was out $50,000. No bail for daddy. Not this time. He'll rot before they let him out of jail.

The police eased their patrols on our street. We kept our own guard with cameras and motion detectors. Thank you, Amazon.

```
Dear Dad:
```

145

This is your son, Andreas. I'm writing because I need to apologize.

I've made fun of you for several months after I found out your gender was fluid. I don't know if they used the term "fluid" when you were alive, but today it is apparently quite the In Thing to be. You could get on any interview show or make a ton of money writing a blog.

Wait. Did they have blogs when you were alive? The whole world has been changing. I've changed, just in the past year.

Nobody told me that gender was anything other than binary: male or female.

In my defense, nobody told me about time flies or Anatole's cage either.

I am married, believe it or not. My husband's name is Mikka, and he took my last name. We got married on the beach in Galveston. I cry a lot now, but the tears are likely to be happy tears. He makes me so happy, daddy.

You may remember him. Mikka Monet is the gypsy kid that Kris and I played with all the time. Kris pissed me off, so I'm still officially mad at him.

My husband is the greatest guy in the world. I wish you and Mom were there when we got married. I wish you were here for Christmas and birthdays. I feel robbed a little. I know that I should have done things differently back then.

So I grew up gay. Mommy once told me that you knew all along. If not, I suppose you just figured that out since I called him a husband.

And you have a kind of grandson. I am completely gay, so my semen wasn't involved. Pasha is gypsy: Mikka's kid brother. He's cute and as stupid as any 15 year old. I have no idea how to raise a 15 year old. I need some help, daddy. I can't screw this up. He's too good a boy.

Pasha joined the family after his own parents turned on him. He made the near-fatal mistake of being truthful to his parents. He told them he's gay, like his big brother. Some parents can't handle that kind of news.

His father put him into the Intensive Care unit at the hospital by attacking the kid with a cast iron skillet. What kind of unimpeded asshole does that to his own son?

I could have used you as a role model several times, when I didn't know the right thing to do. I had to make up solutions on my own. I've had a life of guesswork, without knowing anything about anything. Sometimes I got it right, but I fell down all the time.

I made stuff up because nobody was there to tell me stuff like: no I tried that, but this is easier. Or maybe you can do that but so-and-so is going to go grab a lap post and throw it at you.

Maybe it was something you tried, but the only thing you got was half of Ellis County running after you with pictures of Conway friggin' Twitty.

I don't know how to handle all my new ballistics. I do such-and-such, but I have nobody who can start a sentence with 'I did that but at 2600 meters, it just goes haywire.'

I need all that, daddy. I need to know that a bullet with a boat back will keep the round from going nuts as it reach its outer band.

Mikka, Kris, and I all work for Anatole Austin now. Kristof builds ammunition. I am the ballistics programmer. Mikka does everything else. He is so much fun at work. Mikka is just as much a gymnast as ever. He can do backflips in the front room without touching anything.

My job is programming. I graduated as an English Major, but those jobs don't come around often. Fortunately I have this strange ability to make computers sit up and roll over, and I can find no explanation. My math abilities are a joke. I just somehow know how to make a computer do something. Tell me what the input looks like and show me some examples of the output, and I can draw this imaginary line between the two. I am a computer savant. They all think I'm such a computer guru, but that's just a bucket of hooey.

I still hate guns just as much as ever, but ballistics is what I do. I'm even rebuilding a rifle. Mr. Austin gave me a Remington 700 and a Night-Force Riflescope. I changed it from .308 caliber

to 6.5mm Creedmoor. If they didn't have the Creedmoor ammo when you were here, it's a bullet that
is accurate to a mile or more. I still can't make
that kind of shot, but I'm working on it. Mr. Austin thinks me learning how to murder paper targets
at extreme distance will help me program the computer that helps him tweak his aim.

One fly. One bullet. First shot. Every time.

I got me a sign made up with all that on it: one
fly; one bullet; first shot. I keep it in my work
area at the main house.

Mikka and I go out into the woods, rip off our
clothes, and run and play. We swim in that big
creek on the east edge of the farm. He's taught me
how to live out there with almost no technology.

Did they use the rifle shots back then? If I hear
a shot, it means Hello. I return with one shot. If
I hear 3 shots, we start running back to the
house. Something bad is going on.

Maybe I shouldn't have written to you about rip-
ping all our clothes off. Sorry. It isn't the sort
of thing you tell your father, but you're dead and
all. I assume the kid will join us out there some
day. We'll be fully clothed.

If somebody raises a complaint about two wild guys
rampaging the countryside without a single thread
of 'proper' threads, that's probably Mikka and me.
It could even be Pasha.

I wish I knew you better, daddy. I do. I needed to
learn a bunch more stuff before you left us. My
biggest hope is that you and Mom are together
again. She had an almost unimaginable amount of
pain toward the end.

Wherever you are, I wish you the best. I'm selfish
to want you back here, so one of my character
flaws is selfishness. I will work on that. I promise.

I so hope you get to see this letter. It's out in
the universe, and I don't really know how that all
works. I love you, daddy. I really love you, and I
miss you so much.

So with all the love in the world, I remain

Your son,

Andy

chapter eleven
normative

Q: Why did the bubblegum cross the road?
A: It was stuck to the chicken's foot.

You maybe think your life is tough. Maybe it is. I'm not here to argue.

Milosh Cooper has two gay sons, Mikka and Pasha. The mother is not in the picture, but I don't know if she left or is dead. The father was beyond angry that both children disrespected him by sucking dick. Mikka and Pasha wouldn't be available to carry on the Cooper lineage. He crosses the line into violence sometimes, especially with booze or drugs. All he wanted was a normal gypsy family.

Let me put my English Major hat on for a second.

Two words: normal vs normative.

Some think that being gay isn't 'normal'. Some think that you aren't normal if you don't (or can't) follow society's rule that gender is binary: male or female, with no other gender possible. Those who fail to play by the rule is psychotic, immoral, or both.

I was in that group, and I was so wrong. The word that changed my whole attitude is 'normative.'

There are a few definitions of normative, but the one I'm using is when it means commonplace. Being left-handed is perfectly normal, but it's not even close to being normative.

Bring it, lefties. We got a b'zillion righties who can crush you wrong-handed twits. Back in the 1800s, society decided that being left-handed was the work of the devil. Millions of kids were forced to write with their right hand. The result was millions upon millions of left-handed kids who were taught their natural state was the work of the devil.

Bible-thumping by well-meaning morons is what's the work of the devil.

Sorry. Back to my story…

Are gypsies so evil? The religion Mom tried to teach me that I'm supposed to love everyone, even those who hate me… especially those who hate me. The Coopers make it hard to do that.

Pasha got home after several weeks in the hospital. I had been used to mom's hospital stays. For her, a month was nothing. She was there a really long time. For most people, a month is almost forever. Hospitals try to get patients in and out.

After Milosh Cooper was re-arrested, the police backed off the constant guard at Pasha's room.

The poor kid had the worst cabin fever ever. He took up macramé. When I pressed him, he admitted that he was building a rope to slide down.

"You know the hospital is five stories?" I asked.

"I have all the time I need."

I'm sure it felt like that. Poor kid.

"I love you daddy," he said. Awwwwww.

"Thanks."

"When can I play with your balls?" he asked with a grin.

"Not happening."

"Is he always like this, or did he crack up when he was in I.C.U.?" a nurse said. He'd been listening at the door.

"Hey, you're pretty cute yourself," Pasha told the nurse.

"Not going there," the nurse said. "My wife would have issues."

"Wife?" I said.

"I'm the token breeder in the nursing profession."

Pasha looked confused. It's a good look on him.

The big day was today. The nurse came to help pack all of Pasha's gear It was almost the sum of what he owned. Mikka and I hit Walmart to get him some socks, underwear, and a jacket for "cold" weather. We decided to let Pasha pick the rest of his new wardrobe. And we told him it was going to include trips to Goodwill in addition to retail stores.

An orderly arrived with a wheelchair, which Pasha thought was a game. He planned on doing slalom through radiology or something.

"Okay," I told the orderly, "I'll dash down to get the car. Where should I wait for you?"

"Main entrance is fine," the orderly said.

"If you're uncomfortable to be seen in public with him," said the nurse, "we can do something more discrete."

"Front door's fine," I said.

Pasha was throwing stank-eye at everything that moved.

"Jeep," I said. "Is that going to pull apart any stitches or cause internal bleedings? And let me say that such a thing wouldn't necessarily be a deal-killer."

The orderly was snickering.

The nurse had heard it all before.

I drove around. Pasha and his entourage were just outside the the main door. It was all glass: glass doors, with glass panels on each side of the door. The outer wall of the entire entry way was glass.

I got the kid in the front seat while the orderly piled his gear in the back.

153

"Holy shit, daddy," he said. "You started the truck without a key."

"A. That's correct. B. Stop calling me daddy."

"Okay, father," he said.

"So if I want to go neck with a guy, I just push a start button. Sweet."

"You have to have a fob on your person to use the push start," I told him. "It's mine, and you'll never see it."

"Right," Pasha said, strangely without disappointment. "Like the 9-mil you have tucked away in the small of your back."

Any flinching I did was internal. Outside, I was just regular: "Right," I said.

"What kind?"

"Viper," I said, pretending he wanted to know the make of my magical fob.

"Do I look stupid?" Pasha asked. "No, wait. Don't answer that."

"It's a Glock 43," I told him.

"That's one of those itty-bitty plastic guns."

"It's composite," I said. "It doesn't like being called plastic."

"Does it have a name?"

"No," I said. "That'd be stupid."

"I'll call it Face Gravy or Dilldozer?"

"No."

"Hand job or Lara Croft?"

"No names. Guns don't have names."

"How's about—" he started to say.

When we got home, Pasha wasn't as bouncy as usual. He got himself inside without us helping.

The house was dark, so the kid tried to help…

"Alexa," he said louder than he should.

"Hey, Cortana," he said.

"Hey, Siri," Pasha said, getting a little exasperated. None of it was working.

"Neanderthal's," he chuckled as he went to his bedroom using nothing other than his memory of the house's layout and a wee bit of full moon.

We looked at each other for a second.

Clap. Clap. And the lights dimmed, some fake logs in a fake fireplace in the corner turned on, and some over the top sexy music came out of some small speakers on the mantle.

"Bumpkin," Mikka called out to Pasha.

"Awwwww," I said.

A few days later, we were driving to Walmart to get some jeans.

"Beowulf," I said because I was tired of the silence. "My '43' is named Beowulf."

"What the flying fuck is a Beowulf and why did you name a pistol after it?"

"It's a thousand year old poem about a dragon killer."

He thought about it for a minute.

"What a faggy thing—"

"Stop," I said, touching the brake a little harder than was absolutely necessary. "I'll give you a pass this time because nobody told you different, but that word that starts with an F and refers to gay people… that word never leaves your lips. I mean never. Do not test me on this. Don't say that word. Don't even think it. Your brother would tell you the same thing. If I ever hear it — from you or your friends

— you get swacked. I'm a good swacker, so take this seriously. I already told you this once, so you've had both of your mistakes. You don't get another one."

It was quiet.

"Understand?" I added.

He nodded.

"Understand?" I asked louder.

"Yeah," Pasha said.

"Sorry," I said after we hit a big pothole.

"I'm tough, daddy," he said.

"You know how weird the word 'daddy' makes me feel?" I asked.

"Yup." And he didn't explain himself.

chapter twelve
close counts (sometimes)

"Virtue is persecuted by the wicked more than it is loved by the good."
— *Don Quixote, protector from hit-and-run windmills (1620)*

Over the spring and summer, I got really good with my Remington 700, up to about a hundred yards. I was on the firing range beating myself up about not being able to zero the sight.

"What's up?" Anatole asked.

"I'm fairly accurate, usually," I admitted. "But I'm never precise."

In other words I could eventually put a hole in the paper where I was aiming, but I almost never did it on my first shot.

I kept aligning and adjusting. Nothing worked.

"Okay, I see the problem," he said. "Do the other target down there. Here's how: Put five bullets into the target without adjusting anything."

Bang. Bang. Bang. Bang. Bang. You can read the words faster than I could fire. There's no magazine in my version of the rifle. I had to load each one by hand.

I ran to get the paper. Anatole drew a circle around the group of holes.

"That's called a grouping," he told me. "You can't know what's going on with your sight unless you have several groupings."

So I had a target with a big circle on it. All five holes were inside the circle. It's my grouping.

He told me the center of the circle is where my sight is aligned.

"Take your elevation up a click, and move the windage about 3 clicks right," says the master.

I did that over and over.

And over.

Eventually I got paper targets where the circle was right in the middle of the target.

"What about the size of my circle?" I asked Anatole one morning.

"What about it?" he said. "I mean, your accuracy is getting really good."

"Close doesn't count," I said.

"Actually, it does here," Anatole said, "but we'll get to that later."

My curiosity pegged upwards.

"You are getting nicely accurate. You're just not precise yet. Being precise means you fire five shots, and you end up with as few holes as you can. You put your second bullet through the hole made by the first bullet. When you can do that, you can take on anyone or anything."

"Wow," I said.

"Except Annie Oakley," he told me with a grin. "That woman could knock the wing off an amoeba."

"Amoeba's don't have—"

"Right," he said. "Amoebas have no wings because she shot them all off."

Practice. Practice.

When I was done with my lab work (gun range), I went back to my class studies. Ballistics is really interesting if you're into it. It's also one of the most tedious things in the world. And that's coming from a computer programmer who loves assembly language, the ones and zeros at the most basic level of the computer.

That isn't quite true. Electricity and its electrons flowing through CPUs and capacitors and diodes are a little more basic. This is my book, so I get to say what's the most basic element of computers. Would all the EEs just shut up and sit down? If I let y'all debate me, the quantum nerds will want to go lower, down to strings. There has to be a line, EEs.

Quantum. It's either on or off. Unless it's not. But probably it's either on or off. Then you look at the computer bit, and all the Heisenberg followers jump up and down worried about us looking at the bit.

"It'll change," they insist. "If you look, it'll morph."

Thank you.

One morning, things just seemed normal. I was about to see how irregular a morning could be.

Could somebody remind me to make a sign that reads: "Beware Normal."

My inside ballistics study came to a screeching halt by an eerie rumbling coming from the back of the house. The secret cage is back there, so weird noises always get one's attention.

The rumble grew louder and louder. The house and the ground under it trembled. I thought we were about to be hit by a freight train loaded down with coal and uranium.

Then it just stopped.

That's a weird ending, I thought. If you'd asked me to predict something, I'd have to say it would taper off. Nope, the noise and shaking just stopped. Maybe it was an earthquake.

I saw Anatole. His shirt was ripped, and that was the only clothing he had on his body. It had all been torn away. He'd been attacked.

Whatever is in the cage is dangerous, probably lethal.

Mikka knew what to do. He helped the boss into his private area, where I heard the shower run.

Kris and Hank went into the private area too. I could hear them talking to Anatole, probably through the shower curtain.

After a half hour or so, they all came back to the main room where the rest of the staff was waiting.

"It's okay," Anatole lied. "I'm okay."

The bandages on his face and the sling holding his left arm told a story that was a teensy bit off-center from "I'm okay."

He sat in his overstuffed chair. I'd never seen him in a bathrobe, so his other injuries must make tighter-fitting clothes a bother.

After some idle chatter about the farm in general, he asked everyone to leave... everyone besides me, Kris, and my husband.

Me? Yikes! I'm about to be read in. To what, I hadn't even a microscopic slither of a clue.

"We have a problem, Andy," he said. And let the record show that he's the only person who could call me that without getting his ears popped a few times. That name was reserved for dad.

"These lifeforms can't be killed," Kris said, "not by normal methods. Putting a bullet hole in them just pisses them off."

"What are they?" I asked.

"Dunno," Kris said.

The first secret record of these things dates to the late 1680s. The land here was like a land-locked Bermuda triangle. People went in, but nobody came out. Nobody knew why.

After the Civil War, the Union sent soldiers here. They built the first cover. It was layered steel with rivets. The creatures didn't like their new accommodations, so they broke it. Some dug under the metal walls, and others battered the steel plates over and over. They eventually broke free, which accurately scared the holy crap out of everyone involved.

The original reason the situation stayed out of the history books is that almost everyone who worked here ended up dead. Nobody survived to tell their tale.

In the 1906, an engineer found that the deadly varmint couldn't survive touching metal that had at least 300 volts running through it at 45 Hz or more. That ended up being the temporary solution. It kept the whatever-they-are confined.

And the EE who used experimentation to find all this was (drum roll): Anatole Austin. Yes, my boss was already an electrical engineer in 1906 when nobody actually knew that much about electricity. I mean, they did, but it was still a murky area.

The boss is that old, and it's like he doesn't even know it. Things seem normal to him, but working around the cage gets you close enough to the vermin to alter time.

Nobody seems to know why time gets warped. It just does.

The plan is to keep the creatures contained. That's being done, thanks to Anatole's cage.

The other project is to get rid of them. I don't think Anatole wants to annihilate them. He won't hesitate to do that if he has to, but he'd rather just send them packing.

Kris argues in favor of their complete destruction on the theory they'll destroy whatever they're near.

My theory. I don't have one. Not yet. This was the first I heard about any of this, but I see why we need secrecy. Can you imagine the worldwide panic?

China would send one of their nukes to melt Waxahachie. Some days, I'd probably be in the group advocating that. But, no. A nuke might not even kill the creatures.

There has to be another way, Anatole said.

And for some reason, that's where I come in.

Kristof invented a new kind of .50 caliber bullet that explodes. The concussion is actually an electromagnetic pulse (or EMP). Early tests show that electromagnetism is just as effective as that specific level of electricity.

The trouble is that the pulse doesn't have enough range to do widespread damage. The bullet "explodes" as a double exponential pulse. Any time fly nearby gets all jammed up and hits the ground alive but harmless.

I can live with harmless.

If you don't recognize this kind of pulse, don't worry about it. There's no test next period.

They can't just do a badonka explosion because they couldn't confine the EMP. The good folks in Ontario wouldn't appreciate all their electronics going dead.

To take out the population of time flies, Anatole says they'd need a mondo EMP. The mondo'est EMP ever done.

That can't happen.

So, I'm supposed to make it so the boss can send one of Kris' EMP bullets about a mile off and get it within a foot of the queen. That would make her harmless.

Maybe that would eventually make them all harmless, but that will take monitoring after the queen becomes a dude. Or something like that.

And right on cue, Mikka came back into the room. He had a big box with the word BARRETT in bold letters with a big black rectangle around it.

I know Barrett rifles. They're the bad-ass of military rifles.

The trouble with Barretts is that they aren't always accurate. The rifles are known for their ability to plough through tough steel, turning the metal into grenade-like shards that kill anything on the other side.

If you're trying to kill a drug cartel guy who is in a brick building and in a steel-lined safe room, you want a Barrett.

This is why close sometimes counts in a gunfight. You don't always have to put a bullet hole in the guy's frontal lobe. You can make his safe room explode like a grenade. It's all his protection that kills him.

Anatole wants to use the Barrett .50 BMG (a kind of 50-caliber bullet) for a couple of reasons. First, he's used to the rifle. Second, it can send one of its bullets around the world twice and then peel off to plink Mars. It is the longest-range gun you can find. It isn't accurate or precise, not like my Remington 700, but the boss could take down somebody in Honolulu from the top of his house in Waxahachie.

"You're a fighter, Andy," Anatole said, using that awful name again. "You don't ever give up. If somebody hurts you, you figure out a way to make them stop. When somebody hurts friend or family, you have that same tenacious focus."

So, there it is. It's why they think I add value to their equation.

"The world needs you, son," the boss said.

"The world needs you to figure this thing out," Kris said. I still don't much like him, but I'm warming up a little.

"Are your bullets supersonic?" I asked.

"Yyyyyup," Kris said.

"Do we know what effect supersonic has inside the time anomaly?" I asked.

"Nnnnope."

Great. This is why I keep saying that walking into the office is always a deer-in-the-headlights event. Every day.

Oooo, I could say that there is nothing normal with my normative day.

Mikka took me home early that day. My mind was a big fog. He undressed me and put me to bed.

I slept for several hours.

When I woke up, I was scared. I had to figure out how to make the time fly queen impotent. I had to figure out how to get Pasha a proper education.

Pasha ended up being the simple part. I thought it was hopeless, and I hate hopeless.

There are things called Schools For Troubled Teens, but most of them end up being brainwashing cash cows. If a kid is sent to one of these, he's abused over and over. It isn't sexual abuse. It's the kind of abuse homophobes in Texas employ.

The boss found a school in Oregon. It supposedly is for troubled gay kids and teens. They run K-12.

Mikka and I flew up there to look the school over. We talked to kids and graduates. We talked to administrators and teachers.

We looked all over the place for people with dirt on the school. No school for troubled gay kids can be squeaky clean. The police sometimes have problems with kids from the school, but I expected they would. What I didn't expect was how little in the way of negativity we saw.

The campus is gorgeous. The whole state of Oregon is beautiful. Mom's pot plantation would be legal up there! It's a no-no at the school, of course.

I was sold on it. Mikka thought it was too far away from home. I told him that's probably a good thing. He wanted to think about it, and that was a good start.

A few weeks later, Mikka and Anatole went up to the school without me. I was in charge of Pasha while they were gone.

I don't know what happened, but Mikka was all gung-ho for the place when he got back home.

Pasha wasn't. He refused to go.

"It isn't a discussion," Mikka said.

"Okay, okay," I tried to simmer down the discussion to a milder screaming match than the one that had one side arming their tactical nukes.

"You've always been here," I said.

"So?"

"Did you know some people say "doh-bro-ye uttro" instead of hello?

"Wow," he said, "and I came almost 20 years without knowing that."

I'm surprised that it lasted this long, but a Norman Rockwell page grandmother had torn out of Saturday Night Post finally gave up its hook and went crashing down to the sofa, barely missing Mikka by inches. If he weren't there, the whole incident would maybe be a one liner at a reunion. I knew Mikka: somehow this would end up with 4-part harmony an 8-part invention, and a minuet rammed with in the otherwise unsuspecting middle.

And he barely reacted. I was just about to head over to Amazon or Walmart (better prices) to see if I could find an Oscar or Tiny replica. Junk. Useless. Why do I pay these websites?

Anyway, I crammed 3 toothpicks into the hole and hammered them in with an ashtray that hadn't actually caught tobacco in decades. I pounded on the little points, the toothpicks collapsed.

"Uh," Pasha said, "what the fuck are you doing?"

I looked at him like he… oh the toothpicks. I was completely lost in what I was doing. On and on about one thing or another. Sorry.

Oh, toothpicks. You see, they were no longer toothpicks but are now part of the wall.

"What if the wall was cheap laminate," Pasha said, "like in this case."

"Do not confuse this with gratuitous fact," I said.

"Nail," I said holding out my hand. Mikka put the crumpled nail.

"Extreme whack-it thingie," I said. Mikka put the ashtray in my outstretched hand.

"Bourbon," I said, holding out my hand. Nothing.

"You gotta try," I shrugged.

When I held up the nail. I saw it was worse than I thought. I held the nail against the wall and tapped it with the Supreme Whakit

Thingie (a.k.a. ashtray). I nailed the newly enhanced nail with all it's pre-patina (rust). And returned the Rockwall page torn out of that magazine to its glory on the living room wall.

"God bless, shiplap."

"Stop it, you two."

"Every wall," Mikka said, "In every room is made of wood. The style of wood back then was shiplap. The timber held together with fewer nails, and proper people were frugal."

"Cheap," the youngster said.

We explained to him that I knew about the toothpicks from watching a woodworking show on PBS. There are several. Be careful: one has warnings about safety delivered by a guy missing a finger. I don't know if that's good or bad but...

"Toothpicks," Pasha said. "You used toothpicks to fill the hole."

"My way sounds more fun," I said, "but yeah."

"Let's see," I said. "Oh, "Доброе утро" means good morning."

"What language?" Pasha asked.

"Russian," Mikka said. "It's good morning in Russia. You need to know things, and that's what they'll do in Oregon. You'll know things."

"Can we make a wager," Pasha said, "that I will never need to know good morning in Russia?"

chapter thirteen
partying is such sweet sorrow

"Violent delights have violent ends."
— *William Shakespeare, pentameter fetish (1564'ish - 1616)*

Toward the end of summer, we packed up Pasha and his things. The school gave us a list of things he'd need, and it wasn't much. They'd be providing everything.

"What about rubbers?" Pasha asked.

"Not happening," Mikka said.

"Bareback! Sweet," he said jumping up and down.

The back of my hand brought his attention back to the present. I actually hit a kid with the back of my hand. It wasn't my finest moment.

So we all got in the Jeep for the drive up to DFW Airport. Mine's a 2-door Jeep Wrangler. The back seat comes out, so I had a short SUV. Since Pasha arrived, we put the back seat back in place.

He refused to put on a seat belt at first. I turned. He went click. Life is good.

That poor school is going to have their hands full. They have to tame him without dousing his spirit. They have to teach him all the stuff an adult needs to know but leave the surprise only found in kids. And they have to prepare him to cope with abuse that we all know is going to continue, but that preparation shouldn't make him more interested in fighting than he needs to be.

Mikka and I were arm-in-arm at the ticket counter. We stood back and let Pasha learn how to deal with life. We were sad and happy at the same time. It was sad to see him leave, but we were happy thinking about what he'd be like when he returned.

Parting really is a kind of sweet sorrow. The Bard was really onto something.

We went over to the security line, and Mikka kissed his brother on the cheek. Pasha came to me jumped up with his legs around my waist and tried to stick his tongue down my esophagus. A short jab from Mikka ended that, although I saw that we had worried a couple of uniforms and entertained some of the passengers.

Oh, the Monet family: never a dull moment.

The house was so quiet. I almost couldn't sleep. That teenager is really noisy sometimes.

Meeks walked up to stand right in front of me. We stood there and we stared at each other for a really long time.

"I am so proud of you," he said.

"For showing my restraint at not doing a Cooter on your brother?"

"Yeah, but mainly because you took my brother in stride. You're the one who made him part of our family. You're daddy here. I'm just big bro."

I started to cry.

"Stop," he said. "I think you probably saved my brother's life. He's going to hate you for a few days, but Oregon's going to be the biggest deal in his life. And for that......."

He reached around with one hand on each butt cheek and pulled me to him. So gently. Wow.

We kissed, not as some incendiary trick. We kissed as equals. As two guys who loved each other more than anything in the world. Best friends.

I felt my soul fall into his, and that's an amazing feeling. He picked me up and put me on the bed. With him on top, he unbuttoned my shirt, refusing to let me help. All he needed was fingers and his tongue. It must have taken a half hour for him to get all my clothes off.

By that time, the only things we wore were our wedding rings and a couple of tattoos.

"I love you so much," he said. Sometimes that's hard for me to hear. It feels wrong. It feels like the other person is just saying it for some kind of purpose. When Mikka said it, I knew he was just telling it like he felt it. No moment could be filled with more beauty.

He stretched his legs out, so his body covered mine completely. Both our dicks were hard. I was about to explode just from feeling him on me. He slowly moved his feet together, gently moving my legs apart as we kissed. His hands cupped the back of my neck. Mine held the small of my husband's back.

When my legs were far enough apart, he moved his body toward me. His dick found my hole without a helping hand, and he went inside. No condom. No lube. Nothing but Andreas and Mikka.

My whole life led to this moment.

He made love to me. I did my best to help, but he held me still.

Mikka was so slow and gentle. Somehow we didn't need lube or saliva or anything else. My body wanted him so much that I just relaxed into it. He wanted me so much that he didn't need help to thrust.

And Mikka never did go into any bang-bang. He was so gentle.

We made love for at least a half hour.

And then I felt him. His body temperature went up. His skin became moist.

And I felt his cum inside me because his dick exploded in me. Sometimes jacking off makes a puddle in my belly button, but a few times it hits my eyebrow. That last kind was how Mikka came in my ass.

If I ever doubted Mikka's love, that stopped on our bed that day.

We stayed there. Side-by-side.

Dusk came, and we were still in bed kissing.

I wanted to bottle the moment, but you can't ever do that.

Those moments don't happen often, but their echo remains in the heart.

I should apologize for being so mushy here, but I was more in love with Mikka right then than I have words to describe.

We kissed and giggled, and we didn't say a single word.

I told him I needed to get up. He didn't want me too.

"Bathroom."

It was all I needed to say. Yeah, but he didn't know why.

I made the greatest candlelight bubble bath in the history of mankind, and I invited my lover to join me with the pop of a champagne cork.

The tub was oversized — deeper and a little wider than the modern ones. No music. No traffic noise. Nothing but champagne, bubbles, Meeks, and me.

Our moods relaxed a bit. We were giggling and talking. He told me about some of his escapades off in the woods. I told him about the bright lights of the big city. The woods sounded like a much greater place to be than Dallas.

Dusk became night, and we forced ourselves to get out of the tub and back to bed. We went back to bed for sleeping this time.

That's a lie. He was really drained, but I gave my husband the greatest blowjob in the history of blowjobs. Where our earlier fuck was gentle, this was get-down-and-do-it sex. I played him like it was a flute, and he gave me whatever cum he still had. Personal point of pride: I never gag.

You may have noticed that Meeks is inside me more than the other way around. It isn't a "must do it like that" kind of thing. He's just that good.

But in doing my math, I saw that he came twice with only once for me. One of his was pure love, and the other was raw sex. Mine was that sublime first time.

The universe seemed out of balance.

I turned him over and struck like a lion. He's hung lots better than me, but I think I'm okay.

And BAM, I had my way with Mikka. Pure animal sex with the bed shaking. All I needed was some Beethoven blaring.

I haven't the foggiest idea how straight people have sex, but with Mikka and myself, there's usually some kind of I-am-Alpha play. We wrestle or roll around. We run and tumble.

When he felt me thrust into him, Mikka relaxed. He gave himself to me completely. It's the most intimate gift possible, in my book. He was mine, and I took the gift. That's what "making love" really means. You don't "make" anything, you relax and give it. At least that's what happens with us. I'm not the most worldly slut with so many conquests to be an authority.

With Mikka, it's so fun to be gay.

We started getting postcards from Pasha. His scribbling was so shaky, Mikka had to decipher them.

```
Is it legal for my dad to marry my bro? Kid here
says not. Can I pop him?


PAŞA
```

That was it. Postcards are small. I'm so proud of him for trying. Paşa is how he always writes his name, according to Mikka.

That's the original spelling. In the Ottoman Empire (Turkey), a Pasha was a knight or duke.

We did our jobs at the farm and at home. Meeks was busy making new French maid uniforms and some leather things with rhinestones. I didn't ask. Afraid of the answer.

One of the hens died for no reason we could find. The others were muted for a day or so.

How the fuck am I supposed to do my work. It's like a needlepoint of quandary and brick walls. I am clueless about ballistics, and few of the books agree on anything.

I have to find a way to nullify the time fly queen, but I can't go look at her majesty. I couldn't even write a masters thesis on EMP, and I'm not allowed to ask anybody. Everything is so secretive that if I ever find out what I'm doing, I have to shoot myself.

The scientific method should let me know the terrain and its challenges.

First challenge: I don't hate the time fly queen, although she's most likely the one responsible for murdering my dad. In her defense, he was undoubtedly trying to murder her first. So, the traditional scientific method has 6 steps, and it's always collaborative. I don't get to collaborate, except with Anatole and Kris, and they're both as lost as a gray goose in tall grass.

NOTE: I absolutely promise that this won't degenerate into a science textbook. My science grades in college are fairly clear that this isn't something I should do. So......

Here we go then.

1. See something interesting enough to look at.

    Got that in spades. So far, so good. There are these time flies, which may or may not be actual flies. They may or may not be alien lifeforms who just want to go home or take over the earth.

Maybe they heard of mom's marijuana patch, and they've been trying to score some of that for a... no, the patch is only a few decades old, and the critters have been here for millennia.

I am officially interested at this point, and that's the sole goal of the first step.

2. Find some pertinent questions

Da-fuk am I supposed to do with this? Questions are the summation of the project. It's all I have: questions.

For the first time in my life, I really need to smoke a joint. Rumor has it that one of mom's plants sends the smoker out on a cosmic trip. I don't see any useful questions here, so I need to give that a try.

Bye.

———

Okay, questions.

a) Would a hysterectomy on the queen solve any of the human's problems, or would so much as an attempt so infuriate the time flies that they'll become gonzo-ninja-time-flies? There's a question, and I feel I really need the answer.

b) Is EMP really effective. If so, what percentage of the time?

c) What's the best frequency? And is the double exponential pulse the bad ass that Kris claims it is?

d) An EMP can go from zero to daylight. Did Anatole really test some other frequencies? There could be a kind of EMP that's completely harmless to earth and earth's sentient beings of the indigenous variety? I bet nobody's considered throwing a bunch of AAA batteries into the cage. Or if that doesn't work, how's about one of those 18650 Li-Ion gizmos. Maybe we don't have to go EMP-nuclear as the first step.

e) Lightening strikes are a kind of EMP. Can we do a Benjamin Franklin thingy with a kite, some string, and a key or two. If that isn't festive enough, we could haul in a tesla coil.

f) When a meteor hits one of our satellites, a special kind of EMP gets unleashed. So, would that be effective, or do we have to arrange for a satellite near the cage and wait for a meteor. I have feasibility issues with this.

I'm lots better at doing the dishes and folding the clothes than I am at the Scientific friggin' Method.

The truth is that my science professor at college would have a stroke if he heard that I was doing science, and my science was either going to destroy or save the world.

It's a lot of weight to carry, and I don't feel a bit prepared.

The only thing that keeps me pointed in the right direction is Mikka. He and I have always been together, from the time we both wore Pampers all the way to the point where he made his own leather bustiers for work at Anatole's house.

It wasn't like we met and fell desperately into the hot fires of what we called love. It was sudden, but it wasn't like that. I loved Meeks as a best friend, spending hour after hour talking and walking, camping and wrestling.

Then he said "I love you," and those words were like an irreversible magic spell on my soul. A light switch went click, and there wasn't any way to go back.

I heard Meeks say he was in love with me, and I know how hard that was. He's gypsy from top to bottom. Regardless how much you dig into his psyche, heritage comes out as his most important factor. He and Pasha are the only two Roma I met, but I know how much their spirit needs to be free. Ask somebody to describe himself, some will say they're a Democrat. Somebody else will say they play chess or contract bridge. Activists will tell you they're gay or anonymous or black. Mikka always puts gypsy on the top of his list.

When Hitler was in power, he tried to smash that free spirit by murdering every gypsy he could find. Only the Jews suffered more. In gypsy tales from the 1930s and 40s, it's called the pharrajimos. The word means "the cutting up." I think it was mostly because they were more closely tied to being gypsy than to being the member of one country or another.

We had the Jewish Nation, where Germans were incensed that there could be people in their country who identified with a larger group. It would be a kind of Jewish caliphate. (How's that for a mish-mash of culture?) I think the idea holds.

A gypsy was a gypsy in Romania or Ireland. They were all family, even when their respective countries were at war.

It's what Mikka means when he is afraid of getting stuck. He's gypsy, not Texan.

And that's how wondrous it was when he told me he was in love with me, a gadjo. It's hard to explain, because he's not against any of the gadjé in the world. It's just that he isn't one.

He has a soul chain back to the marrow of the gypsy nation, and that's something that won't ever break. If something bad happened to the gypsy compound in Waxahachie, he'd be right there even if many of them hate him for being gay and (worse) for being in love with a gadjo.

By the way, gadjo is masculine singular. Gadjé, with the e-acute, is plural. Test next period, buster: study study.

Part of me thinks he broke that sinew to the worldwide gypsy nation, but I know he didn't. Not a real break.

That's the sheer depth of his love. He does love me, and it goes against everything he is.

He isn't playing me either. I've known him so many years, that I know exactly when he's gaming somebody. Not this time, when he said he loves me, I could take it to the bank.

And that was my heart's switch flipping.

The mourning doves in Texas mate for life. If one dies, the other is left in complete despair. That's how I feel with Mikka.

175

So, he said the word first (not that it matters in the long game), and that's what made me realize that I'm madly in love with him too. It really was like a light switch. Flip.

I've loved the guy all my life, but all of a sudden, I was IN LOVE with him. There's no place I'd rather be.

We headed out to the woods after work. I'd built a box just out of sight of the house, and that's where we put our clothes and picked up a blanket (for me to lie on because I'm a sissy when it comes to Texas stickers). I also have a pot for cooking and for coffee. I'm the wussy of the family.

"I love the moon," I told him after we stretched out under the clear sky.

"Me too," Meeks said, "but some people get all creepy about the moon."

"Whacha mean?"

"Mother moon?" he said, and I kept quiet about all the times I've used the phrase. "Moon isn't steady. Sometimes it's a slither. Sometimes it's invisible. It makes loops that run on the schedule of a menstrual cycle. Nothing wrong with female things, but I'm gay and don't understand."

He told me that the only time an eclipse is possible is when the sun, moon, and earth are perfectly aligned. He says symmetry is over-rated.

We could sit and talk for hours. He usually seemed so wise about stuff that isn't taught in books.

The next time we were out in the woods on a full moon, he brought a bottle and an eyedropper. He filled up the pot with water from the creek and sat the pot of water right between us. He got me to look at the pot and find the moon's reflection.

Meeks told me to use the eyedropper to pull water from where the moon's reflection was. I saved the water in the little bottle, maybe one ounce.

"There," he said when my bottle was full.

"There's got to be a point."

"Sort of," he chuckled. "Whenever you think you need Mother Moon or Sister Moon, you have it. You got a bottle of full moon, not just some namby-pamby half moon."

We talked about living around nature, and it's the greatest sounding ever. I can see making our clearing home. Winter might be dicey being naked and all.

I got really good at finding edible leaves and berries. We have wild onions out there. I cheated: planted some 'taters. They were good, even if he made fun of me being a fake gypsy.

He always got me to pay attention. We have one moment: now. That's all we ever have.

We have one place: here. That's the only place we'll ever be.

Here. Now.

So many people are "in order to" people. They want stacks of cash, in order to get a car or get an RV. They're so busy trying to get ahead that they miss the scenery of the trip.

Truth: I wasn't going to give up my house. Not even for a daily view of our enchanting, yet shifty, moon. Not even for the miracle of a blue sky.

What he did was teach me to be aware of the bubble I'm in. There are so many bewitching things, big and small.

He once hollered at me for picking a flower.

I liked the flower.

"You murdered a flower just to look at it while it died?"

I felt like an idiot for awhile. His kiss brought me back down.

To make us both aware of what's around us, we started a game. One day, we'd eat only yellow food. Easy: corn, bananas, and so forth. Green was a cinch. Try blue or purple. I absolute detest eggplant, so purple was going to be a problem.

We did a "no kill" day. Nothing could die to feed us. I thought it meant we'd go vegan. Ick, but okay. But no... eating a potato kills the plant. Same things with onions and carrots. I wan't excited about Mikka's no-kill diet. Believe it or not, we could have eggs from a regular grocery store because the eggs aren't fertilized. No eggs from my coop were allowed because of Marengo. Friggin' rooster ruined my breakfast.

```
Some kid took off all shower heads and stuck life-
savers inside. After showers, the whole school was
colored for a day or two. Not me. Swear it.


PAŞA
```

Oh the book on parenting I could write.

chapter fourteen

marengo

"How narrow is the vision that exalts the busyness of the ant above the singing of the grasshopper."
— *Khalil Gibran (1883-1931)*
(Only Wm Shakespeare has sold more poetry. Smoke on that, McKuen.)

To review. I hate guns, but that's what I do for a living. I'm sort of the opposite of a gypsy mentality, but guess who I'm in love with. Back in school, I couldn't even spell EMP, but take a wild guess what my job now entails. And I am an official guardian of an underage kid who really wants to get inside my pants. I'm MARRIED. I mean, I am put-your dance cards down, boys. I am off the market. I still get giddy to think about that.

That's about it. Oh, wait… I also scrambled a bully's nuts with a 9-mil that I happened to have on me (and now I never leave home without it). He had been threatening me and others, so I was saving lives by doing it. I've thought about that over and over. It's the worst thing I ever did. But all the cops and Texas Rangers tell me it was the only thing I could have done.

"I get the whole flower thing," I told my husband (love that term still: the husband, the main squeeze, Mister Man).

"The Masters are pleased, grasshopper."

"What about that moon water?" I asked.

"You think you killed something? Talk to me."

"I froze it in time," I said. "Isn't that what killing is?"

"Yup, your universe isn't catatonic anymore," he grinned.

The next time we were in the woods, I poured my moon water onto the plant I maimed to get its flower.

Speaking of maiming, we had a talk about that No Kill diet.

"Is it really okay to wound a living thing?"

"Huh?"

"We had our No Kill diet, so we ate things that we took from plants that didn't kill anything. We maimed them. That's creepy."

"Wow," he said. "Fucking wow."

He never thought of that. He stood up, put his palms together like he was praying, and said "Namaste."

"Huh?" (Don't you just love my command of the English language?)

"I bow to you," Meeks said, "because I see the work of the divine in you."

I stood up and did the same.

"Namaste," I said, "but can the grasshopper itself be divine."

"It can, it is, we all are," he told me. "All you have to do is recognize it."

"I love you so much, Mikka."

"I love you too," he told me.

And he did. We both did.

It was a moment that was so sweet, but nothing made me want to cling to that moment. I was excited about Now and Here. Tomorrow, I hoped to be ecstatic about that day's Now and Here.

We fell asleep in each other's arms. Right then and right there.

The next morning, when I opened my eyes, Mikka hadn't moved. I stayed still and just watched him sleep. I didn't need sex (which is weird for me: I always want sex). We were under the slight glimmer of the Texas dawn coming over the prairie hills.

We dressed and walked to the main house. Anatole let us use the shower in one of the extra bedrooms.

There was a little excitement. I recognized the noise: Marengo was there going on and on about something. He jumped up and down and rolled.

One of the workers noticed there was a paper stuck to one of his wings. It was hard for anybody to make sense out of the marks on the paper. It was so scratchy that I figured one of the hens was doing some kind of tribal dance on it.

But no, it was English. The author had obviously struggled to get his marks on the paper, and I haven't a clue how the paper got stuck or glued to Marengo's wing.

The rooster held it up to me. He wouldn't let anyone else touch the paper. I think it hurt a bit, but the bird was trying to be brave. When you're blott-o stoned, it's hard to hold onto things. Poor little guy is always stoned, I think. He fell over trying to get the paper to me.

I carefully took the paper off his wing, afterwards the rooster danced around in circles.

Next was the hard part. I looked at it one way: senseless. I twisted it all around: top, sides, and bottom. I worked on the damn thing for an hour.

Kris was beyond impatient.

"Give me it," he said. Marengo walked over and pooped on his perfectly shined wingtip shoes.

Then something caught my eye, almost by accident. A light shown through from the other side. So I turned the paper over to let the sunlight show me the scratches backwards.

181

I could barely breathe. I have never had such a shock in my life, not before or since.

The scratches, best I could tell, said—

```
MORE L M
```

It wasn't just the scratches. They turned on themselves, and they were crazy.

L M — my dad, Laird Monet. That's impossible, of course.

When Mom told him that she loved him, his response was always "more," meaning he loved her more.

If you sat me down and forced me to write out the 100,000 things that might possibly happen, Marengo finding a long-lost note from dad to Mom wouldn't have been on the list.

Dad wrote that note to my mother, and she probably never saw it. The note stayed on the prairie for all those years, until the rooster found it.

Out of the corner of my eye, I saw Meeks bowing to the bird with prayer hands, mouthing "Namaste."

I was grateful for getting the paper. I think. It sure gave me a start.

Anatole sent me home for a week, and he let Mikka come too.

Kris was all business, and he thought some relic from the past was a waste of time. He was probably right.

The past wasn't now, and we had things to do now.

"Stop it," Mikka said. "It isn't the past, dunderhead."

"It's an old scribble from dad," I cried. "It was shaky writing, so he probably wrote it while he was being attacked."

"Okay, maybe," he told me, "but do you really know what the past is?"

"Yesterday, 150 years ago."

"What relationship do you have with the past?"

"I don't understand," I said.

"That's the first thing you said that makes sense. There IS the past. Don't ever say it WAS. It IS the past, and the only relationship you have with the past is thinking about it. And guess when all that thinking is happening."

"Now?"

"Bravo," he said. "It is now. Think about the past, and all your crazy shitty thinking is still happening right now and right here. NOW is the only fucking thing you have. Use it."

"How?" I asked.

"Beats the hell out of me," he said. "I have to do all your work for you?"

I started to get angry with him, and that would have been a first.

What I had was a souvenir directly from dad. It was a relic, probably from the day he died. Considering how illegible the handwriting is, it could have been written as dad lay dying.

I put it in the family bible.

Dear Dad:

Andreas here again. This time I'm writing because I found a note you wrote to Mom. I think it was maybe on the day you died because it was a little hard to read.

She really loved you, daddy. We all did. I still do.

I gave up praying so long ago. I prayed for you to come home because I'm selfish. I prayed that to God every day. Over and over and over. And I never got a response. It was obviously a waste of time.

Deep down inside of me, I know this letter is a waste of time. You will never see it, but I think it does me good. It is cathartic. (See how all that college tuition taught me fancy and expensive words!)

So I write to you again. For me. I know you are gone, but this letter helps me. I want to be with Mikka without dragging him into my secret despair. I need to accept that you're dead and to move on. But your fishing hook is still in my heart, and I feel it being tugged every day. That isn't fair to Mikka. It probably isn't fair to me either.

I stopped praying for the situation to stop. Prayer was wasting so much energy. You must be in a better place, and I will always believe that.

What I stopped believing in was God. All the Christians in Waxahachie hate me because I'm gay. Nobody reaches out to be friends or to be helpful. Nobody even says Hello. The God of those Christians is the most evil thing I know.

Why I prayed to him all my life. I'm a fool for doing it. If there's a God like that, I want to be as far away from him as I can be. No deity that makes people hate is worth pissing on.

Sorry for the language, but I am writing this letter for me. You will never see it.

I had a dream last night. A dog was crying. A poor dog wailing is the saddest thing you can hear. It makes me cry to think of all the misery humans have put onto dogs. They just want to be friends and happy.

In my dream the dog had just run around a corner and couldn't see his human friend. The dog cried. Moaned. Wailed. He called out for the human who he couldn't see.

The human heard the cries, so they still had a

connection. It was the wailing that was the connection. It was the moaning that was this dog's
prayer. That dog's prayer was answered because the
person came running.

What is so sad to me is the millions of dogs who
have no friend. They moan and cry because they
just want a friend.

Mikka and I are friends like that. We are lovers
too, but first we were friends. If I cry, he comes
running, and I do the same for him.

I want to learn how to moan like the friendless
dog, which is the saddest being I can think of. If
I wail like the friendless pooch, I think I will
learn to be friends with myself. I need to answer
my prayer.

When I saw your note, I cried out. I wailed for
the first time in years. I wanted to hold you. I
want to cry out to you, Daddy, to get your attention. And somehow I am also moaning for friendship
with myself.

Daddy, is being an adult always this hard? I see
that I have a bunch of shit I have to work
through.

Love,

Andy

chapter fifteen
the barrett

"Between us, we cover all knowledge; he knows all that can be known, and I know the rest."
Mark Twain (1835-1910) on Rudyard Kipling

> We have a small pool. Senior filled it with cherry jello.
>
> Not me. Swear it.
>
> Paşa

I will say that Pasha's grammar is getting a wee bit more structure. The English major in me doesn't want to throw myself off a cliff reading his postcards.

> Dear Daddy,
>
> Your grandson, Pasha, is in Oregon at a school that specializes in education for troubled gay kids. It is a good school.

187

```
Pasha writes. I think it is most likely a class
project. He is telling us wild stories about what
happens there.


Now, I don't know what it's like where you are,
but if you ever see Allan Sherman, please slap
him.


Love,

Andy
```

Allan Sherman's famous song was "Hello Muddah Hello Fadduh." You should go listen to it on Spotify. YouTube has him singing it on the Perry Como Show.

Perry Como was ….. oh, never mind.

Thanks to Anatole's pointer about grouping shots, my precision with the Remington 700 was coming close to excellent under 500 yards. Over that, it was crap.

And I really don't like the Barrett. It's all scary and stuff, and I don't like it. The thing looks like a long gray pipe with an uppercase T on the muzzle. That goofy thing is called a "muzzle brake."

You know all that equal and opposite science crap that I ignored in school. As it turns out when you cause a boom in a tiny space, it doesn't want to stay confined. The easiest solution for the gun is to send the bullet down the barrel faster than the speed of sound. Bullets are scary-fast and there's an actual sonic boom.

So as the bullet goes out, guess who's the equal and opposite in the calculation. That would be my shoulder.

The muzzle brake gives the escaping gas three exits: front, two sides. The bullet always goes out the front because a bullet bopping along at 3,044 feet per second (2,075 miles an hour) is not going to be happy with the idea of a right turn in the muzzle brake. Not happening.

That isn't the fastest bullet in the world, but it's faster than a time fly flies. Or so I'm told.

And there's a fraction of a fraction of a nano second where the bullet is blocking the front hole on its way downrange. In that tiny amount of time, gas gets expelled out the side. The gas has already done its job of pushing the bullet, so it's just gas at that point. We don't care what it does, so pushing it left or right means... well... Suck it, Newton, we're not going to have an equal reaction.

Got all that? Said another way, without the muzzle brake a .50 BMG firing would move my shoulder from Waxahachie to Peoria, and that'll make me grumpy. Really really grumpy.

It still has a little bit of a kick, but less than you'd expect.

Still, I'm a sissy, so I built myself a rig to hold the Barrett for testing. I don't have to hold it, and my rig doesn't seem to mind the kick.

I did have to drive spikes through the base and into the ground because the rig kept jumping around. I could just see one of my jumps putting a big hole in the boss's satellite dish.

The computer and some assembly language let me bring some order to the ballistics problem. I got to where I could be fairly accurate and always precise (rig did that part) with one of Mr Izod's EMP prototype bullets. They didn't do real EMP, but they were shaped weird like the real thing would be.

Accuracy would have to count, and I was getting close.

I still wasn't convinced that EMP would be the solution. When I mentioned it at our daily staff meeting (Anatole, Kris, and me), Kris always tried to shut me down because I don't have 38 degrees in various kinds of science.

What's an idiot English major going to know about it? He actually said that one day, not remembering that I rarely back down.

"What's Einstein or Oppenheimer going to know about performing a remote hysterectomy on a time fly?"

189

Kris fumed. Anatole grinned.

Point: Andreas. (Still dwelling, apparently.)

"Hey, sweet meat," the woman said at Denny's.

"Mo-mo?" I said, "What are you doing waiting tables? Aren't you—"

"Yup," Monique Thompson said. "Sis is out of town, but she really didn't want to be docked pay. I got a health card."

"I never doubted that for a second," Mikka said.

"How's married life?"

"Don't you know?" I asked.

"Do not go into that pothole, dear," she said with a snap. "Just leave that lie."

We ordered. Monique refused to let me order the chicken fried steak.

"Just don't," she said with the kind of finality that isn't to be discussed. I don't know why, but I got a burger instead.

When she brought the food out, she asked about Milosh Cooper. Mikka's dad had been missing since he tried to attack Pasha at our house.

"Figure he's dead then," Monique said. "Crispy critter or floater, maybe."

I pointed to the burger, like she's talking about stuff not intended for lunchtime conversation.

"Taste that fucker, love, and then tell me about what's befitting this sumptuous feast, motherfucker."

And she was off.

That's Mo-Mo. I love her to death.

"Death?" she said from the kitchen. "I heard that, bird-brain."

How could she hear exposition I just wrote in a novel? Jeez.

"It's fiction, Sherlock," she said as she passed us to get to the next table.

As we paid, the phone rang. Hank told us to get back to the farm.

"Nothin' serious," he told Mikka. "Boss just wants the two of you."

chapter sixteen
how it has to work

"A lot of hacking is playing with other people, you know,
getting them to do strange things."
— Steve Wozniak (most righteous hacker ever) —

K ris and Anatole were already in the big, front room of the
farmhouse. I know they were just waiting for us, but it somehow seemed ominous, like an ambush. My guard went up. It
didn't need to. (wiping forehead)

There was another strange note. This time, Marengo had it in his beak.
It was the longest message of any. They spent hours trying to decipher
it, and finally they all knew — we all knew:

```
Dog pray so goes heavin. Love you 'n Miks 'n Pash.
L M
```

I could feel all four of our hearts stop when Anatole read what
he'd deciphered.

"If this is some sick joke," I said, "stop it now."

Mikka hugged me tight.

"Agreed," Kris said, "but it was neither Anatole nor myself."

This changed everything. I mean everything.

The first sentence was the old pithy saying that just says "All dogs go to heaven." It's the name of an old, crappy movie. The flick came out in 1989, so it's likely dad would have known the title at the time of his death.

"Anybody know what the praying dog reference is?" Kris said.

"Maybe," I said. "I wrote a letter to dad that said when the dog cries for his master, it's a kind of prayer. It is, and I believe that, but dad never knew that."

"When?" Anatole asked.

"The note? I wrote it a couple of weeks ago."

"Where is it?" Anatole pressed.

"At the house," I told him.

"No, it isn't," Kris said as he produced that letter I wrote to dad.

"You went into our house?" I pressed strongly. If so, Anatole crossed a line.

"No," Anatole said. "I found the two notes together."

This was the goofiest thing ever.

"Am I supposed to hear eerie music and get palpably wet with fear?" I asked.

"No," Mikka said, "but maybe we can figure this thing out."

It was Kris who finally stated the obvious: "So we have a letter to a guy killed in the cage, and we have an answer scratched out somehow. And the whole back-and-forth comes special delivery by a rooster that's always stoned on pot seeds."

We all sat there, soaking it in. But, yeah, that is pretty much what we were being led to believe.

"Are these time flies intelligent?" I asked.

"I don't know," Anatole admitted. "They're intelligent enough to outsmart our attempt to kill them for a few hundred years. Yeah, in some way, they have to be intelligent."

According to the letter, "L M" (Laird Monet, my dad) knows about Mikka and Pasha.

I didn't see anything specific that we needed to do, other than being freaked out and royally pissed at whoever was doing this. The letters were a cruel joke being played on me. Kris has been such a dick for the past year, that he was my person-of-interest.

"What kinds of sensors are around the cage?" I asked. Look at me, getting all scientific all of a sudden.

"There's some work there," Kris said. "One case is a touch panel. The sensor works on several frequencies that could mean somebody is pressing the panel."

Why do science wonks make everything sound so complicated?

"Radar receivers understand a range of frequencies," Anatole said.

"Could we — meaning you, of course — build something that scans a wide range of frequencies?" I said. "Couldn't spend more than a fraction of a second on each frequency."

"What frequency range?" Kris asked, like he was annoyed.

"What is the theoretical range of frequencies coming out of the cage?"

"Then no," he laughed, "there is no machine like that available, and it'd take years to develop one."

"Chop. Chop," Mikka said with a grin.

"You've got audio, light, ultraviolets, radiation," Anatole said. "I'm afraid Kris is right. That would be an almost insurmountable project."

"How do we make it simpler?" I asked. "Has anybody ever heard anything from the cage."

"Boom," Mikka said. "Things explode."

"There a buzzy thing sometimes," Anatole said.

"If there's a recording, could we speed it up or slow it down to see what's inside the buzz."

"Kris?" Anatole said.

"On it." And he left us, sneering at me.

I mean, we used to be the best of friends. Now, he treats me like I'm slime off some neglected pond. He acts like there's no amount of wax that could polish me into anything acceptable to the Halász family.

In a few minutes, I was in my little work area. My Remington 700 rifle, chambered at a reasonable 6.5-mil Creedmoor cartridge was there. My big honker — the Barrett bazooka/rifle thingy that blew out an insane bullet a half inch in diameter — was there. I had stacks of ballistics books, a wind portable gauge for the firing range. I had two different gizmos that you use on the range to determine the velocity of the bullet. All my paper targets are in a shed next to the range.

And there was me. I had no clue what to touch first, but the whole lot didn't seem useful for the time flies. The Remington was the only thing that was actually fun. It was like one of those cars from before computer chips. You could actually understand what the engine was doing with a few simple monitors and tools. I never hesitated to work on the Remington 700.

Need a new barrel? Not a problem. All I need is the barrel, some shoe polish, and epoxy, because I'd bed the barrel just like I did the Picatinny rails.

Trigger too heavy? Take it apart and adjust whatever made it a easier pull.

I could do things with the Remington.

But what the fuck do I adjust for a creature I never saw. Big bullets with built-in EMP (which still is as weird as it sounds) didn't seem promising.

And my whole adventure was as dangerous as it sounded. People got killed working around the cage. That includes my father and several others in the past couple of centuries.

I was at such a loss that I broke the rule about being close to the cage.

There's an airtight room with thick steel walls, and on the far side of that mini-fortress is a metal door with a lock like you'd find on a bank vault. I could see inside the cage because lots of the rest of the wall was that metal screening. Scary signs warned about certain death just by touching the screen.

The whole thing was scary: the bugs, the electrified screen, that cranked up cray-cray Barrett bazooka back on my desk.

There was a bench in the metal room. I thought I maybe should have brought some kind of weapon, but which one? And how exactly are you supposed to defend yourself against something that does freaky things to time?

"Andreas," I said to myself, "grow a couple and deal with it."

It was where my dad was killed, and I felt some kind of spiritual connection with him, faint memories of a long-dead man.

So, I made a decision: I would sit on that goddam bench until I figured the whole thing out, or my ass fell off. Smart money would be on the second option.

So I sat. And sat.

And when I was done with that, I sat some more.

The room was my new roost.

I noticed a few odd things inside the cage, but they were all trivial. That said, I got all scientific one day and started writing things down.

- Limb moved with no wind, which was kind of trippy
- Rain came with no clouds, which made me go "noid" for some reason.

197

I mean, it was a whole new level of bat shit crazy. But I had to do it. Nobody else could figure anything out (and I was beginning to put myself on that unfortunate list). People depended on me, says Anatole.

The time flies could destroy the entire world. Oh, sure, we have an extinction level something-or-other, so... I don't know... let's put the idiot who can't even multiply or divide in charge. That makes perfect... it makes perfect bat shit.

I didn't feel any animosity. Usually when there's a group of people who want to put you down, there's some level of hostility, maybe antipathy. The other guys, at a minimum, aren't going to like you. But I just didn't feel them.

It wasn't like the Brits, when they came over to put us in our place for all that outlandish talk of freedom (limited to white men who owned land, but it was still a kind of freedom).

There was a guy named Patrick Henry back then. He was your basic politician, but the time he lived in wasn't basic in any form. It was dangerous and desperate. In the build up to the revolution, Patrick Henry gave a speech that I had to memorize in history class.

The famous line in that speech was "Give me liberty or give me death." He absolutely was a politician, which tells me he was always trying to game the system one way or another. The speech was about a tax that the king way over on another continent tried to impose. Henry and others said, oh hell no.

So was that part about liberty or death just a platitude? Yeah, probably. I think so. It was years before any fighting, but he said it. They didn't have YouTube or the WayBack website, but the king's supporters had their memories of what he said.

He knew they knew, and they knew that he knew they knew. See, they were all smarty-pants about knowing stuff.

So what he said was just a political statement, but when the shit hit the fan a decade later, he was certainly on somebody's list. Some folks really wanted him dead, and it's the kind of dead where you really stop breathing. It just stops. You're there, but you aren't breathing.

"Can I be so bold as that?" I said out loud.

"You have to be," Anatole said. He made me fall off the bench. I didn't hear him come in.

"Something is there," I said. "Maybe it's deadly and maybe not. And you picked me to figure it out?"

"I can't figure it out," he said. "Your dad is dead, so it isn't him. It can't be."

"I'm not a scientist," I continued, sort of talking to myself, "and I don't understand scientific methods. All this is is science. The cage has no poetry or music. There is no round ball to be kicked, and no walls to be painted.

"I can do all those things," I said. "That's not what you need here."

"Says who?" Anatole said.

"Whom," I corrected, mostly by some kind of grammar police inside.

Anatole ignored me: "I picked you because of all those things, believe it or not. Science has done nothing productive here, not for centuries. We haven't done anything, other than get good people like your dad killed. You don't do science, not the regular type, but you never give up. Never. We have to have you to break all the rules here. You have to nail jello to an old tree."

"Jello to a tree," I laughed. "You've gone batty-batty bomo."

"Bobo," he corrected.

"Bobo, sorry," I said. "One thing's for sure, no more letters to dad. That's just too weird."

"No, let's try another," he said like he was in the middle of putting a thought together.

"Okay."

"We know that whatever is scratching out these notes isn't your dad. I'm fairly sure Marengo is just the delivery-bird—"

"Not airmail," I said. "He doesn't fly."

"How's about a letter asking how we can communicate."

My entire being — body, spirit, psyche, soul — had a Holy Shit moment.

```
Dear Whoever You Are:


I am Andreas. We wish to converse. How do we
"talk" without using these notes?


Andreas
```

I left the note near Marengo in the chicken coop of my house. Sure enough, within a week there was another note.

```
Bird is our friend, Andy.
Look for barometer.
```

Da-fuk?

chapter seventeen
hurry up and wait

"Ah but if you go from Moscow to Budapest you think you are in Paris."
— *Gyorgy Ligeti, Hungarian composer, and hysterical human being (1923-2006)*

All I can say is daaaa-yum. Damn, I'm good. All the big-brain squad has been working on the problem of the time flies for centuries, like more than 2 centuries, without so much as a clue.

It took me less than a year.

And what do I have to show for that year

And we have time flies — alleged time flies. Nobody knows what they are or what they can do. People suspect they eat time. Unless he's lying, Anatole has gone through something involving time.

We have had no theory on how to observe or communicate with the time flies. (Yeah, me. Yeah, me. Ra. Ra. Ra.)

For reasons that will forever baffle me, they are somehow friends with my rooster, who is 24/7 stoned out of his little rooster brain on pot seeds from mom's weird psycho garden.

I am in the middle of the most fucktafied life in history, but I am sharing it with a man whom I love, and who has that primo wisp of hair on his stomach — his treasure trail.

So I am simultaneously completely fucked and totally / blindly / wholeheartedly the luckiest guy ever.

Mikka and I packed up our gear. We were taking Miss Jeep to the coast for a couple of days.

Pasha was safely in Oregon studying and coping. I think. I hope.

Anatole gave me a satellite phone. I didn't even know you could have a phone that went directly to a satellite. It was for emergencies when we were out of cell phone coverage, which is very precisely where we intended to be. The boss reminded me that actually using the phone was incredibly expensive, so it really was for emergencies.

I knew a place. Matagorda Island is one of the barrier islands that run the entire coastline of Texas. To the northeast is Galveston Island, and Mustang Island is on the southwest end. (Note to snarky Texans: yes, I am ignoring San Jose Island because it's puny.)

So what's so special about a hunk of sand in the middle of nowhere? Well, for starters... it's a hunk of sand in the middle of friggin' nowhere. There aren't any people for miles, and there's little danger from apex predators like we have around Waxahachie.

There's pure danger close-by: sharks. The islands along the Texas shore go out so gradually that you think everything is okay, but there's a shelf. The islands all drop off from knee level to really deep. You can see the color of the water, so it isn't like you're surprised by it.

The shark population really increases the further south you go. Galveston has some sharks. Matagorda has a few more. From Corpus Christi on down to South Padre, it's party time for the fins.

Just off the shelf are sharks and lots of them. The nasty one is the bull shark. There aren't many attacks in Texas, but it's the bull shark that is usually playing the part of the bad guy. We have tiger sharks, too, and they scare the crap out of me. I've seen bonnet-head sharks, which is sort of like a hammerhead but with bonnets instead of hammers.

Oh, don't snicker at me. Do I look like a fish expert?

We have lots of black-tip sharks. By the way, when you see something labeled "black-tip shark" in a grocery store, they're probably lying. It's commonly mislabeled, and not by mistake. People are willing to pay more for the black-tip, even the tip is gone long before the consumer is involved. Supply and demand. Pull in a sandbar shark and pull off the skin, and voila.

When I'm out on one of the islands, I can see hundreds of sharks. I think they can probably see me too. They almost never come in off the shelf. Maybe they're waiting on me to come out there. That isn't happening.

Somebody told me they thought sharks were the stupidest fish in the ocean. It's that fin. If they're intent on sneaking up on you, would the silly fish swim about a foot deeper?

Matagorda is a little weird as a destination. It's a long sandbar, 60k acres worth. I can't take the Jeep there. The Miss Jeep could handle the sand just fine, but it's against the law. Texas lets you drive everywhere. Not on Matagorda. There are zero bridges. No ferries. Nothing.

The only way onto the island is by boat. Humans aren't barred from being there, but the state government has taken away all the machinery that makes it simpler to destroy a sand island.

Every inch of Texas coastline is owned by the people of Texas. They can't even keep gay people off the beaches. If you build a house near the beach, you can't do anything to keep people from using the beach. If a hurricane blows through and eats up all the sand between your house and the gulf, you no longer own your house unless you can convince somebody to truck in sand or dredge it from wherever the stuff grows wild.

Mikka and I drove down to Port O'Connor, which is about the size of a zit on the end of your dog's nose. We both got fishing and hunting licenses, mostly to keep the Wildlife uniforms calm.

I brought my Remington 700 with no intention of using it. It was a just in kind addition. Matagorda is far from anything civilized, so we're on our own. By the time we could get DPS onsite, whatever happened would be over. If we're playing out on the sand, some ruffians might pop up. They won't. They never do, but the rifle makes me feel better. It's one of those "just in case" things.

I also have a World War 2 mortar launcher and a big treble hook on a long winch line (metal "wire"). If we get hungry, I can put a big fish on a couple of the hook's points and fire it with the mortar. Instead of fish line, it's a winch line designed to pull on stuff. Boom.

First of all, this is perfectly legal. There's even a "Shark Hunter Association of Texas."

Second, there are plenty of sand-sharks, tigers, and bulls. It is not any danger to the balance of nature. Not with those sharks. Not along the Texas barrier islands.

Each person could catch a shark a day, if they wanted to. Meeks and I could eat one shark for a whole week, longer maybe.

It's my sinful pleasure. I don't like causing pain, but the treble hook is a quick kill on the shark.

Hauling the thing in is where the real problem is. On any other island, the line would be coming out of the winch I have on the front of the Jeep. No Jeep here. It isn't allowed, so I have a little generator and a portable winch that I "lock" (sort of) down to the sand. If I ever hooked one of those great white sharks, the fish would… I don't know what would happen. My winch and line would be gone in a hurry, and I'd have one really pissed off shark.

By the time the typical shark gets all the way to the beach, it's tired and ready to give it up.

Bottom line: I never hurt an animal just for sport. Shark meat really is awesome. I eat what I catch. Mikka always wants the fins for a friend of his (whom I've never met, so he's undoubtedly Roma). We take the teeth to the bait guy up in Port O'Connor because he can make a few dollars with tourists, and he's a super-nice man.

It was a quarter moon, so the skies were fairly dark. There weren't any clouds or lights, so we got the full show of stars and the fluffy star-gas of the milky way.

We were out of our clothes as soon as we got to the shore. There's something about setting up a mortar and a treble hook in the buff.

Mikka and I just played. All day. All night. We hugged and ran and swam. While the sun was up, he made sure to keep my lily white skin slathered in SPF-b'zillion. For some reason, he likes me without a suntan. If he likes it, I like it.

Meeks has naturally tan skin, even though he's obviously not Hispanic or Indian (American or otherwise). He just has his gypsy skin. He's been on the receiving end of some Waxahachie hatred of all things non-cracker, like they assume he's one of those religious terrorists from the Middle East.

We fell asleep without having sex. It was just a play and romp day. We slept on the sand near the boat, with my rifle nearby.

The night sky on Matagorda Island is the most stunning I have ever seen. The sky's fullness always gives me a jolt, and I've seen it dozens of times. Getting to share it with Mikka for the first time made me cry. I don't think he saw my tears. There are so many stars that are hidden by city lights.

"Uncle Boldo died," Mikka said softly.

"You okay?" I asked.

"Yup," he said. "Rattlesnake bit him."

Under Mikka's always-cheerful attitude sits quite a bit of pain. Uncle Boldo raped him when he was a kid. It happened more than once, but Mikka never wanted to talk about it. The uncle was one of those in the Roma compound who used the F-word to Mikka. No love lost there. It was so bad that he started staying in the woods.

"That usually isn't fatal," I said.

"Yup, but dear old Uncle Rapist thought it was so minor he didn't need to see a doctor."

"He did, apparently."

Anatole discovered the teenaged Mikka and heard the stories about gypsy homophobia. That's when Meeks started working at Anatole's house. He never had any college education, but he was good keeping the house organized. Best I can tell, Mikka never slept with the gypsies again.

He squeezed my hand as we lay under the gorgeous starry sky.

"Are you still pissed at your dad?" Mikka asked softly.

"Pissed? No way."

"Way," he said. "Ever since you found out he was gender-fluid, you've ragged on him."

"Oh, okay. My bad," I said, thinking out loud. "I didn't phrase myself... it was a shock to me. I never even heard of it before I found out about Dad. I had to work things out."

"You're saying you're a work-in-progress."

The next morning, we built a little campfire using some mesquite wood we brought with us. We planned to take all our ashes when we left. Campfire coffee is awful, which is why Mikka brought his French press. Can you imagine being on a deserted island that's absolutely silent except for tiny waves lapping at the sand, drinking the best coffee in the world? I can imagine it. There's roughing it, and then there's what we do on deserted islands.

I worked on the mortar and made it go boom. It shot my big treble hook all the way off the shelf and into the deep water. I had brought some "junk" fish from the boat rental place in Port O'Connor and kept it cold in an ice chest. You don't catch good shark with crappy bait.

After only about 10-minutes, I had a hit. I pulled on the line hard to set the hook, and then let the winch do the heavy pulling.

It was my favorite thing to kill: a tiger shark, medium size. I am terrified of tigers, but they sure taste good. Tiger sharks aren't too picky about what they eat. The one I caught had a couple of fish in its stomach. It also had a partially digested toilet seat. There had to be a story there, and I am happy to report that I don't know it.

Mikka was surprisingly good at preparing the shark. We got all the edible part into the ice chest, to keep cold but not frozen. We wouldn't be needing any more bait, so I threw all the unused fish into the gulf. They'd be somebody's breakfast in no time. He prepared some great shark steaks. I made him a necklace out of shark teeth, so the bait guy won't get all the teeth. We really tried to use every bit of the animal that we could.

All our meals that day were shark, and we'd still have some to take back home. Frozen shark steak is okay, not as good as fresh, but it's soooooo tasty.

After breakfast, we laid out some beach towels and then raced to the water. I wanted Mikka inside my mouth. I mean NOW. Given the choice, I'd rather swallow salt water than sand. Personal choice. We weren't going to waste our supply of fresh water just for a blowjob.

Only it wasn't a blowjob. He wanted to be inside me, just not in my mouth. I felt that line of fluffy hair from his navel to his pubes. It's the most awesome feeling ever.

"I am so madly in love with you, gorger" he told me, and I wrapped my arms around him and pulled him close. Fucking wow, is all I can say. I feel him so sweetly and gently in me every time he makes love. That's what he was doing: making love, not just having sex.

When he came, he kept repeating "arva." I'm sure it's a gypsy word, but don't ask me what it means. I'm fairly sure it's a good word, though. He stayed in me and kept his arms around me in a strong bear hug. I was about to get up, but he was still up my butt. He was getting hard again, so I reached down to urge his balls closer. It was me saying, "go for it, lover." And he did.

Right then. That moment when he took me for a second time is the most perfect point of my life. I relaxed into him. I used that phrase before: relaxed into him. I don't know if it makes sense, but it was me giving myself to this man. My best friend, and the best husband any guy could have.

I know. I'm all mushy. And I promise you my word processor keyboard is about to short out from all the tears.

207

The thing is that it was perfect, and I saw the perfection right in that moment.

Life just can't get better. It's tried to get better, and maybe we've hit that same level, but...

Oh, hell... I over analyze everything. Sorry.

chapter eighteen
barametric pentameter

"America at its best: edgy, experimental,
open-minded — and brilliantly diverse."
Fareed Zakaria, Washington Post 11/08/2012 (b 1964)

Anatole and Kristof worked hard while Mikka and I were on the beach. We hadn't needed the satellite phone once, which was kind of a bummer because I wondered how they worked.

When we got back to "the office," Anatole was excited, but Kris was completely frosty. It was late in the day, so we just said HI and went home.

"What was that?" Mikka asked.

I just shrugged.

That night, it was one of my college bud's birthdays, and the party was up in Dallas.

It's impossible to say how Mikka actually convinced me to wear a friggin' kilt in public, but that's what I was in. It was Mikka's olive green kilt. Commando, because my husband is a total wackadoodle. And for the shirt... what are you kidding?... no shirt. My "top" was a leather harness. For the half hour drive to the city, he did let me put on a t-shirt. And the shirt he insisted I wear said, "I'm not gay but $20 is $20."

See, this is what I live with. I will be under the constant supervision of a psychiatrist before our 10th anniversary.

We got to Dallas way early with plans on a nice dinner. My favorite gayborhood restaurant was closed. It was one of those Forever Closures, so sad. I once had a date there. He ordered Chinese and some ketchup.

In case you missed it: the guy wanted ketchup for his Mongolian Beef. Seriously.

There was no second date, and I don't even think that makes me a snob. I do have standards. Low standards. But standards, nonetheless.

Mikka and I (and my kilt, which was already getting butt pats and whistles) had burgers and dogs at Hunky's, one of the long-standing restaurants on The Strip in Oak Lawn (gay part of Dallas). The Strip on Cedar Springs is the main commercial part of the gayborhood. I always feel comfortable there. It's like home, despite all the straight couples moving in. I think we should have an ordinance that says they have to act gay in public.

Mikka had a Hula Burger. It has a burger patty: check. Pineapple slice: ick, but okay. Bacon: check, check, and check again. And mayo: Oh, no, no, no, no. Mayo doesn't work on any burger that touches the inside of my mouth. Ick. I get all the white creamy stuff I need from Mikka.

I had one of their Chili Hunky Dog, which is like a Coney Island but made with actual chili. It has mustard, onion, cheddar, and it's slathered with a credible recipe of chili. Don't even get in the same zipcode as me with yankee chili. I ordered something alleged to have chili on it. It was Dennys. The chili came out with beans. Oh, no, no, no. That isn't chili. You might call it "chili with beans," but it certainly isn't chili, not in Texas. We do a lot of stupid stuff, but chili isn't one of them.

There's a diner near Oak Lawn — Market Diner (because it's near the Apparel Mart) — that offers a chili and cheese omelette. I am practically getting a hard-on thinking about it.

The bars on The Strip are mostly corporate (read: boring), but that's where my friend wanted to go for his birthday. I hadn't been in the Round-up Saloon in years. It's the place you want to go to show off your latest ginormous belt buckle. Not really my style, but this wasn't really my night.

If you want to visit a real, honest, authentic western gay bar, you go over to Fort Worth. You trip over gay cowboys over there. There's something special about a gay guy's butt that's agreeably wrapped up inside Wrangler-brand denim. (fanning face)

I suspect the Round-up was opened by the corporate bar owners for tourists. I don't know that, but it seems that way. That isn't necessarily a bad thing, especially if you're a tourist.

So, into the Dallas idea of a western bar I walk, and don't forget that my honey had me wear a kilt and a harness. There's lots of shit you can wear into a gay bar. There's nothing illegal or immoral about a kilt, but this was a western wannabe place. There's no kind of PR spin you can put on a kilt to make it cowboy. Meeks says he loves my legs and wants to share the view with others. Awwww (I think).

Oh, and I was commando at Mikka's insistence. Nobody wears underwear with a kilt, he says. It's like socks under sandals, he says. It's just not done.

I can tell you that it will be done if I ever go out like this again. It's like I was wearing a big sign "Grope Me" on my ass. I guess I was flattered, but still—

We were still a little early. No, we were on time according to regular timekeeping rules. Gay time means you're fashionably late. I don't know why that is. It seems rude to me. My friend wasn't even there for his birthday.

Mikka and I headed to the bar. He got a scotch, and I ordered red beer. Does anybody drink that outside Texas? I may seem gross, but I really enjoy it. It's just beer with either tomato juice or Bloody Mary juice. I like the spice.

As soon as I looked up, I saw Kris just a couple of stools down. He gave me an icy stare.

What is wrong with that guy? I didn't do a damn thing to him.

211

He was with some man I never saw before. I'd never seen Kris doing anything gay in my life. I'd known him all my life. We grew up together, and I thought he was one of my best friends. And I never knew he was gay until a few months ago.

But there he was, talking gibberish.

"Ante, apud, ad, adversus," Kris said to the man he was with. Apparently with.

"Circum, circa, citra, cis," said his new buddy.

"Contra, inter, erga, extra," Kris continued. Whatever, he was grinning so much, I thought he was going to tear something on his face.

"Infra, intra, iuxta, ob," they both said together.

So that was one of my best friends growing up in Waxahachie. I assumed Kris had found another Hungarian, but Mikka said they were speaking Latin.

So what we have is Kris, the consummate education elitist, was in a touristy cowboy bar on The Strip in Oak Lawn. He was doing some kind of responsorial ditty in a supposed Dead Language, Latin. And they were starting to get lightheaded from all the... I can't imagine how a Latin something would make anybody giddy.

I tried to be happy for them.

Carlos, the birthday boy, showed up finally, and it was so cool to see him. We dated a few times in college, but that was something that was never going to be. We're friends to this day, and I really like him. If Carlos ever gets married, that other guy is going to be one of the luckiest men in the world. I hope to be his best man.

I love Carlos so much. Always did. If you've never had Arroz con Pollo (rice with chicken), oh my goodness. I watched him make it once.

Carlos likes it with plenty of cayenne, but he always toned it down for me.

Cook some cumin seeds in a hot dry skillet. Then grind the seeds to powder.

Get a meat-only chicken that's cut-up.

Put salt, black pepper, cayenne pepper, cumin, garlic powder into a plastic grocery bag

Add chicken and shake

Cook chicken in a little olive oil, say 6 minutes per side

Remove chicken

Put chopped onion and pepper (bell pepper or stronger if you want) into the skillet, 6 minutes again, stirring

Add rice (long grain is the authentic one here) and garlic (2-3 cloves)

Cook the rice dry for about a minute

Add water to cover the rice

Add a little tomato sauce

Bring to a boil, then reduce to simmer

Add the chicken, a handful of chopped cilantro. Cover, and cook for a half hour (until chicken and rice are cooked)

Remove skillet from heat. Don't remove the lid for 10 or so minutes

Oh, man that's good. Carlos sometimes used Sazón spice mix, but I like the other better. Plus, Sazón has MSG. He might add frozen peas or carrots, just so the dish is a little different. Please don't take my recipe as gospel. Carlos grew up in a house full of Latinos and Latinas, and so he probably learned the recipe from a family member. I make Carlos' Arroz con Pollo just like this whenever I can.

Carlos and Mikka seemed to hit it off, especially after I told Mikka that the chick and rice he so loves is Carlos' recipe. We ended up with an invitation to come up for one of Carlos' famous meals of something-or-other.

The entire birthday entourage of party peeps had started the party without us somewhere else. We took over one corner of the Saloon.

I danced until closing. There's something really different about doing the Two-Step wearing a skirt with absolutely nothing to slow down your balls slamming into your legs over and over. That part was really kind of fun.

I'm not proud to admit it, but don't knock it until you've tried it.

I felt the leather harness tighten up a little from all the sweat, but that was just part of the fun. Before the night was done, almost everyone had their shirts off. I caught several guys drooling over my husband's body hair. Meeks is not a hairy guy, but he has those thin strips of fluffy hair that look so enticing.

When I dance, I never lead. Mikka likes to lead, but he took the time to teach me that side of dancing. It wouldn't be a regular thing for me, but he wanted us to be equal at everything. Following in dancing doesn't make you less of a person. It does make you stuck on one side of the party, and we know about Mikka's pathological fear of getting stuck. So, I think he just wanted to follow for awhile, and he wanted me to be on the other side of the dance.

I tripped a couple of times because the footwork is backwards from what I'm used to. I had to pay attention. After a couple of red beers, paying attention to anything was getting tricky.

The next day, Anatole had news. I dragged myself down the street to work, way more hungover than I should have been. I didn't have very many red beers, but they hit me.

Anatole got readouts from the barometers we placed near the cage, and there was something regular in the changes. The barometric pressure in there actually changed. Rapidly. It was almost like an ultrafast Morse code.

They couldn't make any sense out of the flutter.

"I can do the analsys," I said, "but we need a bigger computer than we have."

"Would a quantum computer help?" Anatole asked. He was nonchalant about it. Maybe he didn't know that the phrase "quantum computer" would give me heart palpitations.

"Oh, wow," I said, "Would it ever, but they're like a b'zillion dollars."

"I know people," Anatole said.

He made some calls. Within a couple of hours, a helicopter was landing at the farm. Anatole and I were on our way to a private jet to Brazil. There are some of those big boy machines, but the one in Brazil was run by one of his buddies.

We landed at the Jobim airport. I don't really know what the locals call it, but that's the name plastered on everything. I don't know Portuguese. Wouldn't it be awful if Jobim translated into "bathrooms" or something? I think it's the name of the airport.

We went through customs, and got back on the jet to head inland. His friend is in Campinas, a really big city that I never heard of. Did you? If so, my hat's off to you for doing all your geography homework.

Their quantum computer is made by a company called Quantum. Clever folks.

Apparently, the Chinese are the real stars in this technology. Anatole knows people there, but he trusts his friend in Campinas.

This is going to be a rough fly-over of what I think is going on. It all seems interesting and totally trippy. Their setup uses the Quantum as a way to store and access data. They also have some kind of supercomputer that does non-linear decision making that falls through a neural net.

See what I mean about being whacked-out trippy?

I mean, I have no idea what the analysis might do, but I can program the supercomputer to do the work. To tell you how gonzo the whole thing is… did I use one of those IBM terminals? Nope. I didn't even use a powerful desktop to do my part of the work.

In Campinas, they gave me the choice of an iPad or a Microsoft tablet. Seriously.

So I have this storage device that's faster than anything on the planet, and it works directly with a supercomputer that's measured in "teraflops" rather than bits per anything. And the genius college kids who thought up all this shit figured I'd want to use a tablet for my part of the whole operation.

I felt like I was locked inside a high tech mental institution, where the real loons are the ones in lab coats.

There were uniforms everywhere, and all the uniforms carried assault rifles, pistols, and tasers. This has very little similarity to the computer lab back at college.

Basically I had some profiles for the Supreme Think-it Machine to consider. I wasn't sure if the time fly messages sent by barometric pressure… (I am already feeling the need for professional counseling)… was it a kind of Morse code, where everything was spelled out in letters of the alphabet (English, if I'm lucky). Or was it actual speech, where I needed to be looking for vowels and consonants.

What makes it possible is that people have done research on what vowels and consonants are used most often. There are at least two studies I found that do the same with sounds. The time flies have spent hundreds of years in Texas, so if they're using some kind of country twang, I'm going to be really pissed.

When you're typing in English, the most common first letter of a word is a T. The second most common first letter is an A. I'm hoping that all the neural net stuff can use that kind of information to find word delimiters. I fed all the statics into my tablet, and it somehow moved the data into Maxine (what I named the supercomputing quantum matrix net thingy).

In the middle of words in English, the letter E is by far the most common. The other vowels are next in the list. By the time you get to Q and Z, it's almost a rounding error. And if they threw any umlauts at me, there's going to be trouble for the time flies when I get back to Texas.

What I didn't expect was encryption. That would really fuck up the statistics because a T isn't represented as a T when things are encrypted. Again, I would be going back with lots of cans of RAID if we were unsuspectingly dealing with encrypted text.

And don't even get me started on what I'd do if the barometric flutters were really images. If they fluttered me a copy of the Mona Lisa, I was going to go nuclear — sorry, nook-you-lar.

But damn I'm good. This is where the English major was paying off. I absolutely love what's called corpus linguistics. No, that isn't the dialect they speak in Corpus Christi. It's the body of language used in real life. So, you wouldn't consider things like "ain't" and "fixin' to leave now" in proper speech, but reg'lur folks use those words and phrases all the time.

Playing around with words is my happy place. No, loving Mikka tops that, but you know what I mean.

So all that's for written language, and Morse code is a kind of written language. It's a letter-by-letter way of representing the language.

When you talk, it's a whole different thing, especially in Texas and Alabama.

The study of this is phonology. I'm kind of getting a hard-on talking about this. So much fun.

So you have your consonant sounds and your vowel melodies. Unfortunately, you also have twangs, and General American (like you hear on radio/TV), and Received Pronunciation (which is the hoity-toity way the Brits describe "General British" uppity pronunciation. Ah, but they also have Cockney, Manx, Ulster, and so forth.

What I'm counting on is that the dialect won't change the frequency of the sound. If you use the word DOG, the "o" might be an "aug" in New England, but the "o" is always going to be "aug" there. So unless the asswipe flies are messing with me, it'll be standardized enough to figure out.

So job one was to find out if they're typing or speaking. They were speaking. I don't know what dialect, but Maxine found patterns common to phonology, not some kind of written language. What we had was definitely not a copy of the Mona Lisa drawn by changing the barometric pressure of the room. And all I can say, those time flies should be very happy that they weren't messing with me.

So it's a kind of speech. It isn't speech like anybody ever considered, but it was speech. From the phonology and a quantum storage system full of every word in the world, Maxine found that it's most likely General American English with a dash of Texas twang sprinkled liberally on the top.

Then I moved one line of code, and holy moly! There it was.

"Found it," I said louder than "You can run from Andreas, but I will find you."

I can deal with that. Damn, I'm good... it isn't bragging if it's true. I'm not some all-powerful genius scientist or computer guru. I just love words and language structure.

It's really fun stuff. Like this: Wales and England are next to each other, but there are more English words that come from Arabic than from Welsh. That said, we get lots of our strange word structures from Wales.

I eat this stuff up, so this is a fun trip.

With the help of one of their pimply faced kids in the lab coat, we started to see actual words. It was the most amazing thing ever to appear on any iPad in history:

> MARY HAD A LITTLE LAMB

Da-fuk? That fly is dead meat when I get home.

chapter nineteen
wordage

"To err is human. To really foul up requires the root password."
— Paul Ehrlich, speaking with the authority of personal experience

Anatole made some kind of deal with his friend that let me use Maxine from home.

Maxine, the expertly crafted silicon that does more advanced calculus during its power-up phase than the city of London has ever done in its existence. How can you not be in love with such a creature? It means I can do my work without an abacus.

I had to be really careful not to say or do anything that let anybody know what I was really doing. The lab coats would have shit their pants if they knew about time flies, and I'm fairly sure that supercomputers don't run well with Brazilian feces in the circuitry. Fairly sure, not totally certain.

```
Dear Whoever you are:


Mary had a little lamb, little lamb,

little lamb, Mary had a little lamb

whose fleece was white as snow.

And everywhere that Mary went

Mary went, Mary went, everywhere
```

that Mary went

The lamb was sure to go.

You gave us a laugh here. Now tell me what is really going on.

Love,

Andy

I gave the note to Marengo. He did a somersault. This really is surreal stuff, and it never settled into anything that sounded normal.

Kris, meanwhile, had turned into Mr. Frosty for reasons I couldn't imagine. It was like he was mad at me. With his bullet-making skills needed less… wait, that's probably why he's so frosty. I made him less of the center of attention. I didn't mean to, but being a bullet maven just isn't what it used to be around here. His fame kind of had the flight characteristics of a glob of frozen yak shit. I certainly never got the kind of education that you'd need to knock Kristof off a pedestal. I'm an idiot most days, and I don't know how to fix this one.

Why don't I ever know how to fix anything? I damn good at agitating anything, but I'm crap at calming things down.

Kris was into his Aussie football. The Premiership (main season) was coming to a close, and the Finals were about to start. He's crazy for the Sydney Swans. They certainly have more than their fair share of adorable men on the field, but this year they're struggling to win. That gets Kris in a foul mood.

I remember this time of year at his house. It was always tense because of a red card or the goal tender kicking the ball into the wrong net. It sounds crazy, but I've seen it on TV.

We were in the big room at the farmhouse one afternoon. Mikka was wearing one of his French Maid uniforms, dusting some crystal figurines. I was standing, deep in thought, when Kris walks by. He hit my shoulder in passing, almost knocked me off my feet.

I saw the look in Mikka's eyes. Danger.

"I got this, lover," I told him.

"What's wrong with you?" Mikka asked Kris. "Are you suddenly 12 years old?"

Silence.

More silence.

Kris turned and walked up to me, when he should be apologizing to Mikka. Our bodies were inches apart, and he just starred at me.

"I have loved you, since 7th grade," Kris said so softly that Mikka probably didn't hear. "You're the most amazing man I ever knew, and I'm scared of you."

And that was it. In a few seconds, he turned an walked out the front door. When Kris walks, it's almost mechanical.

He still has a perfect body that ought to be on the cover of some fashion magazine. This time, he left me speechless. I didn't even know how to tell Mikka what he said. I didn't know why somebody as smart and great-looking as Kristof Halász would be scared of me.

I just stood there, like an idiot. My mouth was probably open, motionless toward the door Kris just walked through.

"Let him be," Anatole said softly from the far side of the main room. I didn't see him come in.

I turned my head a little.

"Give him time," Anatole said so calmly that he brought down the tension levels.

"Time for what?" I asked.

"He's trying to find his place in all this," Meeks said. "You solved a problem that's taken genius scientists centuries, and they all failed."

He paused a second.

"No offense," Mikka told Anatole, who responded with a mixture of grin and grimace to mean "none taken."

"Let me work with him," Anatole said.

The school season was about to break for the semester, so Mikka and I got all our wildest sexual gambits as far and as fast as we could. I wasn't used to living around a kid, but I knew Meeks and I probably shouldn't fuck with me hanging from the chin-up bar. It sets a bad example.

It was late summer when we picked Pasha up at DFW Airport.

My ward had morphed into quite the young man. He was still Pasha through-and-through, and he was still the consummate gypsy. We sent a boy to Oregon, and we picked up a wonderful young man. They didn't seem to use military school tactics, which is great.

Pasha was more dangerous, of course. His love of mischief was intact, but Oregon added skill sets that made us know that he'd become a man— a fun-loving man, but one who could function outside the gypsy compound.

His talent, strangely enough, was microbiology. Seriously.

If things continued, we were going to have a proper scientist in the family. Microbiology. I can barely spell microbiology.

After unloading all his gear at our house, we drove to Anatole's farm. Pasha was never invited to go there, but it's what he wanted to do. I secretly called ahead to make double-sure it was okay with the boss.

Pasha just wanted to hug Anatole and thank him. He planted a sweet kiss on Anatole's cheek.

"Thank you so much," Pasha said. "I think you probably saved my life."

"You are most welcome, Master Cooper," Anatole said. "Just don't ever forget your roots."

"Huh?"

"You're part of a culture that the rest of us can only imagine," the boss said. "The school in Oregon will help you move around in all parts of society, but you have your own ancestry. It's like your pedigree, and I'm practically jealous of you for it."

"Wow," Pasha said. "Thanks, Mr. Austin."

I looked over at my husband. He had the most wonderful smile, and tears were streaming down his face. When Pasha turned toward his brother, Mikka tried to wipe the tears before Pasha could see him crying. The Monet family cries a lot.

"Don't be going all sissy on me," Pasha said with a grin.

The brothers hugged for about two minutes, and then we were off.

We locked up the house and headed to South Texas in the Miss Jeep. The brothers called it a good old-fashioned gypsy caravan. I imagined those were always in wooden wagons with rounded canvas covers, but apparently that's for previous generations and Hollywood.

We were going to Matagorda Island, against my better judgment. Before I agreed, we set down the ground rules to keep me from going insane.

Pasha is of legal age, but he's still a kid to me. I am his legal guardian.

The first rule: no sex. None. Not with anybody.

"You can't even do a menage a moi," I said with a grin.

"Five knuckle shuffles are a no-no," Pasha laughed. "Yup, okay."

(A) He understood my fake French; (B) He picked up on the reference to a popular saying; and (C) He threw back a cool comeback that was far away from proper.

"We play by all the state rules," I said. "That's rule two. If we take something to the island, we leave with it. If we fish, we all have licenses. I'll have a couple of guns just because there's no law anywhere. If we get attacked by beast or human, Pasha is the one who stays in the background."

If that happened, I secretly knew it would be something that Mikka could handle. He knows how to hurt or stop or disarm a person with his feet and whatever he finds lying around. Yeah, I studied martial arts, but I'm unsure of myself. If it even looks like harm to my kid is possible, I'm going straight to firepower. A 6.5mm Creedmoor bullet will take down almost anything from human all the way to cougar. We don't have grizzly bears, crocodiles, or leopards. My Remington 700 and a few boxes of Creedmoor rounds ought to be more than enough to handle what I hope won't ever happen.

When we got to Port O'Connor, we loaded up with supplies. The store owner said there was a squall headed in. I decided it was prudent to stay in a motel for the night, and it's a good thing we did. The place was hammered by the storm. Sometimes when a thunderstorm moves across the Gulf of Mexico, the wind gets out of control. The wind is what we call a squall.

I assume other gulfs, seas, and oceans have squalls. In Texas, it can be a big deal because of the warm air hitting the jet stream.

By morning, the storm passed, and we went back to the store for supplies. Poor guy had a mess on his hands. The squall blew all his windows out.

Nobody asked, but Pasha just started sweeping up glass. We all helped the guy. By mid-afternoon, the store was back to a reasonable shape. There's actually a Home Depot there, so we used the jeep to haul plywood to cover the holes where the windows once stood. He'd eventually get insurance money, so he let us just take supplies for the trip out to the island. He threw in a larger boat for the trip. We left the Jeep in his parking lot.

The sun was starting to set when we got to the windward side of Matagorda Island. It's mile after mile of sand beach with some sand-loving greenery up about a hundred feet from the shoreline.

The first thing to go: clothes. As I insisted, we all wore swimsuits. In Pasha's mind, I became Public Enemy #1, #2, and #253.

It was a little creepy at first because Pasha was there, but he was really into the whole nature thing. I was so proud of him: he did almost nothing that was overtly sexual. Pasha and Mikka both wanted to be naked, and they showed me how annoyed they were all day. I had no idea what to do. I hadn't studied that chapter is Adults for

Dummies. We should have discussed it before the trip, and I was sure Mikka and I would talk about it. Family meeting: on the agenda.

I just wanted to do what's right. Beats me what that is. What I came up with wasn't going down well with Mikka or Pasha. Growth sure is complicated sometimes.

We swam and fished and laid back on the sand. Pasha cleaned and cooked all the fish we caught. I was surprised when a red drum ended up on my hook. Redfish is the best fish in the universe. It isn't for those squeamish about "fishy," but it's wonderful in my book. I don't know if he used special gypsy seasoning, but the guy made us one of the best meals I ever had while stranded on a deserted island with no roads or bridges.

Around the campfire that evening, Pasha filled us in on the school. He told us that he was offered for a full scholarship to Stanford University. He loved that he'd be living so close to the Gay Mecca of San Francisco.

He went from idiot delinquent to scholarship material at one of the best microbiology universities in the world, and he did that by himself. It wasn't like we could help him with his homework. Anatole Austin is what made it happen, of course, and I love him for it.

"Both y'all are cryin'?" Pasha said, but this time he started crying too. This kind of thing just doesn't happen, not to me, not after I grew up in fear of all my bullies.

The whole state of Texas, from the government and laws, to all the preachers who knew nothing but how to dish hate, to the homophobic bubba assholes with too much testosterone and not enough IQ.

Who knew that any of that could lead to this: gay family around a campfire, sharing lives like a family and eating the best goddam redfish ever cooked?

"I am so proud of you, kiddo," I told Pasha.

"I have one little request," he said.

"What?"

"If you call me 'kiddo' again, I'm going to do what you did to Cooter Keith's nuts."

I looked up. He was grinning with the shiniest white teeth I think I ever saw. He'd gotten dental work somewhere.

"Promise," I said, and I meant it, more-or-less.

"My other request," Pasha said, "can I call you daddy?"

And that's when I just lost it. They both had to come over to hug me, to get me calmed down. I cried and grinned at the same time, as I shook my head.

"Of course you can," I tried to say. "Of course you can, son."

"I think 'boy' might fit better," Mikka said through his own tears.

That night, we fell asleep on the sand without any beach towels. The sky was absolutely clear, like it is after a squall moves through. There were too many stars to count.

"I love you both," I said quietly as we started drifting off to sleep. I was lying between the brothers, which meant Mikka had Remington 700 duty. He didn't need to do anything with it, other than have it close and in a way some human robber couldn't come up and take it quickly.

"I love you both so much," I repeated.

"We know," Pasha said.

"We love you too," Meeks added.

chapter twenty
queen'ish

"Windows Vista: It's like upgrading from Barack Obama to Donald Trump."
— anonymous

We got a noisy start to the morning. It was the satellite phone that Anatole always makes me carry when we're out of reach of any cell phone towers.

"Matagorda here," I said.

"We need you here," Anatole said. "Pronto."

"It'll be most of the day," I said.

"No, can't be."

"We're on Matagorda Island, boss," I said with the tone of voice you use when you have to explain trigonometry to a 10 year old. "You can only get here by boat. The Jeeps up at a store in Port O'Connor."

"Not a problem," he said. "I have your GPS off the phone, and a helicopter is on the way."

"What about the Jeep?" I asked.

"I'll call you back. The helicopter is minutes away, so gather your belongings."

And with that, the phone went click.

I told my family (and isn't it cool I get to use the word "family" here?) what was happening. What's happening is… uh… I don't even know. So I just told them to pack up and be ready to move in a hurry.

"You rob banks and they just found you?" Pasha asked.

"No."

"What do y'all do for a living?" Pasha asked. "You're starting to scare me."

"It's microbiology crap, Pash," Mikka said. "You wouldn't understand."

"Microbiology is what I do, daddy," he told Mikka. "I understand that."

"Not this kind," I said.

The phone rang again.

"Helo is on the way from Galveston," Anatole said. "There'll be the pilot and one other person. That other person will get all your gear and your boat and return it back to Port O'Connor, and then he'll shuttle the Jeep back home."

"Ok," I started to say, but he wasn't stopping his end of the 'conversation,' using the term fairly loosely.

"The chopper will get you to Galveston. By then my jet will be waiting. Ok?"

"What's wrong?" I asked.

"No tragedy," he said. "Don't worry. There are events unfolding, and you need to be here. I need you here, and I promise it's all good."

Mikka was concerned by the activity. Pasha was about to pass out. I gave each a gallon of fresh water.

"Quick shower is in order," I said. They poured the water over their heads, and then got towels from the boat to dry off. We had to hurry. I knew enough math to figure out that a helicopter that's hauling ass could be here in a half hour.

And there it was. We were all ready, and there it was.

"Holy shit, that was fast," Pasha said.

As fast as I could, I told Mr. Martinez where to take the boat. I gave him my Jeep fob.

"Go," Mr. Martinez said. "I got this."

"Bueno," Pasha said, "y gracias."

"Adios," the man said as I closed the door of the helicopter. Spanish is more common here than French is way up north. Our Spanish is "Tex-Mex" or "Spanglish." So far as I can tell, it's roughly the same as what's spoken in Mexico, but you can throw in an English word if you don't remember the proper Spanish word.

We were in Galveston in a half hour, which means they were redlining the chopper's engines. There was nothing leisurely about the trip. The pilot was pleasant but not really talkative, which is okay because I'm a little squeamish in helicopters.

He put down at Galveston Airport within a few steps of a Gulf-stream. A split second after we walked up the jet's stairs, I heard the engine's start up. We were rolling before any of us could sit down. Is that what happens on Air Force One when the president arrives?

"We're going up fast," said the fight attendant, "so sit down, buckle up, and hold on."

"Who are you people?" Pasha asked his brother.

Mikka just smiled.

"What I'd like to hold onto is the stewardess up there," he said.

"I heard that," the man said. "I like you too. When we're air-borne, we can talk if there are no objections."

There weren't. I gave them a "go for it" gesture.

"Topic one," the steward said, "will be steward versus steward."

When the steward got up, he asked if we wanted anything to drink. Without even waiting, he pointed at Pasha: "I know what you want, so let's stick to soda pop right now. K?"

"K," Pasha said with a big, made-up frown.

We all just took bottled water.

"Hi," the young man said, "I'm Chase."

"I'm Pasha, that's my brother, Mikka, and my dad, Andreas."

"Dad?" Chase said, "You started making kids really young."

"Guardian really," Pasha said, "and he's married to Mikka. I am their ward."

Chase and Pasha moved to the back of the jet. A G650 isn't all that big, so "the back" is a relative term. For a private jet, it's big with room for a dozen or so, maybe 20. The back had sofas instead of chairs, so I was guessing that the jet was made for sleeping.

Correction: a G650 is gigantic for a private or business jet. It isn't a 747. [Note to self: never employee a pilot as a fact checker.] [[No worries, at what you paid.]]

"Don't get too comfortable," Chase said from the back. "They've got us on a hurry up schedule, so we're clipping at Mach zero-point-8."

"Holy shit," Pasha said, "that's... uh... 650 miles an hour?"

"Ding, ding," Chase said. "We have a winner. Pasha, you are just adorable. You're functional and decorative."

Mikka and I talked about Pasha and Anatole's farm. I knew there's a concrete strip way off to the side. That's probably where we were heading. But what were we supposed to say to the kid about the cage?

We didn't have a clue. We couldn't even come up with a believable cover story. Hopefully Anatole had that under control.

"Should we call?" I asked.

"Who? Why?"

"The boss, because we have an extra passenger."

"No, Anatole knows that we have Pasha in tow, so he'll have something ready."

So I just sat there holding hands with Mikka with his head on my shoulder.

"Oh, that is soooooo sweet," Chase said from the back.

The guys were really cutting up back there. Kids do that. Chase was about Pasha's age, maybe a year or two older.

I kept telling myself that: it's all natural. He's just growing up. Almost in friggin' Stanford University, for gods sake.

But I wanted to go back there to chaperone. Maybe wrap Chase in duct tape and superglue.

No, they're just talking and enjoying each other's company. Pasha's been away for what seems like 8 years. All he's known is fellow students and teachers.

I think that's all he's known, and I'm so proud of what he's grown into. He seems like a great kid, unlike the urchin we sent out to Oregon. He's able to hold his own in conversation with Chase who is clearly educated and proper. I don't mean stuffy-proper. I just mean he knows the difference between and adverb, a watermelon, and pink-ing shears.

When I turned around, they were kissing.

Part of me wanted to say "Awwww." Part of me wanted to throw Chase off the jet.

WWMD? What would Mom do?

Crap: pregnancy. Yes, Pasha's gay, but I still wanted to talk about women. Like know about that? Maybe Hank hires out for chats about pregnancy.

She had me to deal with when I was near college age. Hor-mones were rushing around inside my head, and I'm sure she knew it. Yet, she gave me space. We had our ground rules, which we'd even-tually review with Pasha, but I could go out and date. Presumably she knew I wasn't a virgin, and that was okay. Mom was always talking about safe sex and condoms. If I didn't know about them from else-where, I'd know about them from her.

"Strap yourself in, guys," Chase said from the back. It was only about 10-seconds later that the wheels touched down. I saw an SUV screaming down the runway after us.

We all got out of the jet. I saw Pasha and Chase kiss, which was wonderful and terrifying at the same time.

"We have a kind of situation," Anatole said. "Pasha, you're about to hear some things that your brother and guardian have known for a long time. You okay with that?"

He nodded.

"No," Anatole said, "what I mean is that you are about to be read-in on a black-ops site run by the government. Once you hear what I have to say, you can't ever tell anyone. You can talk to anyone who works here but only while you're on the property."

The SUV was racing back toward the house. It was there before Anatole was done.

"If you agree to silence," he continued, "I'm going to create a trust fund for you. It will have $5-million in it."

I could hear Pasha's bowels twitching, which made me giggle, which made Pasha's left fist hit my right arm.

"You will have a monthly stipend from the trust fund for the rest of your life. You never get to touch the principle. All these financial words making sense?"

Pasha nodded.

"Great," Anatole said, "the school in Oregon's reputation remains solid. So you never see the principle, but you will have a really handsome income for your entire life. You'll never have to work, if you don't want to."

"I want to," Pasha snuck in quickly.

"I figured," Anatole said. I reached over and held my son's hand and squeezed it.

He went through the whole time flies story and the centuries of time-related anomalies. He said that I was the first person in hundreds of years who was able to communicate with the creatures.

"Marengo helped," I said.

"Later," Anatole said. "The main thing is what we found yesterday."

And it was earthshaking.

First, the time distortion is because the creatures can change gravity. That's somehow related to Einstein's space-time continuum. If you are looking for an explanation of Albert Einstein's theoretical papers, that's not what you'll find.

Anatole made my eyes glaze over. Pasha seemed to keep right up with him, which was one of the scariest things that ever happened at the farm in all my time there.

"Let me just say," Anatole said, "that the creatures — and nobody has been able to get them to talk about their history — do stuff to gravity. They don't intend to do harm. My secret theory that day was they fuck so hard, they pound the earth's gravity. QED. Thanks to Andreas, we know that we can live with these critters. They're apparently quite happy to be in the cage. It's a huge place, when you're a tiny creature. They say they have more interesting things to do than destroy the world. I'm not sure what those things are right now."

The SUV came screeching to a halt at the back door of the main house. We went into the front room.

In the main room, I could see that Pasha's eyes were bigger than a soccer ball. His reaction was just the opposite of mine. I still think the explanation of time flies has some element of hooey in it.

Pasha accepted it immediately because of the space-time connection. He was almost giddy with the excitement of seeing it in action. The whole thing made absolute sense to the kid, and that fact was an endless source of amusement for my husband.

"Everybody sit down," Anatole said. "There's a bit more."

We all sat down. I got my standard lump in the throat. Fight vs Flight will always find me ready to run. I hate confrontation unless I have to do it.

"Andreas," Anatole said, "Laird is alive."

"Dad?"

Anatole nodded. Mikka and Pasha both ran over to the over-stuffed chair I was in to put their arms around me.

"He not only survives, he has flourished. I have no idea what happened or in what order or anything like that. There's time to learn those things, just know that Laird Monet is alive and living inside the screen. He doesn't want to leave it, but he desperately wants to see you."

I just sat there. Is this guy shitting me?

Pasha was ready to go for it, but that's not me.

My dad was a gender-fluid special ops soldier who was killed on a secret military mission. Only he wasn't. He went into the cave and decided to stay.

"He also wants to meet you, Mikka," Anatole said. "He is thrilled that you guys are married, and he wants to see his grandchild."

It took a second.

"Me?" Pasha said with a quick rattle of this head. "Grandfather? I got one of them now?"

"Not really a grandfather," Anatole said. "Pasha, do you know the term gender-fluid?"

"Yeah, sure."

"Andreas' dad was always gender-fluid, although he did a really good job of hiding it from everyone. His wife never even knew."

"She knew," I said. "Yeah, she knew. So what are you saying?"

"As bizarre as it sounds, the person you know as your dad is what we've been calling the Queen of the Flies."

And there it was. What do you call it when "the other shoe" falling is more like Mount Everest deciding to lob itself onto Australia?

That was it for me for awhile. They went on to talk, and they filled me in on what was said while my entire life was shut down for processing and re-programming. My dad was a time fly and was elected their queen. I know of guys whose dads are gay, and they joke that their father is queen of the house. But really? This was different.

I let out a long guttural growl of anger at the world, as I walked to the front door. Mikka followed to join me. We sat on the front steps. Surroundings were fuzzy and ran together. Trees looked like trees. Prickly pear cactus looked so ordinary. There was nothing ordinary about any of this. When Mikka put his an arm around my shoulders, I lost it.

"I got you," Mikka said.

"Ain't got much then," I cried.

"True," he said with a grin, "but it's enough for me."

"What the fuck am I supposed to do?" I asked, totally confused.

"I got a pithy saying," he said, almost whispering.

"Oh, goodie. An ancient axiom to the rescue."

"So an old guy said that serenity is inversely proportional to my expectations."

I was in no condition to parse a pithy saying. Fortunately I didn't have to—

"When you got your mind set on something, reality wants to knock it down. Somebody comes up with another reality, so you're pissed. You think 'A' but here comes 'B,' and you're hopping mad. You know 'A' is right."

"Dad's a time fly," I said, "a creature that's murdered people and stolen time itself."

"Yup."

"And I'm supposed to accept all that?" I asked.

"You want to attack your dad," Mikka said, "or do you want to learn what's going on?"

We just sat there.

"The universe threw up some really weird shit, and you're saying you want to destroy it before you understand it?"

"That cannot be my father," I insisted. "It's unacceptable, and I don't have to accept what's unacceptable."

"Yup," Mikka said. "You got that right. All I'm suggesting is that you learn about your enemy. Maybe after you understand, it won't be so black-and-white."

I put my arm around my husband's waist and laid my head on his shoulder.

The door behind us made some noise. I didn't look, but it was obvious somebody was there.

"Hey," Pasha said.

"Andreas is 'processing' things," Mikka said. "Give us a minute."

"Mr. Austin wanted me to bring the iPad," Pasha said as he handed the tablet to his brother. I nodded.

Meeks and I sat on the step. I processed things— kooky things. After about 5 or 10 minutes, I held my hand out, palm up. Mikka gave me the tablet.

> Prove you're my father.

> Remember Trinkets? She picked you.

OMG. Trinkets was the name of my Rough Collie that dad got me for Christmas when I was in the 2nd grade. Not only did she pick me, she was the most loyal dog I ever knew. She'd hear me coming from school and got into a frenzy of excitement. We could play catch or wrestle or run or whatever I wanted to do. I was safe when I was with her: no bullies, no bobcats. Trinkets was a collie, but she was almost completely white. She had brown markings on her face and tail, but the rest was white.

If this was somebody trying to mess with me, it's a good one. It could still be bullshit, so I picked a random question from when Dad was still alive.

> 2nd grade science fair. My project was what?

> I am shocked by this.

"Daddy?" I asked.

"Yup," he/she said.

Here's what happened: in the second grade, we had a science fair just for second graders. Dad helped me create and understand it. We made electricity out of a lemon, a galvanized nail and some wire. I could really feel the tingle when I touched both the nail and wire that we inserted into the lemon.

What was the deal maker was his response. We used to joke that my project would be the most shocking exhibit at the fair. Nobody else would know (a) the project and (b) our inside joke.

I asked why the time flies want to kill us. He said they don't— not anymore. There was a big civil war in the pit, but that was over in the late 1700s. By then, a few people assumed it would always be a murderous creature in the pit. Dad said they will always defend them- selves, but the creatures don't want to go looking for trouble.

chapter twenty-one
perchance to dream

I dream of a better tomorrow, where chickens can cross the road and not be
questioned about their motives.
— *Anonymous*

I had a long conversation with the creature on my iPad, covering a week or so. Kristof made it so those inside the cage could see my iPad's display, which made it simple to type a reply. Whatever I typed into the tablet would appear on a big display that Kris pointed to the cage.

To get their flutters translated into English, the iPad sent a stream of barometric readings to the quantum computer in Brazil, and it did the translations quickly. In fact, that computer was so fast that I figured I could program a Mac or PC to do the translations in Texas: rainy day project.

Somewhere along the way, I started calling the creature "Dad." He kept calling me "Andy," and my father is the only on who got to use that name without getting their teeth and nose rearranged.

He liked the way I handled my bullies. Dad said what my martial arts training really did was give other bullying victims hope. If the school won't protect them, Andreas found a way where we could protect ourselves (with the occasional suspension). He was particularly fascinated with Milosh Cooper and the cast iron skillet. I know the creature was angry because we could all hear the fluttering in the cage.

No, not "creature." I meant "Dad." I had (and still have) a fairly steep learning curve.

He didn't want me to use "he" or "she." He said he learned a better word: "sie." In German, it's pronounced "zeee," and it's the pronoun for both she and they. I messed up a few times, but I started trying to switch to sie. I found out later that sie is what lots of our genderqueers use. The transgender picked "sie" after Dad disappeared, but sie wouldn't tell me how sie knew the word. There had to be contact with other genderqueers.

Sie told me he needed to stop our daily chat for a week or so. I didn't know what the time anomaly would treat "week," but it seemed important to the queen.

The others left me to continue learning about the time flies. Either this whatever-it-is has assimilated Dad perfectly, or it really is my father in the cage. I kept a log of all our conversations. Somebody will want them someday in the future.

Okay, this really is a thing, and I am completely stupid about the whole thing.

> **Why did you wait to make contact with me?**

No answer. I asked that question almost every day, but Dad wouldn't answer. It was a mystery.

I asked if they really were flies: no. I asked if they really ate time: no, the time anomalies happen when there's lots of fluttering, such as during mating. Mating… you get horny just to kill time. Get it: kill time?

Their cage shares a wall with the main house. All of the other sides are hardware cloth that has an electric current running through it. When it rains outside, the cage should get wet. It doesn't, but I can see a wide variety of vegetation inside. One day I plan on asking Dad about that. I see no water, no soil, and not much sunlight. How do plants grow in there

Dad went on and on about me giving hope to others. I didn't see it that way, but okay— whatever. When I was bullied in elementary school and nobody came to protect me, I took charge of my own protection by learning martial arts. Dad says that gave hope to other kids who were facing things that no kid should have to tackle. Sie loved to hear about all my encounters with Cooter, and he seemed to stay furious about how Milosh treated Pasha and Mikka.

The kid proved useful. In his spare time, he got lumber, screws, and nails. Pasha repaired the chicken coop and the house facia that had gotten dry rot over the years. The kid was awesome, and he did it without being asked.

It's nice to chat with whatever my Dad became. That said, I am having a wackadoodle life. You may think you're in a rough spot, or you're being bullied, or your politicians hate your guts... I will trade you. Whatever you have, it isn't in the same league as the cage. My life is a whole new level of batshit crazy.

I mean, I taught myself how to protect myself from bullies. I got interesting digital photos for politicians who get too aggressive against LGBTs. That's all like dandruff on the shoulder. I will trade your bullies for a father who's a genderqueer time fly.

As Summer worked its way toward Autumn, we got Pasha ready to go back to school in September in Oregon. We got him non-school clothes, for when he gets to leave the campus. The school includes his school clothes in the tuition.

Pasha was excited about the new semester.

Mikka suggested we do an extended outing on Matagorda Island. A week on the coast sounded wonderful. Chatting with Dad was awesome, but I had to pay close attention to everything. The technology had lots of moving pieces,. So, when something tiny happened, the whole apparatus would stop working. I discovered that even iPads can produce a BLUE SCREEN OF DEATH, the dreaded display when any Mac or PC crashes or locks up. And iPad isn't always "user friendly," and it's a half day's job to recover from that.

I was tired and needed a week on the coast. By the time we were ready to drive, my poor Jeep Wrangler was bursting at the seams with supplies: clothes for the three of us, fishing and cooking gear, and so on.

With more than a little effort, Pasha got us to let him invite Chase, the flight attendant. They'd started regular chats on the phone

241

and with an instant messenger. Pasha swore an oath that he'd always use protection. He also promised to make lots of noise if he found out that Chase was a serial killer. And so forth. And so on.

Chase was supposed to meet us in Port O'Connor. Mikka and I already had a chat about Chase. I wanted to put down some tough ground rules, but my husband stopped me. The State of Texas says the kid is old enough to consent to have sex, so everyone would be old enough to do whatever the "kids" wanted to do. That scared the crap out of me because I had a clear picture of myself at 17.

On the big day, we got a big wrinkle. The street in front of my house was all abuzz with police lights and firetrucks. Apparently somebody was attacked by a bobcat or coyote. The cops told me there wasn't much of the body left. It was so messed up they were going to use dental records and DNA to make a positive ID. I went to check on the old man next door: he was fine.

Great. Do I have to start open carry on my own street? I'm a sissy and definitely allergic to mountain lion bites. I guess it's all one of the things to deal with living on the edge of the woods.

We loaded the jeep with everything we might need. Yes, including duct tape and WD-40. We had to feed four for up to a week, so there was plenty of canned goods and tuna (in case fishing was off). We had plenty of clothes and towels, mortar and treble hook (sharks), a first aid kit, my Remington 700, Mikka's .480 snub nose Ruger. In 480-caliber, the bullet is almost a half inch wide. The snub nose means there's not all that much weight, so it's easy to carry in your pocket. It's no fun to fire! He let me try it on one of our trips. I sent a round out into the Gulf of Mexico. I mean, holy shit— the damned thing knocked me back on my butt. I never wanted to fire it again. I might change my mind if there was a javelina (wild skunk-pig) was coming. So, yes I could fire it and make a dangerous animal's head explode, but I never want to touch the trigger ever again.

Pasha's hormones were in some danger of exploding on the drive south. I wondered if my car insurance would pay to clean up the Jeep after a teenager exploded inside. It's a long 5-hour drive, assuming there's no traffic in Austin. There was a wreck on the Interstate in Austin, so we actually spent almost 6-hours.

It was evening by the time we got there. Chase was there, and I apologized for being tardy.

I suggested we camp out at a motel overnight because I didn't want to steer a boat in the dark because we had a New Moon. The kids were a little bummed, but they cheered up when I got two rooms instead of our usual one. Pasha and Chase would have their own space.

Before I let them go to their room, I did a small lecture about safe sex. Chase and Pasha both held up condoms. Each had brought a supply. Point for the boys.

When I saw them the next morning, they were still all huggy and kissy. I assume everything went okay overnight. Pasha snores a little. Chase didn't give any sign that he had a problem with the noise.

We piled into the Jeep and got a quick breakfast at Mama's Kitchen. They define morning a little differently. Breakfast starts at 8:00, so we had to wait a half hour. The kids wanted to take a quick walk to the water. We were just a few blocks from a bay. They promised to be back by 8:00, and they were only about 2-minutes late.

Chase actually paid for everyone's breakfast. With the trust fund, Pasha most likely had more money than Chase, but it's nice to see costs being shared.

At the bait shop, we got bait, ice, and boat. The owner was happy to see us. I guess we're regulars now. If he minded seeing two teenage boys hugging and kissing, he kept it to himself. Point for him, and I watched to make sure the guys didn't cross any lines into unacceptable displays. It was PDA but not u-PDA.

The owner said the best bait was going to be shrimp— live bait shrimp. I got a pail. And I bought myself a new net for scooping fish out of the water, mainly on board a boat. Mine was old and was tired of my repairs, so I retired it.

And with that, we were off.

"Ahoy, mateys," Pasha said. I got us way west on Matagorda Island, several miles further than we usually went. Maybe it was for extra privacy. I don't really know why, but that was where I beached the boat. Pasha knew the drill, so he jumped out and tied our boat to a stake he slammed into the sand. He rejoined us to get everything off our ride.

"Mikka and I talked," I said. "If y'all want to make your camp aways away, it's cool. That's for sleeping. We're still here as a family during the day."

Chase jumped up and came over to give me a really big hug. He even knew how to make a campfire from some of the mesquite wood we brought from Waxahachie. It was small to make sure the wood could last awhile, and he left it ready. We'd light it to cook or if it got chilly. It was August, so chilly wasn't going to happen in South Texas.

Mikka and I caught enough sand trout to feed us all. Chase cleaned them, and he seemed to know what he was doing. Trout isn't my favorite fish because it's small and has little bones that are almost impossible to get out. Put a trout filet in front of me, and I'll assume it has bones. It's usually a valid concern, too.

We told the guys how to cook the fish, and then we sat back to relax. Chase and Pasha did a really good job. It wasn't the best fish I've had, but it was credible for sand trout.

They first went off the beach and came back with enough rocks to encircle the fire. Then Chase got creative and stuck a couple of mesquite logs into the sand, one on each side of the fire. Clever boy: he used the sticks to support the fish basket. I have this cooker tool that's basically two grates on a hinge with long handles welded to each grate. When the basket handles are together, there's about a half inch between the two grates: hence the name "basket." It makes it turning the fish simple. He tried to put all the fish on the fire at once but found that the cooker couldn't hold that many filets. They ended up doing 3 batches, with the first going to Mikka and me. Awwww…

That night, the kids went off to their own space. Mikka gave Pasha his handgun just in case. They might need protection quicker than Mikka and I could wake up, grab a gun, and run to wherever they were.

"Y'all okay?" Mikka hollered.

"Oh, yeah," Chase called back.

"I can take him out, you know," I told Mikka softly.

"Yup."

"I mean, if Chase turns out to be a serial killer. Remington and my scope. 50-yards is nothing for me."

"Yup."

"Am I overreacting?" I asked.

"Yup."

The next morning, Chase and Pasha were already up and splashing around near the shoreline. I relit the fire and started cooking scrambled eggs.

When they were ready, I called the boys. They ran to our camp. Plumb nekkid, they were. I started to tell them to go get shorts on, but Mikka stopped me. He stopped me by standing up and taking off his shorts.

"Okay, okay," I told him as I stood up. Four men, naked as a jaybird (or seagull), on a deserted hunk of sand. I threw some sunblock to Pasha. He made sure Chase's dick was protected. We were way outside my comfort zone, even though we were all of legal age.

"It's only nasty if that's what's in your mind," Mikka told me later. "Go with it be natural."

"Is it okay we're all naked?" I whispered.

"Yup."

"Am I overreacting?" I asked.

"Yup."

"A year ago, I was a 20-something guy," I said. "No cares. No worries. Now I've got responsibilities, but I'm still that guy on the inside. I have no idea what I'm doing."

"You're making America fabulous again," Mikka said.

After we finished eating, I told Mikka that I wanted the boat to do real fishing. What we did the previous day was fishing, but I wasn't going to spend a week eating little trout. I wanted something more substantial, and apparently that was going to mean putting the hook in the water further than I could throw.

Mikka came with me. The gulf was a little choppy. Thank goodness I don't get seasick.

I had my deep water fishing rod with one of the live bait shrimps. Nothing happened. I thought I felt something and went to haul it in. What I found was an empty hook. I bought somebody breakfast. It happens.

My second shrimp worked, and it was one hell of a tug. Fish went *Giddy Up*. Whatever was on the hook wanted to drag us to Florida or Cuba or something. Mikka showed me he was ready to help or take over. It took me about 15-minutes, but I finally got the fish close enough for Meeks to net.

It was a sailfish. Its dorsal fin was massive, and it really looks like a big sail. I freaked out at the look of its bill. Like all the fish in the marlin family, it has a big sword instead of a nose. I was intimidated at what was on my hook.

It was an athlete. I know sailfish are fast in the water, so that helps explain its long fight against the hook. He almost turned us over fighting that fish with the net. I was so glad I bought a new net, because the old one wouldn't have been able to scoop such a large and muscular fish.

Mikka hit the fish in the head before he tried getting it into the boat. It didn't help. Even with the fish dead, the thing wouldn't fit in our little boat, so I slowly turned it around and drove back to shore. We basically were dragging shark food along side, so I pushed boat as fast as possible. Mikka told me to slow down a few times because he was close to losing the sailfish.

When we pulled the fish to shore, the kids gave me a standing ovation.

"We went skinny-fishing," I said.

My sailfish was almost 6-feet long. It's a good thing we brought the big cooler with plenty of ice. The boys cleaned the fish, saving the sword-bill and sail. I told them about sailfish not being Kosher because it has skin instead of scales. They pretended to be interested.

I had them make filets out of the meat close to the tail.. For the main body, they cut steaks straight through the fish.

Thank goodness, I treat life as a boy scout: I had plenty of Kosher salt, sugar, and fresh water. That was all for a brine. I don't know what sailfish is like without a brine, and I don't really want to find out. We brined just enough for the next meal, with the rest going into the cooler for later.

Chase found the potatoes and did a really nice potato dish:

Potatoes, cut into large chunks

Onion, coarsely chopped

Garlic, minced

Salt, pepper, herbs (like rosemary, thyme, and/or oregano)

He gave me his recipe later. I was beginning to like that guy, even though I was still going to cut off his dick if he ever hurt my kid. Just sayin'.

Chase's parents lived off-the-grid in Mendocino, California. He was home schooled and knows Spanish and French.

"Off-the-grid," I said. "And now you work for a charter jet company?"

"I learned all about cool places in geography lessons," he said. "Now I get to see them."

"So you knew about Matagorda?" I asked.

"Close," he said, "if Galveston and Padre islands count."

"They do," Pasha said defensively.

I asked if he ever wants to go back off-the-grid. Nope, he didn't. He said there are places in Oregon and New Mexico that sound interesting. When I mentioned that Oregon gets snow in the mountains. He told me there are hot springs where he was looking.

"But, no," Chase said, "I'm okay with cell phones and electricity for now."

The boys squeezed each others shoulders.

And that's about how it went. Mikka lay on his back with both arms outstretched, palms down on the sand. He adopted a grin, a contented smile. That made me happy.

If they stay together, I think Chase is going to love the woods in Anatole's estate. He won't like all the grass burs. No sane person could ever like stickers.

chapter twenty-two

ay, there's the rub

"Once the game is over, the king and the pawn go back into the same box."
Italian Proverb

The noise was a jolt. We'd spent almost a week where splashing waves were the only sound. Now the satellite phone was ringing.

"That can't be good," I told Mikka as we tried to follow the ringtone into our stash of gear.

"I was hoping the ``teries were drained," my husband said.

He found the phone and answered it. I could only hear Mikka's side:

"Hello."

"Are you fucking kidding me?"

"You need us back now?"

"Okay."

The call was over.

"Pasha," Mikka called out. The boys came running from... oh, okay... they seemed to be welded together like a human bowl of spaghetti. Legs and arms were entwined.

"What's up?" Pasha asked.

"It's Dad," my husband told his brother, as I saw Pasha's blood pressure spike. "The body in the street in front of the house. That was what's left of Dad. Cops used DNA and fingerprints to identify him."

Milosh's DNA and fingerprints were in the system. I'm shocked. (Not!)

I reached out to put my arm around Mikka's shoulder, and I saw Chase doing the same for Pasha.

"Should we go back home?" Mikka asked softly after waiting a minute or so.

"No," Pasha said fiercely. "He fucked up my life over and over. He's not going to barf on our vacation."

Mikka did a quick nod to show he agreed. Chase looked a little confused, but he didn't say anything. Pasha would fill him in, if he wanted to.

"Write what you remember about the last time you saw him," Mikka said as he gave his brother paper and pen. "Cops are going to want a chat with all of us, so you need to log what you know."

He got up an started walking back to the kids' area.

"Shouldn't we go back?" Chase asked.

"Nope. Tomorrow's fine," Mikka told him. "It'll be okay. Anyway, it's too late today."

So Chase started walking to his new lover.

When I looked their way later, they were siting in the sand, staring at the water's horizon, and talking. Chase was obviously holding Pasha, and Pasha put his head on Chase's shoulder from time to time.

The kids said goodbye to each other after they helped us move all the gear from the rent-a-boat to the Jeep.

"I'm sorry you had to be in the middle of our family... uh... situation," I said to Chase.

"Sorry?" he said. "Are you kidding? I got to see— finally see— a family that isn't dysfunctional. You were all great, even when there's a bump."

Then came what had to be the longest goodbye kiss in history. Awww—

I had a hunch that we'd see Chase again someday. It could be awhile: Chase invited Pasha to come to his parent's house for Hanukkah. He's Jewish? I wouldn't have guessed. It looks like I need to get up to speed on what Hanukkah is. Piece of cake, or piece of latkes. Whatever. I figure if I can get up to speed on time flies, a Jewish holiday would be simple. I'm embarrassed to say that I know almost nothing about Judaism, but I'm ready to learn.

We talked about lots of things on the drive back home.

"I'm not getting my dick sliced," Pasha said. Converting to Judaism means circumcision. I don't blame the kid.

Mikka told us about some of the Roma/gypsy customs for death and funerals. He was worried that his father didn't leave a happy spirit behind. Apparently being eaten by a bobcat or coyote can agitate one's soul, and there's nothing worse than an agitated ghost.

"Marimé," Meeks said. "It's the contamination a death leaves behind."

"He marimé'd over our lives for years," Pasha said curtly.

"Fuck burial," Mikka said. "Gypsies don't get cremated, but this one will. We want him burned up."

"And the ashes thrown in the trash," Pasha added. "Maybe down to a sewer."

Mikka turned in his seat. I saw they did a fist bump, although I was really trying to keep my eyes on the road.

"With Uncle Boldo dead," Mikka added, "we're the only family. Dad wasn't popular with others."

251

"The only thing asswipe daddy taught me was how to make a bender tent," Pasha added. "That's the only skill I got from the old mahrim."

Mahrim means unclean spirit in the Romani language. I really wish public schools taught Romani.

The police back home were really interested in Milosh Cooper's cause of death. Their crime lab reports an unknown organic substance. They found nothing to suggest it was a bobcat or coyote. It was something else— something unknown to the crime lab.

> Dad. Did you kill Molosh Cooper?

Days went by with no response. I asked the same question over and over.

Then one day, I found a weird message from inside the cage. It was a kind of computer algorithm, similar to C++…

```
While (!0) {

    With Dad {

        Love();

        Protect();

    }

    With Marengo {

        Fight_for_you();

    }
```

So my rooster killed Milosh Cooper? I never knew Laird Monet to be anything less than precise. When sie uses a word, it's always a word he picked because it was exactly the correct fit for what he was saying.

I tried to get sie to use more words or different words.

The thing is I haven't seen my iPad deliver any messages from the cage, and it's been over a year.

Finding Help

GLBT Help Center
Coming out • Relationships • Bullying
888-843-4564
www.GLBThotline.org

The Trevor Project
Suicide
866-488-7386 (toll free)
www.TheTrevorProject.org

Stop Bullying
www.StopBullying.gov

This information was valid in 2017. If someone or something broke one of the websites shown here, try these terms using your favorite search site:

- Gay bullying
- LGBT bullying
- Trans bullying
- Coming Out help

The Blooper Reel

This Marengo didn't make the cut? Nor did this:

The quotes at the start of each chapter sometimes relate to the chapter's plot. Sometimes. Other times: not so much.

Here are a few of the quotes that didn't make the cut:

- If Python is executable pseudocode, then PERL is executable line noise.
- Programmers are tools for converting caffeine into code.
- Yo moma is like HTML: Tiny head, huge body.
- If you think you need to twist the knife, you're using the wrong knife.
- Life is made up of marble and mud. (Nathaniel Hawthorne)
- Evening news is where they begin with "Good evening," and then proceed to tell you why it isn't.
- If you think nobody cares if you're alive, try missing a couple of car payments. (Flip Wilson, the devil's patsy (1933-1998))

About the Author

"A foolish consistency is the hobgoblin of little minds,
adored by little statesmen and philosophers and divines"
— Ralph Waldo Emerson, cocksure, transcends Thoreau (1803-1882)

by Rik Wallin

This is the point in each novel where a publisher hires a PR dude to scramble the author's life into something that sounds cool. They asked me to do that for Time Flies, and I have a unique point of view on the subject. I've been in love with the man since the 1980s. Now I sleep with him as Wynn's husband.

Wynn Wagner   Rik Wallin

The first thing you have to know is that writing is just one of the things Wynn's done, but writing is one of his favorite things to do.

When you ask him about writing fiction, he denies it. He says he's only the stenographer for the voices in his head. I find that really troubling as his husband.

Time Flies is the book he wrote for himself as a defiant celebration of life. It's his angriest novel, and yet the main characters overcome tribulations. They even flourish.

As he worked in corporate America, he saved up for retirement, planning for a catastrophic disease. He won the lotto and got two: HIV and pancreatitis. The weird thing is that – thanks to agitation from the likes of my friend Larry Kramer, HIV is the easiest conditions to manage.

Pancreatitis is an entirely different matter. It never gets better. It never goes away. He makes no insulin for himself, and he can no longer make digestive enzymes. I wouldn't wish it on anybody.

We almost lost him in 2010 from pancreatitis. Since then there hasn't been a single day that he wasn't in so much pain that we'd all be jumping off cliffs.

Thank goodness for software like *SCRIVENER* (which he curses hourly), but it lets him pop around to joggle his mind.

If you didn't already know, every one of his novels is written in a first person point of view. That always means the plot is incomplete. If the narrator knows it, you know it. If the narrator is inept at something, it may seem like Wynn is an inept storyteller: read on, he'll get to the explanation. All of Wynn's books do that.

Wynn started being a professional singer in the Texas Boys Choir, as a boy soprano not the baritone voice he has today. His first paycheck was from the Lorimar company for singing on the *Ed Sullivan Show*. He also sang on a Perry Como special produced in Dallas to calm the nation after JFK was murdered (#285, 01/23/1964). His boy soprano voice is on albums of Christmas music and hymns. He was on the last recording of *Persephone* conducted by the composer, Igor Stravinsky. He was a soloist with the choir. When they did Mendelssohn's Incidental Music to *Midsummer Night's Dream*, Wynn was picked to be the Fairy King, Oberon (who resurfaces in one of his *Vamp Camp* books). He had really wanted to be Puck, but nobody was moved by his kinking the carpet. So he got an early start being a fairy, speaking the words of William Shakespeare from the Dorothy Chandler Pavilion to Carnegie and Town Halls in New York City.

Wynn was to be the soloist for a one act opera, *Bartolomeo Bonifacio*, about a boy soprano whose voice started changing. It's when Wynn's voice really started to change. It was in rehearsal, and his voice cracked at the wrong time. That was the end of his days in a boys' choir.

He was so tired of singing that he didn't sing for years, and he was so tired of being on tour for long stretches of time that he didn't leave Texas for a decade.

So back home in Fort Worth, he needed spending money. That's mainly because he had fallen in love with fast cars, and those take coins. He taught piano. Not well, he'd say, although one of his students ended up at Juilliard. He played in restaurants and piano bars for several years and was on the keyboard at a French Bistro when Frank Sinatra walked in for supper. Wynn says he practically shit in his pants. He was only 17 years old then. Before Wynn could play a single note, Sinatra came up and put a $100 bill in the tip jar. "Just don't play any of my songs," Sinatra said.

"But you've recorded every song that's been written," Wynn told Sinatra. "You're leaving me with a paper thin songbook." The crooner suggested "Chop Sticks," which Wynn started playing, first as a Debussy arabesque then as a Bach invention. When everyone was sick of "Chop Sticks," he moved on and played: "Alice's Restaurant," which was greeted with hoots and hollers from the Sinatra table. He also did "Steppenwolf," and Tiny Tim's "Tiptoe Through the Tulips." At that point, a waiter brought another $100 bill from Sinatra. A note said: "point noted."

He started working in theater (backstage, not acting), radio, and TV. Full disclosure: Wynn tells me that the scene in *Time Flies* whose setting was the Scott Theater in Fort Worth really happened.

Theater doesn't pay much of a living wage, so he got into broadcasting. His Dad owned radio stations on and off, so it's a business he grew up in.

Radio was fun, and he was excited to be hired by one of the Biggie Networks. Union Scale in New York was poverty level, so he came back to Texas, moving from the music side over to the newsroom. Broadcasting was changing. Real journalism was being pushed aside by pimply-faced kids with that day's wisdom printed on fanfold paper with little holes running down each side. The rule at his station was to lead with a "feel good" local story. When some students in Tehran, Iran, took over the U.S. Embassy, Wynn felt that was too important to bury. He led with it, and was promptly fired for it.

Wynn needed cash (a recurring theme), and he saw the only creativity was in computers. The thing is that he didn't know anything about computers. That slowed him down a bit, but he made things happen. His boyfriend at the time bought a shiny new gizmo called an Apple][. Its floppy drive had a 6 digit serial number and 3 or 4 of the leading numbers were 0. So Wynn just sat down and poked around. They kept the Apple in a closet in their apartment, so yes, he really became a closet programmer. The interesting thing is that he just knew how to make it do things. He can't even multiply or divide, but Wynn can make a computer do anything he needs doing. He started taking in the odd job at programming, ending up with two employees. He got so frustrated that he found work for his employees and then closed his business. He went corporate, and that felt like a defeat for his free-spirit life. But the big business pay was okay, and they didn't mind that he attacked problems in his own unique way.

At one company, everyone was using the C programming language. Wynn thought it was silly because assembly language was much more direct, but he agreed to give C a shot. His boss eventually bought him a Nerf bat so he could hit things without doing any real damage to the equipment. He was in his own little world, grumbling that his hippie days were done.

He rode his Harley to work every day when it wasn't wet. It was about 20° one day. When he passed another biker in a hallway, the other man said it was too cold to be on 2-wheels. Wynn gave it about 2-seconds after they passed each other and said, "I'm supposed to be the sissy in this place, and you're making that really hard."

One story I've heard repeated from several is about a guy where he worked saying he was going to reveal some of Wynn's personal secrets. Without missing a beat, Wynn said, "So you're telling somebody I'm queer? Let's see: my manager knew it before she hired me; my whole team knows I'm gay; the president of the company knows, too. My Mom knows. My dad knows. And my boyfriend is beginning to suspect." Going back and forth with Wynn, you have to know he plays real close to the net.

Then the 1980s came, and his friends started dying. Beautiful men with wonderful personalities were getting horrible diseases and dying. His whole world crumbled, and he couldn't do anything about it. Nobody could do anything. He was ashamed to be alive when everyone else was dying. The entire gay community was terrified.

And nobody helped. Parkland Hospital, the big hospital in Dallas (where JFK died), opened a ward for diseased gay men. Many of the doctors and nurses refused to go into any of the rooms. They refused to do the job they swore an oath to do. The US government had Ronald Reagan who dismissed the whole thing. To this day, Wynn says Ronald Reagan and George H.W. Bush are the two assholes more responsible for the AIDS pandemic.

Nobody did much of anything. There was the SHANTI project in San Francisco and Larry Kramer's GMHC (and Act Up later) in New York, and that's about it.

Wynn knew we had to do something, and we had to do it ourselves, and we had to act right then. He and I knew each other through a fledgling group of computer operators. There was no internet, so computer operators ("SYSOPS") had to connect their computers through regular phone lines. Wynn kept noticing the lights on his telephone modem flicker. Send and it flickers. Receive and it flickers again. When the lights were dark, nothing was coming or going, but the phone bill was still ticking along. He was always annoyed by that.

Wynn started writing a computer program to let computers exchange messages and have forums on lots of topics. It was like the Internet before there was an Internet (outside of secret DARPA military installations). Wynn got busy and figured a way to send with the light on constantly. When the transmission starts, it doesn't stop. If the line has noise, the transmission continues and fixes missed blocks as it goes. If the line is dropped completely, it just starts where it left off the next time the two computers are connected again. It saved individual SYS-OPS, including me, lots of coins.

He called his program OPUS. At the height of its popularity, 90% of the connected personal computers in the US were running Wynn's software. Nobody does that kind of thing. And he never made a single nickel from anyone. He asked SYSOPS to donate money to a local charity that works with AIDS patients or HIV research. They raised millions of dollars around the world. One charity listed "OPUS SYSOPS" as their biggest "corporate" contributor. Elizabeth Taylor's AmFAR came along fairly late in the pandemic, but they've done so much good, and they recognized the pioneering work Wynn's OPUS did for HIV charities.

Wynn is neither a scientist nor medical professional, but he knew he had to do something. He has no clue (and no desire) to rub elbows with the richy-riches of the world, trying to get them to write checks. He did what he knew, and that raised millions of dollars around the world. Even big corporations and US governmental agencies that used OPUS for its dogged reliability sent money to these charities, despite of what Ronald Reagan said. Wynn made that happen, without getting anything back. Few even know of his work, outside the BBS community, because he is always in the background.

Then came *AEGiS*, which became the largest Internet website in the world. Based in San Juan Capistrano, CA, it had millions of articles that were reposted with permission, and it was all about HIV/AIDS. I know about *AEGiS* because

I was one of the original engineers, helping *AEGiS* Founder, Sister Mary Elizabeth. She's not my sister, she's a religious sister. Like Wynn, she saw a need and went to work.

AEGiS got so unwieldy that it was ready to collapse under its own weight. Building the database used for user searches took more than a day. We brought in Wynn to work some magic. It was the only time I saw him intimidated. Turns out, when Wynn realizes the situation is hopeless is when he does his best work. He put a buttress here and a splint there.

When his engineering was done, he spotted another flaw. He'd looked all over the Internet and found almost nothing written for people diagnosed with HIV. What was available was done by medical authors, and it was confusing to the new patient, who was terrified at the death sentence he or she just received. Wynn sat down at a word processor, and when he stood up "Day One" was on that computer.

I'm just going to share an excerpt. *AEGiS* has since gone off-line because others (with big budgets) are able to do the work of a repository of data. You can still see "Day One" in a number of versions. The versions came about as the science in treatment changed. *AEGiS* had a staff of professionals who kept changing (or "ruining" according to Wynn) his original piece. Medical strategies changed, and "**Day One**" had to keep up. But you can go to the WAYBACK MACHINE website at archive.org to see his full article. Go to their snapshots of aegis.org and pick a date to see the full article. Here's an excerpt from a 2006 version:

Day One

by Wynn Wagner

You are in the right place if you just found out you have HIV.

Yeah, me too. This web page is the beginnings of your Survival Kit. I'm not a doctor or professional counselor I'm just a person with HIV, and I've gone through the same thing you're going through.

My plan here is to give you five pointers that I think are Big Deals. Then, I'll show you where you can go get whatever information you are ready for.

Five Pointers for Survival

1. Use a specialist. Make sure you find a doctor who specializes in HIV. That's a Big Deal. Studies have shown that your survival depends on you being treated by a doctor who deals with HIV on a daily basis.

Your regular doctor may be great, but you don't need general medicine right now. You need a specialist.

Those who get treated by an HIV specialist live longer. Period.

If you can't afford or locate a doctor, find an HIV/AIDS organization that can help you directly, or help you find public assistance.

2. Be good to yourself. That means eat right and take vitamins, and it means finding somebody to hug you from time to time.

It also means stop beating yourself up over being HIV-positive. Oh, okay ... do some self-pity for a day or two, if you want ... but remember to snap out of it.

[etc]

[This is my favorite part:]

Hearing you have HIV is like hearing a death sentence.

It can ruin your day.

It ruined my whole week.

[and so forth]

Yeah, parts of "Day One" are so funny they catch you off-guard. The newly diagnosed patient needs some grins. I used to hear Wynn say that you can be serious without being solemn. Damn wordsmiths like to shave a definition with a scalpel. Playtime with grammar and words is his Happy Place.

AEGiS got Thank You notes by the hundreds: "Thank you so much." or "You saved my life."

"Day One" is direct and to-the-point of a newly diagnosed patient. It tells the new patient to take charge. At one point, he told the patient to fire his doctor if he didn't like him.

What surprises most people who don't really know Wynn is that line: "Yeah, me too." Wynn almost ever talks about it, but he's one of those long-term survivors. He suffers from what's called "survivors' guilt" which is a kind of PTSD.

Does he complain? He goes beyond complain several meters into whine. Oh, you'd better believe he complains. All the damn day, somedays. But that's only around the house.

Outside the house, his main point is hope. You don't complain. You fix. When others see that the impossible isn't so impregnable if you stick to it.

You see the pattern again: Wynn sees a situation, and a solution is completely impossible, so Wynn chips away until there's some kind of something we can do. It's always forward. We live in a dangerous time. Nukes abound. Sorry, this is Texas… noo'cleer. People hate gays. Gay people, many of them, hate those who are HIV-positive.

Look what we've overcome. Until the 1800s, it was legal for a white landowner to own a human being. This was at a time when our indigenous people thought it was wrong even to claim ownership of the sacred earth. In the 1940s, crazy people like Mussolini and Hitler hypnotized whole populations into genocide against Jews, Gypsies, gays, and others. In the 1980s, we lost a whole generation of beautiful gay men because of creeps like Ronald Reagan and George Bush.

Today, when the majority of a country's population is Muslim, being gay is likely a death sentence. If another religion is in the majority, it may not be pleasant or easy to be gay, but at least it isn't a capital offense. The world should be ashamed of that statistic, but we rarely hear about it.

Those things aren't going to change, not by themselves. There's nothing in it for Saudi Arabia or Iran to treat their gay citizens with the respect they deserve.

Wynn's idea is that ordinary folks are the ones who have to bring change. You have to grow some balls and do something. If you can write: write. If you can schmooze: fundraise. If you're hopelessly corrupt: get into politics. (Just kidding on that last one.) (More or less kidding.)

He says we have to be our own hero. If you look at every one of Wynn's novels, including this one, you find a person who learns how to love himself and to be his own hero. You find characters who face a situation that has no solution, and they go make one anyway. The man is far from perfect. He undercooks beef, which he swears is a Texas thing. But his Tex-Mex food always comes out with a French twist.

I sometimes think his corpus is "ours" because I'm the first one to read everything he writes. I'm his alpha tester, and he makes me cry and laugh. He also makes my dick hard because he really knows how to write a sex scene. This book was supposed to be his PG rated novel, like that was ever going to happen.

If you want to know more about him, good luck. He has dementia, and he says J.D. Salinger used to ask him for pointers in staying anonymous in everyday life.

He did several interviews back in the OPUS days, but he only spoke once about his novels. He talked with John Selig about writing. It was for his "Outspoken" podcast. Go out to a Google near you and look for "John Selig Outspoken." Wynn is in there somewhere. Wynn agreed to sit down only because John's such a good friend, and he likes skating on the wrong side of the ice (whatever the hell that means).

Today Wynn has no pancreas after a Whipple Procedure in 2010, which is also part of the plot of this book. He got pancreatitis from an adverse reaction to an the early HIV drug, ddI.

When he writes about diabetes and addiction (*Commitment Issues*), Non-Hodgkin's Lymphoma (*influential*), HIV, Pancreatitis, Whipple Procedures (*Time Flies*), know this: Wynn walks those walks every day.

I never thought this book would happen. He hadn't written since 2010, but lookie here.

What you'll always get in a Wynn Wagner novel is hope. Shit hits the wall all over the place. His characters are bullied, cruelly turned into vampires, kidnapped. Each time, they refuse to wait for help. If somebody's going to be homophobic, he'll will find a way to kill that character. If somebody picks on a kid, heaven help that character. He loves killing off homophobes: like the vampire Hamlet flying over the Swiss alps picking apart a bully who just killed a gay kid. One leg at a time: he loves me, he loves me not.

Take our history and be grateful. Gays don't have family history, so we have to be careful to tell kids about what's already happened: Oscar Wilde, Alan Turing, Harry Hay, Rachel Maddow, Patricia Nell Warren (especially Patricia Nell Warren), and so many more. None of those is a finishing point. We need to learn about them so we can build a better future for our LGBT brothers and sisters. We're the only ones who will do that.

Martin Luther King, Jr pushed us when he said nobody's going to give us justice, we have to take it.

Rev. Jesse Jackson is right: hope is alive, but we are the ones who have to keep it alive.

Dan Savage does so much good work with his "It Gets Better" campaign (and his *The Real O'Neals*, which is Wynn's favorite show right now). Savage does everything with such panache that he does good while leaving a smile on your face. *That's* the way to make things better.

You have to put it together and be visible to LGBT kids. We have to show them it gets better. We have to show them every day. We have to seize justice and resist homophobia.

Hope and love are uplifting, and they're both hard work. Mark this: hope and love only happen when we give them to others.

Wynn says we have to be the face of hope. That's on us.

Meanwhile, please send him healing energies. Not having a pancreas isn't exactly a walk in the park. Neither is being "poz" almost forever.

Love you, hubby,

Rik

BRENT THE HEART READER is cosmic, tender and funny.
It's a New Age romance in paperback, e-book, hardcover, and audio book.

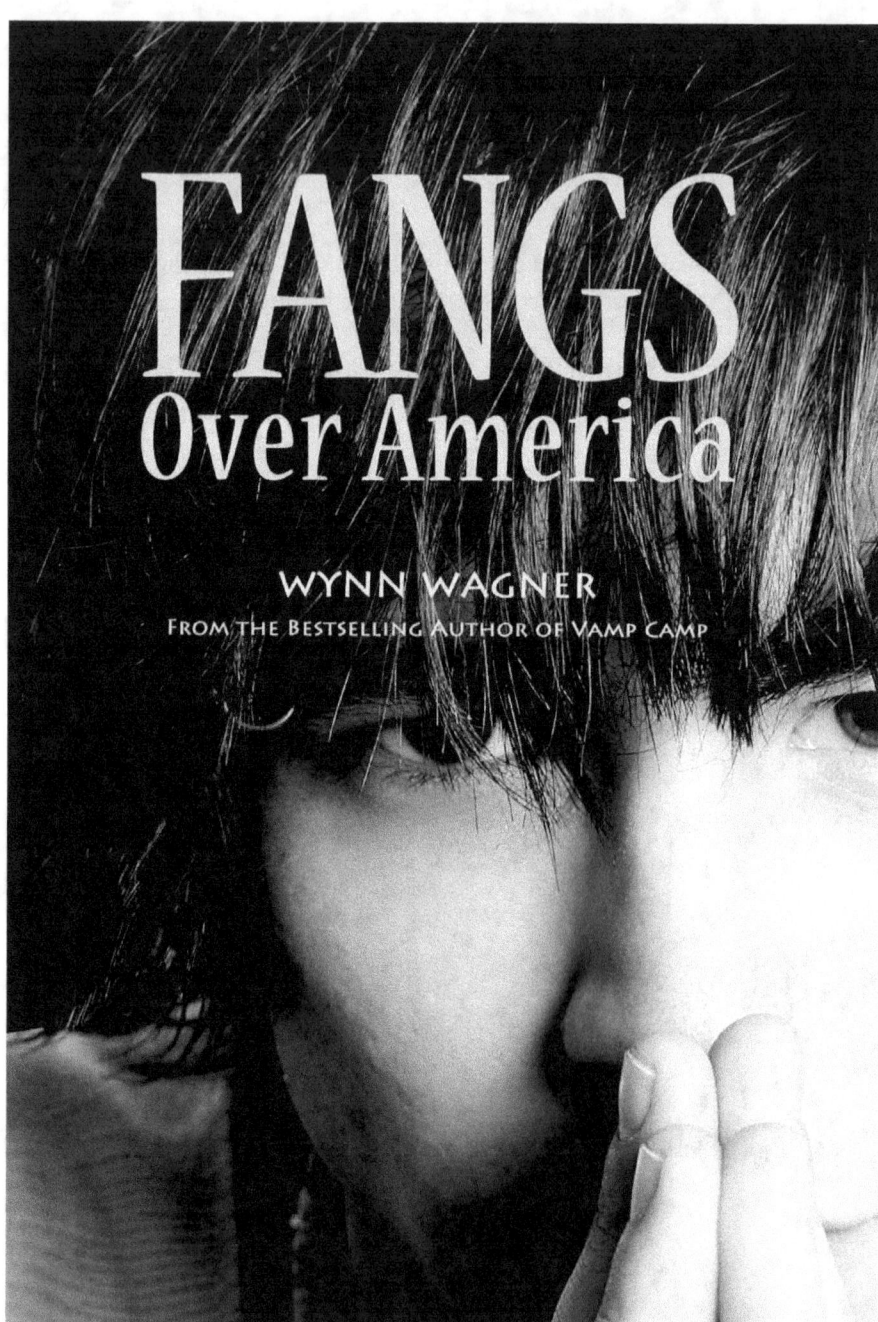

FANGS
Over America

WYNN WAGNER

FROM THE BESTSELLING AUTHOR OF VAMP CAMP

The latest in the VAMP CAMP series.

www.ingramcontent.com/pod-product-compliance
Lightning Source LLC
Chambersburg PA
CBHW070856250626
47159CB00003B/1086